ACROSS FLORIDA STRAITS

From Cuba to Key West

Marvin Cook

Cover art and maps by the author.

Lyric excerpts from song, "Memory of Florida Bay," copyright Mark Andrew Smith (www.marksmithsongs.com), are used with permission.

ISBN: 979-8-9886083-0-1

Printed in the United States of America

The author thanks, first and foremost, Lee Cook for proofing, editing and encouragement. Test readers of the draft provided valuable comments and suggestions that are most appreciated. Thank you to Sue Doker, Pat and Frank Hankins, Pat and Judy Ball. Doug Bailey, Anna and David Grossman, and Maxine Glenn. The author is also grateful to Pete and Pam Scalco, and Ernesto Reyes Mouriño for insights on life in Cuba.

Marvin Cook has travelled throughout the U.S. and Caribbean working to connect people to natural and cultural history at parks, museums, and wildlife refuges. Fiction has liberated his imagination, allowing him to invent characters maneuvering through dramatic circumstances in interesting places. When not writing or painting Florida and Maine landscapes, Cook sails the coast of Florida and spends summers aboard a boat in Downeast Maine with his wife, Lee, co-author of Blue Goose Passport (ISBN 978-0967129211).

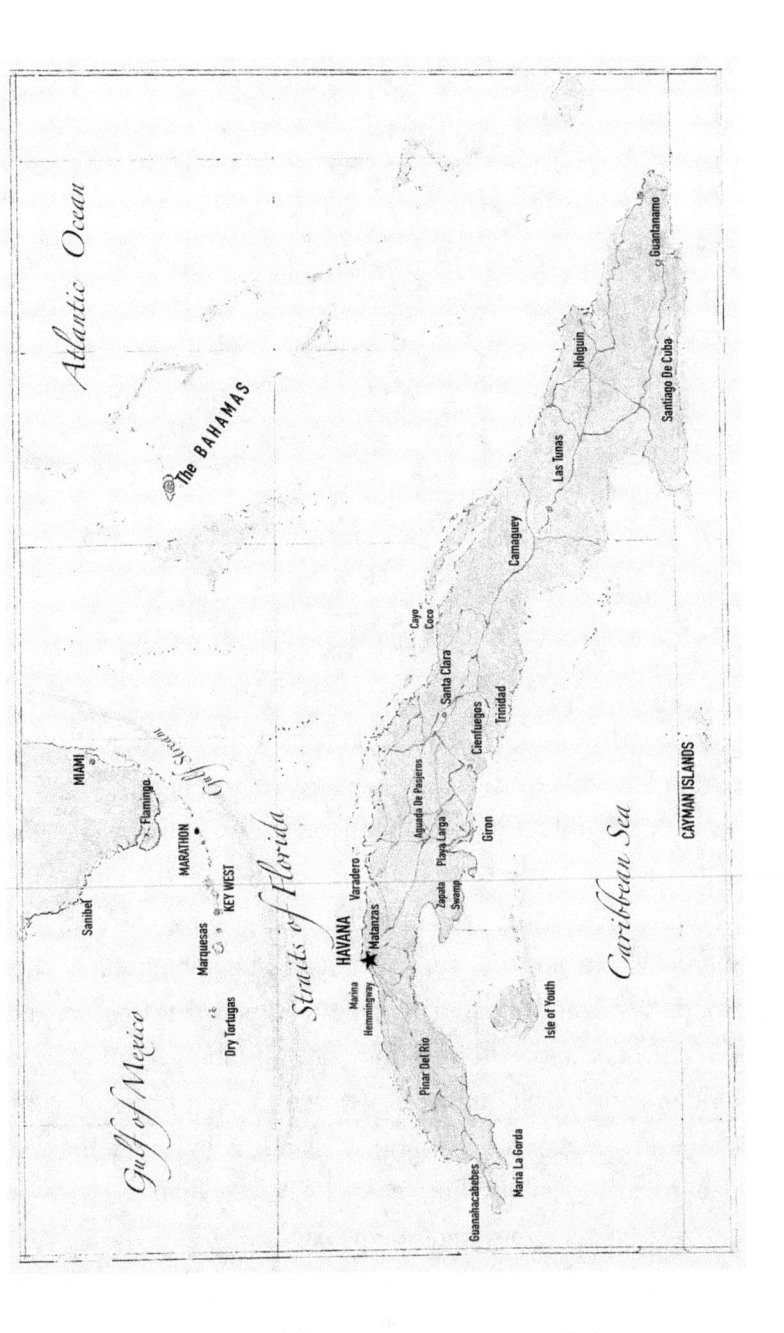

ONE

It is the welcome night reception for the new arrivals to the Cuban resort. Vacationers come to enjoy a week of relaxation, full of expectations of exotic fantasies in the Caribbean. A sumptuous buffet is set up on the patio by the pool. Artistic displays of tropical fruits, pastries, chicken, and plantains are laid out for the guests' consumption. A chef stands by a whole roasted pig still on a spit, ready to carve and serve. Ironed tablecloths drape cocktail tables in an elegant casual setting. The guests are wide-eyed and excited in the heady ambiance of a Caribbean island, with balmy breezes under swaying palms. Illuminated by colored lights, the palms create a blue, yellow, and orange canopy.

A band plays classic popular tunes, nothing current or political, but all infused with a distinctive Cuban flair and incorporating Cuban instruments. A marimba player imitates a steel drum pan. A talented vocalist sings in English, tinged with a Spanish accent. The set list includes world-wide jazz favorites like *Just Take Five* and *Girl from Ipanema* and others that were popular in pre-Revolution times. Nearly two decades past the Revolution, prohibitions on imperialist music and musical instruments have moderated. Besides, the resort rules are a little more relaxed than those imposed on the Cuban populace.

Every opening welcome night includes a walk-through by a stately figure, elegantly dressed, with the carriage of an ambassador. A tall Russian with crystalline green eyes and blonde curls combed back into rippling waves, Ivan Volkov is the resort's general manager. He strolls among the tables, smiling and shaking hands, only nodding in acknowledgment to guests as if he knows who they are. He says little, especially in Spanish that he struggles with even after five years working at this Soviet-sponsored property. He only breaks from his stoic role when a beautiful young lady catches his eye. He might make eye contact, but only for a glance, before he reverts to his disaffected aura.

The staff refers to him as El Jefe, the boss, partly because he IS the boss, but mostly because of the aloof distance he keeps from the staff. He does not invite conversation with the workers. He is El Jefe, but to his face, the staff addresses him as Señor Volkov.

His right-hand lieutenant is a short, heavy Cuban woman who is fluent in Russian, German, and French and, of course, her native tongue. She is unremarkable, in juxtaposition to Volkov's imposing figure. She is a female Sancho to Volkov as a Russian Don Quixote. Maria is a constant fixture at Ivan's side, always ready to translate or handle problems. Quiet and unassuming in his company, her temperament is anything but when she is on her own to address whatever needs attention. She is deeply feared by the staff of the resort, not just for her closeness to the top, but primarily for her bullish temperament and vindictiveness.

The resort workers have a name for Maria. She has been dubbed "Maria la Gorda", not to her face, of course, only in their private conversations. The original Maria la Gorda lived long ago. By legend, she was a pirate whose base was on the far western shore of Cuba or, some say, a prostitute. It is a fitting insult tag for fat Maria. She is El Jefe's whore, his mercenary who will do anything for him. And, she is vicious in the administration of her authority.

Sometimes, Ivan takes a seat at a table brought near the front stage upon his entry. The waiters quickly bring the table and chairs and a fresh tablecloth to his prominent grandstand. There, he feigns enjoyment of the band and dance production for a song or two, and then exits with a dismissive wave to the audience as if he were royalty. In some ways he is royal. As the Russian overseer of the partnership venture with the Cuban military, he wields power; power over the property, staff and the guests. The resort is his kingdom and his prison.

To the staff, Señor Ivan Volkov is an enigma because he has little interaction with them directly. Maria is his interface, who executes his orders and directions as the manager's emissary. Her job is a fitting reward for her heroic role in the Revolution and faithful devotion to Fidel Castro. Doing this job with zeal is her patriotic tribute to the cause.

On this welcoming night, Ivan sits at his table, ordered a Havana Club 15, lights a cigar and leans back in his chair. Calm and aloof, he surveys his kingdom from his prominent perch.

The band resumes with a drum roll. To a flourishing fanfare of the band, two dancers swirl onto the front stage. Spotlights flash on to reveal their arrival. Julio and Juanita are a spectacle to see. When they enter, the dance floor clears like a drop of oil spreading its sheen across water. They have such charisma, such presence, they seem to float. The band hit a fast-tempo Cuban salsa tune and their synchronized choreography is mesmerizing. Close gyrations of their hips are suggestive moves that attract the attention of both the men and women in the audience. For many, it is a moment, watching with their eyes but with minds wandering in lustful amorous day-dreams.

Julio is dressed in a black form-fitting tuxedo, with no tie. Juanita wears a simple black dress, slit up the leg to her hip and spike heels. Her necklace is sparkling paste that glimmers in the glow of the spotlights.

Their show is a journey through Cuban dance culture. It starts with the local style of classical ballroom dancing called contradanza, followed by rumba, mambo, and even a ballet leap and lift, ending in a hot salsa segment. To finish, Julio wraps Juanita in his arms, releasing her to spin into a fluid pirouette. She twirls back to his embrace. Then, both raise their arms to invite the applause from the vacationers at Girón Beach Club Resort. They strut off the dance floor with the same elegance displayed during their entrance. Juanita's hips swing in a model's accentuated gait.

Taking the microphone, the band leader announces, "Señoras y señores, aplaudan nuevamente a nuestros bailarines de Girón, Juanita y Julio, y sepan que ellos están disponibles para clases de baile todos los días por la mañana."

What the white-tuxedoed emcee announced in Spanish was "Ladies and gentlemen, please applaud again for our Girón dancers, Juanita and Julio. And know they are available for dance lessons every day in the morning."

The dancers return to take a bow and turn to applaud the band. The audience applauds politely, not necessarily understanding the Spanish, but getting the idea that it is a call for acknowledgment, perhaps for the band, perhaps for the dancers.

When the band takes a break, the audience of mostly eastern Europeans, sprinkled with couples from the UK and Canada, go back to browsing the buffet. The noise of the crowd is a mixture of languages, growing to a background din. Attentive servers wander the tables to take orders for drinks and clear the tables.

Under the strings of lights on the patio, under a dark sky, the illuminated palm fronds sway in a gentle Caribbean breeze. This is a heady experience for the visitors, who feel as if they are a million miles away from their lives in temperate climate zones.

The resort functions as a self-sufficient enclave segregated from the surrounding community. No gates or fences are necessary. All the local residents know that the resort is off limits except for the few who have jobs gardening, cleaning, in the kitchen or taking care of maintenance. The key staff are provided small apartments and are considered privileged. Although they have access to good food and simple accommodations, most importantly, they receive tips from guests. Small gratuities make a big difference in their personal standard of living.

While gratuities are generally discouraged, as is intimate contact with the foreign guests, the management usually overlooks small transgressions. But sometimes management would intercede to keep the practice of tipping in check. Fear of losing the advantage of being staff workers with housing is a powerful motivation. Having a job at the resort means workers have a little extra money to purchase goods on the underground market or contribute to their families who have only the basic subsistence provided by the OFICODA, the jurisdiction that issues supply booklets for each family.

TWO

The Girón Beach Club Resort was patterned after other all-inclusive resorts in the Caribbean. Cuban and Russian planners and representatives visited several vacation destinations on stealth excursions to experience how the other resorts operated. Some of the resorts they visited were American, but others were operated by companies from other countries.

They travelled separately and together enjoying the amenities each resort provided and then rendezvoused in Cuba to discuss their findings. They surveyed everything: furnishings, pools, service, and food. Architects made notes of the buildings. Hoteliers checked out the procedures and pricing. It was a perk for the undercover surveillants to enjoy the western-style resorts as tourists.

At the time the resorts visited by the Russian and Cuban representatives were developed, the all-inclusive tourism model was new to the large hotel companies with properties in the Caribbean. The design of the all-inclusives was generally patterned after large hotels in the States, but adapted to the tropics. The architecture rarely respected the local traditions. The aim was to create a sense of a stereotypical vision of an island paradise. Colors inside and outside were pastel shades of blues, greens, and pinks. Bamboo furniture and ceiling fans were common.

The all-inclusive resorts were conscious that, because of racial prejudice, some guests, primarily Americans, may be uncomfortable and anxious for their personal safety in a foreign land. Operators of the resorts were sensitive to these fears, so guests were isolated in sanitized, artificial properties. The resorts were designed as enclaves, separated from the local communities, with security to keep local people out and foreign guests in. Their staffs were trained to interact with the guests in a deferential colonial manner when providing services. The menus featured traditional midwestern food rather than local Caribbean cuisine, partly due to the preferences and comfort of the guests but more to maintain a dependable supply of food. Buying from local sources would require too much effort to maintain a regular meal plan.

The Cuban representatives observed that the resorts were full of well-paying guests, mostly upper class, but not extremely wealthy, who arrived for predefined stays. Some local tours and programs, such as diving or fishing excursions, or cultural trips to see the "real island life," were offered at additional costs to the all-inclusive package price.

The Cuban and Russian intelligence teams took all of this in. They used their research to adapt their resort plans for new developments in Cuba. They merged what they liked at the other Caribbean resorts with the Cuban style. The existing inventory of nationalized hotel properties developed before the Revolution, some dating back to the Mafia times, were folded into the new business operation which was under the control of the military. Their market would be Europeans and USSR clientele who were not bound by the U.S. embargo restrictions. Perhaps the embargo would end someday but, until then, the Cuban all-inclusive resorts would need to market to clients who could navigate travel rules to come to the island.

The Cuban resorts were competing with the all-inclusive properties that the West had scattered throughout the Caribbean. The U.S. tourist market to Cuba had been closed since the blockade instituted during the Russian Missile Crisis in 1962. Subsequent punitive restrictions by the U.S., meant to instill hardship and foment discontent among the Cuban populace, provided a convenient and believable reason to deflect responsibility for any failure of the Castro regime.

Girón Beach Club Resort was one of the first resorts developed by the Soviets in a secret partnership agreement with the Cubans. It looked like any 1960s Holiday Inn built on a Florida beach but with adjustments for the climate and culture of Cuba and the non-American clientele.

Large open-air atriums and lounges bridged the hotel room buildings. Poolside bars and dining areas were located on tiled patios overlooking the Caribbean Sea. Girón Beach Club Resort was painted a rich coral accented with forest green trim, something like an exaggerated watermelon color scheme. In time, it might fade to a more subtle coloration that fit in better with the geography but, being newly opened, the color scheme was gaudy.

Large gardens and open spaces with mowed lawns were carved out of the native scrubby coastal forest. Blooming bougainvilleas were woven into gateways and used for hedges. Their orange, white, pink and fuchsia blossoms were a festive tropical fringe to the plantings of elephant ears, bananas, and bird of paradise. Tropical fruit trees were planted throughout the resort and most of the year something was bearing fruit; mangos, avocados, guineps, soursop and key limes. To the delight of birdwatchers, native birds frequented the gardens, but were unnoticed by most of the tourists. A few iguanas roamed the resort grounds, startling guests who encountered these miniature dragon-like reptiles lounging wherever they liked.

The resort's programs were designed for the guests' entertainment, using the talent of the Cuban people, including dancers, jugglers, and, of course, musicians. The result was an exotic venue that met the romantic notions of the guests who came from temperate or even frigid climates to enjoy a week in paradise.

Juanita and Julio were brought to the resort early on to create a floor show and offer dancing lessons to guests. A magician and a gymnast were also part of the entertainment. The band was assembled from local performers. Only Julio and Juanita had a place to live at the resort, due to their night-time shows and morning teaching schedule. The gymnast rode a unicycle and juggled maracas. His featured act was riding a modified bicycle on a taut wire suspended 6 feet above the pool. The magician had a small repertoire of slight-of-hand tricks for his show, but mostly he wandered through the guests to pull pesos out of their ears or make balloon animals for the few children who were on vacation with their parents. The entertainment was an amenity that most guests enjoyed.

When completed, the resort was promoted and guests arrived. With the availability of Cuban labor, and management by a Russian administration, the resort flourished. Girón Beach Club Resort became popular and the foreign currency was beneficial to Cuba. It was capitalistic entrepreneurialism with Communist partners.

On the day after Julio and Juanita's opening night performance, the morning sunlight streaked through the bright blue of the tropical latitude sky. White cotton-candy clouds were tinged with yellow.

The Activities Director led a group of guests to the poolside courtyard for the introductory lesson to Cuban salsa dancing. The coral-patterned concrete deck was still damp from the morning rinse by maintenance crew. Mostly, the group was middle-aged matrons whose husbands were not able to be persuaded into joining a dance class. A couple from Canada, on their postponed honeymoon, were among the group. An older couple was joyfully enthusiastic about learning Cuban dance.

Julio said in his best English, "Welcome sirs and madams, we are so happy you have come to learn to dance the salsa."

Juanita added in Spanish "¿Cuantos de ustedes entienden el Ingles?" How many of you understand English?

Only a few raised their hands, while most just looked around for sympathetic gazes from the others.

"OK, OK, tak skol'ko ponimayut po russki. How many of you speak Russian?" As most of the visitors were from the Soviet Union, many in the group smiled in relief that there was a familiar language falling on their ears.

"Bueno, we will address you in Russian and English, but we are not so good in speaking as we are in dancing. So, let's just begin."

Julio and Juanita motioned to the group and gently shepherded them into a line facing the pool. Then Juanita pushed PLAY on the boom box to start a cassette tape of salsa. They assumed a start position and slowly moved to the beat to demonstrate the dance moves. In chorus, they counted "One, two, three. One, two, three." Pausing for the three-count beat, Julio then counted in Russian, "Raz, dva, tri. Raz, dva, tri."

Breaking their pose, Julio went to a woman in the line and Juanita picked an older gentleman. Taking them by their hands, they continued with the simple steps, saying "One, two, three. Raz, dva, tri."

"Now you!" The dance instructors moved their students to pair with one another, gently guiding hands to hands and hands to waists. The older unaccompanied women were paired with each other, who nervously smiled at their unfamiliar partner.

The music continued and before long the student dancers were jiving with the salsa rhythm in the simple back and forth step. Now it was time to add a hip movement, then a side step, then a turn. The group was having fun and making progress, with giggles on frequent missteps.

"Now, that is the end of our first lesson. You must practice for tomorrow morning, when you will learn more."

Julio and Juanita thanked the guests for attending and invited them back for the next day. When the last guest left the poolside, they walked down to the beach, hand in hand. They took off their shoes and strolled at the water's edge. Their life was good.

They were "children of the Revolution." Each came from privileged families, but neither was affluent. Their youth was informed by the new regime as they were too young in 1959 to know what was happening in the turmoil that rocked Cuba. Their only knowledge of the past or the world was from the rhetoric of the government. Their lives were what they were.

They met in the National Dance Academy. Julio was from Cienfuegos, the port city on the south, while Juanita's home was Havana. Their talent and passion for dance led them to be selected for the prestige of the academy, where they found one another and were inseparable.

It was fortunate that they made their way to the resort at Girón, even though they each would have preferred to be in the National Ballet troupe, but only if they could be together. They might have been assigned to be teachers, to enrich the cultural education of students, or made their way to jobs that had nothing to do with their training. Their timing was just right to be tapped to dance at one of the new resorts the Soviets were building in partnership with the Cuban government.

Walking the shore, holding hands, their feet were massaged by the warm sand and washed by the lapping waves. Their bodies were their currency and staying healthy was important. They had each other, a better place to live than most Cubans, and a little extra money from gratuities happy guests bestowed upon them.

Juanita and Julio were not political. But there were Cubans who cared about politics. There were people who idolized Fidel Castro and those who were critics, but most just accepted the regime and lived within the bounds that were established by the government. Their concerns were living and surviving in the system they lived in but had no ability to control. That was the place where Julio and Juanita lived and they were comparatively well off. For them, life was indeed good.

THREE

Juanita heard a knock on the door to their studio apartment. A bellman was there to summon her and Julio to see El Jefe.

Curious and a bit frightened she asked, "Why does El Jefe want to see us?" Julio was away. She told the bellman, "Julio is not here. He is in Cienfuegos with his mother," hoping that this might postpone a meeting with the big boss.

The bellman shrugged and said only, "He wants to see you now. You better come. Maria "la Gorda" will be angry if you don't come now."

"Un momento, por favor."

She quickly freshened her makeup and combed her dark hair, checking her appearance to be presentable to the powerful General Manager. She then followed the bellman to the main office which she had never been admitted to before. Juanita didn't know who she feared more, El Jefe or Maria. The office was a forbidden domain for the staff. While her confidence was unshakable on the dance floor, her knees trembled in the anxiety of being called to the office.

The bellman opened a huge mahogany door and motioned for her to enter. In the foyer a secretary sat at a small table and gestured for Juanita to be seated across the room. She lifted the phone and whispered something into the handset. She paused and said, "I don't know, only a woman is here."

Maria opened the door to El Jefe's office and said, "Entre," in a polite, yet seriously firm tone.

Juanita had barely entered the office and glanced at El Jefe behind his large formal desk, seated in a large leather chair, when Maria barked "Dondé ésta tu esposo?" Juanita felt a spasm flow through her body and a chill race up her spine.

"Julio is in Cienfuegos to see his mother today," offering as an excuse, "She is not feeling well."

Maria huffed, knowing that she only had one fish in her net and there was nothing she could do. She had not remembered Julio had requested permission to leave the resort to go to Cienfuegos.

That's when Juanita noticed what was stacked on El Jefe's desk. She saw their VHS player and several pirated videotapes of *Grease* (1978), *Saturday Night Fever* (1977), *Sweet Charity* (1969), and *West Side Story* (1961). She knew immediately these were from her apartment. Her mind raced, thinking "I thought these were well hidden. Somehow, they found our tapes and player. Was it a maid, or repairman, or, worse, the secret police who found our private hiding spot?"

Juanita and Julio had used some of their tips to purchase, in the underground market, the prohibited technology and tapes of American dance movies to view privately and quietly in their time off. To be connected to what was going on in a world they had no access to was exhilarating for them. They sometimes studied the videos and re-created the dance moves. These movies were forbidden fruit and it was exciting to be so risky.

But being caught was a terrifying reality. Maria said, "Sit!" and rattled a heavy mahogany chair directly in front of Señor Volkov.

"I'm sorry…. I'm so sorry." Juanita was frightened, crying, and saw no reason not to be honest. She was clearly caught in something that was not permissible, even in the resort, where standards for mostly foreign guests were more relaxed in contrast to outside social regulation.

El Jefe was quiet, his eyes pierced her soul and wandered to her youthful figure. Her form was not an hourglass but a sleek egg timer, the well-toned body of a dancer. Juanita could not look him in the eye, and averted her focus to anything else in the room: the lamps, books, paintings on the wall, even his pen and pencil set and engraved gold nameplate "Ivan Volkov, General Manager."

Maria began the inquisition. "Do you not know that this equipment is prohibited? These imperialist movies are poison to our culture and an insult to the Revolution!"

Juanita nodded. Maria continued to berate Juanita, who was heaving with sobs, her vision blurred with tears.

Maria said, "I am disgusted! It will be up to Señor Volkov to inform you of the consequences of this horrible mistake. You have such privilege here to be with your husband, to dance and entertain our guests like celebrities … and now this?"

Ivan finally spoke. "Maria, I believe Juanita and Julio can learn from their mistake, so there must be something we can do." He leaned back in his chair, looking over Juanita, who was clearly vulnerable and at their mercy.

"Maybe we do not need to report this to the Ministry of Interior?" Juanita, like all Cubans, feared the G2 unit of the General Directorate of Intelligence. Getting in trouble with the G2 could be very bad, especially if the crime was counter-revolutionary.

"What do you think, Maria?" Maria's face turned to an inquisitive scowl.

Ivan glanced at Maria with a look that told her Juanita should wait outside. All that from a glance, but Maria understood and directed Juanita to the foyer couch, almost humanely giving her a tissue to wipe her tears as she took her by the arm to the door. "Wait here," Maria instructed.

It seemed like an hour that Juanita was in the foyer, but the clock only moved five minutes. The secretary made every effort to avoid looking at Juanita who was still sniffling. The secretary knew something was up, but it was her nature to avoid any involvement in activity that she was not directed to participate in.

Juanita jumped as the phone rang and the secretary said, "Please go in Señor Volkov's office now." As Juanita opened the door to enter, Maria stomped out of Volkov's office.

El Jefe said, "Please sit. I think we have a way to avoid serious punishment, if you are willing." Juanita nodded, hoping for leniency.

"We can take care of this." He leaned back in his chair and sprouted a malicious grin, his eyes fixed upon her cleavage.

Juanita quivered in her chair, immobilized in nervous anticipation of the situation. She felt alone, so vulnerable, and powerless to avoid whatever punishment he would deal. Even having Maria in the room would be welcome as a hope that this uncomfortable situation would end soon. His eyes pierced her dress and she felt naked.

El Jefe stood and walked behind her. Juanita closed her eyes. She felt his hands gently embrace her shoulders. She instinctively recoiled and he took his hands from her shoulders.

"I thought you might want to avoid any problems, but it is your choice," he said to her. Tears filled her eyes, but she nodded, "Sí, no hay problema, por favor."

El Jefe smirked a wry grin and brushed the back of his hand on her neck to move her hair from her ear. His other hand cupped her breast. She closed her eyes tightly. Juanita hoped Maria would come back into the room to interrupt this assault, but she never returned.

It was over quickly. El Jefe might have been an imposing figure but he was not a sophisticated lover. She could not look at him. He said, "I think we are done, for now. But I will see you tomorrow to decide what to do."

As she quickly dressed and fled the office in humiliation, her thoughts were "Oh, my God, this is not over!" Succumbing to El Jefe's desires had not exonerated her and Julio, but only extended the peril.

She retreated quickly to her studio with so much confusion swirling in her head. "What would El Jefe do tomorrow? What would he decide? Had she allowed him to violate her for nothing?" Now, she would continue to agonize over her fate.

She was traumatized with guilt, fear, and worry. She took a shower to wash away the disgust, sobbing as she tried to scrub off the smell and touch of her assault. She wished Julio was with her instead of being with his mother. She needed him. What would she tell him when he returned? How could she know what he might do? There seemed no way out.

El Jefe sent for Juanita again the next day and repeated his vile act. Every day, for the week Julio was away, she was a helpless victim without a champion. Juanita came to insulate herself from El Jefe's actions, still hoping that when Julio returned this would stop and things would return to normal.

FOUR

Julio returned from Cienfuegos. His mother was sick and his father was not well either. Julio stayed longer than he expected to help get his sister established to live with them until something better could be worked out.

Juanita cried when Julio returned. She hugged him tightly and took his hand to lead him back to their apartment. Julio was very concerned, stopping her on the open sidewalk. "What is wrong? Please?"

Juanita only cried, and said, "We are in trouble. Let's go to our place so we can talk. There are too many ears here."

Once the two of them were in their apartment, Juanita breathlessly told Julio what had happened. She told Julio about being called to the office, of her meeting with Maria and El Jefe. Through her tears and sobbing, she explained how she had been confronted with the things they should not have, the contraband tapes and player. She did not tell him everything, only about being caught with the videos.

She could not bear telling Julio that El Jefe had forced her into sex. Her humiliation and guilt could not be put into words. She was afraid Julio's reaction would be violent and get them into even deeper trouble. Her deal with the devil was still her secret. This was the price she had paid to keep them out of trouble. Now she hoped they would face any consequences together.

Juanita told Julio that Maria and El Jefe would not turn them over to the G2 for punishment, but she did not know what would happen. Neither knew what the punishment for their "crime" of having foreign videotapes and a player would be, but their imaginations of harsh treatment were fostered by rumors of the jail. Fear is a powerful tool for any government to wield to reinforce power. That fear was a powerful tool for El Jefe, too.

Julio comforted Juanita. He could not imagine how just having the prohibited movies could be such a big problem. He thought it ridiculous that the foreign movies were a threat to Cuba, but he knew they were contraband. He knew the imperialist propaganda was illegal, but they really had done nothing wrong except purchase bootlegged VHS tapes on the black market. Julio said, "Let's try to say we are sorry and endure whatever El Jefe decides. We can do this together and everything will be fine."

Juanita was a little relieved by Julio's confidence that this was no problem, but he had not been in the office to be scared into submission by Maria and El Jefe. Having already paid a brutal price for their violation of the rules, she feared the punishment so much more.

Julio's reassurances that everything would turn out okay helped to calm her. He told her, "We just need to do our jobs and wait for Maria and El Jefe to talk to us again. For now, we must go on, as if there is no problem. Maybe we won't have any problems."

Despite his optimism, she didn't really believe their punishment was over. She had endured being berated and abused, but accepted Julio's consolation. She put on her dance costume and he unpacked his bag.

That evening they entertained a new group of guests, dancing the same show they had danced a hundred times before. Although Juanita's performance was a little off, her entertainer ethic of "the show must go on" carried her through their routine. The audience was happy. Happy to have Julio back, she temporarily put aside her anxiety.

The next morning, they had good attendance for the pool-side dance class. Maria intercepted them at the end of the lesson and commanded them to go to El Jefe's office once they changed out of their dance costumes. Juanita was relieved that she would have Julio with her this time. Certainly, El Jefe would not force himself on her again with her husband there.

When they went to the office, El Jefe was not there. Instead, Maria sat at his desk, in El Jefe's chair, exuding the authority it represented. What Maria and El Jefe decided was to separate Juanita and Julio as punishment for their cultural violation. In this way, the Girón Beach Club would not permanently lose their popular entertainers. Maria had made a call to the resort that was opening at Cayo Cocolobo in the northern keys.

"I have some news for you," Maria said through her teeth, while she sneered at Julio and Juanita.

They looked at each other and then back to Maria in anticipation of learning their punishment.

"You have committed a crime against the Revolution. Señor Volkov and I have decided that we will not report you to the G2 Police, because this was the first time we have caught you having the illegal materials. But your act has consequences."

Without empathy she blurted, "There is a new resort opening on the Atlantic side of the island and management has decided to send Julio to this new resort for several months to work with a team of dancers. Julio, you will help them set up the same kind of program we have here, for the guests there."

Turning to Juanita, she said, "You will stay here to keep our guests happy and entertained. You must work up a new solo routine for the entertainment, perhaps something like the avant garde dancing of the 1920s. You studied ballet, no?"

Both were shocked by this sudden change. Julio said, "When will this happen?"

Maria glared, "This is immediate. Mañana. You will travel on the bus with our guests who will be returning to the Havana Airport and transfer there to the Cayo Cocolobo bus taking their first guests to the new resort. I will have papers for you tomorrow morning, and you will meet the events manager when you arrive at the new resort. Perhaps some time apart will help you both learn to respect the laws of the Republic." With that, she was done, indicating, with a flick of her hand, it was time for them to leave the office.

29

They retreated to their apartment. This was devastating news for them both, but more so for Juanita. She would be left without her partner. She would have no escape from El Jefe. She hated Maria la Gorda.

Juanita was quietly despondent at this news. Almost catatonic, she sat on her bed and stared at her feet.

Julio seemed to better accept this turn of events. He was always the optimist, but still he was very unhappy that he would leave the familiar life they had at Girón Beach Club and the wife he adored. They had been inseparable since school days at the dance academy.

Trying to make an awful situation seem better he said, "This is bad, and I hate to leave, but it will only be a short time. At least we will not go to prison or a re-education work camp. There we would be separated and who knows what would happen."

Though Julio outwardly was consoling, he was fuming inside; angry at whoever turned them in, angry with the resort for separating them, angry with having to leave for a place so far away from Juanita and distant to his family in Cienfuegos. Still, he reasoned this punishment was a little relief from what they imagined could be a penalty for having contraband materials. They had been worried about losing their jobs, being sent to a work camp, or something worse, something that they could not even imagine.

"Now we know the punishment. This will be over soon enough," Julio thought. But he did not know the secret Juanita kept from him. Without Julio for comfort, if not defense, Juanita feared that the sexual harassment would continue and

El Jefe would dominate her. She wept. But she could not bring herself to reveal her true fears to Julio.

The new assignment was arranged quickly. In what felt like only a moment to the loving couple, Julio was packed and gone on the bus to the northern keys resort. He was on a new course and Juanita was trapped at Girón Beach Club Resort. El Jefe was her jailer and torturer and Maria was the prison guard. Alone, she would have to endure this separation. She prayed it would be over soon. She dreamed that when Julio was back, they could leave and do something else. It did not matter what, anything. Anything would be better than continuing to endure the insult of her situation.

In resignation, she accepted she would have to endure her fate until Julio returned. Then maybe they could escape together. She reminded herself that Julio loved her, that he would understand how she was forced into this awful situation and he would make a plan for them to get away together. They would be together and happy again.

Weeks passed and Juanita bravely faced the frequent calls to El Jefe's office. She endured the compulsory violations. She tried to leave her body emotionally to find a safe place in her mind. She just passively submitted to his vile acts with detachment.

Juanita came to fear hearing the footsteps of the bellman and jumped whenever she heard a knock at the door. El Jefe would send for her almost daily; her visits to his office were brief. She felt shame every time she walked back to her apartment to shower. The water could not wash away her anguish. Because this kept happening, she quit crying and became empty of feelings. She hated how she had become El

Jefe's private toy. He was stealing her body and her self-worth with each encounter.

Juanita continued her dance performances and lessons. Her inner glow had faded and her once energetic routine became a rote iteration of practiced choreography. She missed Julio so much. Wanting to be free from her captor, she dreamed of running away but didn't know how to escape, even if she had the self-confidence and courage to do it.

A few months after Julio had been taken away, she began to feel sick. She thought that perhaps it was her broken heart but, in reality, her maladies were not merely the result of the situation she was in, but from a new life forming in her. Three months passed. The changes in her body told her she was pregnant.

This was a new problem; a very big problem. Pondering what she could do, her sleepless nights and morning sickness were adding to her stress and depression. When she overslept, or was too sick to make her morning dance class, Maria would come to her room and bang on her door.

As with most days, today Juanita jumped and ran to open the door, only to be humiliated by Maria.

"¿Que pasa? What are you doing? You have guests waiting for their morning dance lessons! This is unacceptable! You are lazy. You are worthless!"

Juanita felt worthless indeed.

"I am sorry. I am sorry, Maria. I am not feeling well."

Maria glared, "Again! This is happening too many times. You are not a princess! You are a tramp. Get dressed and to the poolside quickly. Then, we will see Señor Volkov for what to do with you."

This made Juanita wretch and her vomit shot out in a spurt to land directly on Maria's shoes. Stunned, Maria looked down at her shoes and then back at Juanita in shocked disbelief that the spew had soiled her feet.

"Andele!" she barked. Slapping the back of one hand into the palm of the other, Maria stomped off, shaking her feet like a cat that had stepped in water.

The delayed morning dance lesson went well, though Juanita was functioning subconsciously, half asleep, only bolstered with adrenaline from her encounter this morning with Maria. The guests seemed to be pleased and accepting that the delay was just the Latin custom of time being a general concept rather than a specific moment and always being late.

Maria waited at the edge of the pool. She had cleaned her feet and shoes with a hose at the pool. Taking a pool towel she sat wiping her feet and shoes, fuming with anger.

Maria la Gorda took great pride in her shoes. They were Italian pumps with 3-inch heels. Although in her own mind she believed she looked fashionable and stylishly elegant, her heavy torso made her waddle more like a duck than the runway model she imagined herself to be.

As soon as the dance lessons were over and the guests were gone, Maria approached Juanita and escorted her to El Jefe's office. Maria was more agitated than usual. Juanita followed behind her, dreading what might come next.

After shouting instructions to Juanita to sit, Maria went directly into El Jefe's office and slammed the door. Juanita sat waiting. The secretary at the desk averted her eyes, as was usual. This felt different from the routine visits for the sexual gratification of El Jefe. This was an angry meeting with complaints from Maria and suggestions for harsh discipline. Through the door, Maria's animated shrieking was muffled and not understandable, but the tone was telling. Moments of silence would pause Maria's outbursts. These pauses were El Jefe's measured responses or questions on what Maria wanted him to do.

When the tempestuous protest calmed, the door opened. It was El Jefe who opened the door, beckoning Juanita to enter and sit in front of the imposing desk, the desk he had used for his gratifications at Juanita's expense. Maria was seated in a side chair, fuming, but silent.

El Jefe spoke in his broken Spanish. "Maria tells me you have been late and missed your dance lessons many times. She says that you are insubordinate." Not knowing the word for insubordinate in Spanish he stumbled on his words, and said "malo" or bad. "Muy malo. You have been muy malo."

Juanita was exhausted, physically and emotionally, and she was backed into a corner. Sitting in front of the desk, a symbol of her exploitation, she had enough of being abused, berated, and demeaned. Her perturbed mood exceeded her fear. She thought, "I am miserable and pregnant. I do not need to be treated this way."

"You cannot treat me like this! I am pregnant!" she blurted. Then, surprised at her sudden temper, she added, "This is because of you! And you are the father!" she exclaimed with a fierce passion that shocked Maria and El Jefe, but even more herself.

"Calm down, calm down," El Jefe said as he gestured, pushing the air beneath his hands toward the floor. He had to think a bit on how to respond. This was a surprise and now it was El Jefe who was perplexed.

Maria's eyebrows furled and her face turned to look to El Jefe for some direction. Then she lowered her head to look at the floor.

"Well, let's stay calm," he said again.

Silence descended on the room like a dark cloud and the tension was oppressive. El Jefe sat in his chair as if his knees had buckled from underneath him and he held his forehead in his hands for a moment. Then he assumed an upright posture in his chair and looked around the room, avoiding any eye contact with Juanita or Maria.

In what seemed like an hour, El Jefe finally spoke. "Juanita," he said in a tone that was more humble than his usual manner. "It is obvious that you cannot continue to be a dancer or instructor in this way. If you are pregnant, you will need to take care of yourself and the baby you and…" He paused because he could not recall Julio's name. He continued "…the baby you and your husband are having."

Juanita heard, but did not listen. She was still focused on what she had just said and the truth she had spoken, in an outburst, to power.

El Jefe continued, "We are sympathetic to your situation, so we will let you continue to work here and keep your room. But you will be part of our housekeeping staff instead of performing and teaching dance. As time goes by, we will help you and your husband get back to your dancing jobs."

He rose from his chair, and said, "We now understand why you have been such a bad worker at your job since your husband left."

Turning to Maria, he said, "Please make the arrangements," as he motioned towards the door. They were both dismissed.

FIVE

Juanita was relieved to have a new job at the resort. While she would not be the privileged dancer, she thought her new job would allow her to hide within the midst of the working staff. Most lived in the nearby settlement; only a few lived at the resort. She longed for anonymity and promised herself she would be diligent in her duties.

Her maid's uniform hid her growing middle. She cleaned rooms, did laundry, made beds and removed the trash that guests left behind. Her days started early with making beds and daily cleaning. When guests left to return to Havana, the housekeeping staff prepared the rooms for the next arrivals. The work was hard, but honest, and the harassment from El Jefe was diminishing. She always made certain she would smell of cleaners and bleach so El Jefe might be offended by her fragrance.

Occasionally, Julio would send a letter with a tour bus driver, hoping it would get to Juanita. She would answer in the same way. Neither was sure that their letters were received by the other.

In his letters he told her his job at the new resort in the north was keeping him busy. He said his dance partner was not as talented as Juanita, but likeable enough. He assured Juanita of his lasting love and mentioned that he thought his dance partner did not like men. Juanita was happy that he was doing well at the resort, but missed him terribly.

She wanted him back with her but, at the same time, she worried about his return. He knew nothing about her pregnancy or her change of jobs. She had kept El Jefe's indecent abuse from him, and she did not how she could tell any of this to him or how he would react.

The day her baby decided it was time to come, she was working at the laundry. Her water broke and a puddle pooled at her feet. She knew she must go to the hospital. "Call Maria!" she said stoically. "I am going to give birth and need to go to the clinic."

Her labor was long, but the delivery was uneventful. The midwife announced, "Tienes un bebe! It is a boy." In Juanita's eyes, the boy was beautiful. The midwife measured and weighed the little child remarking, "He is a very big boy, and so long too."

Juanita's joy and euphoria crashed when it was clear that it really was El Jefe's child. The timing of Julio's departure, the birth date and the size of her belly during pregnancy were telling. Julio could not have been the father. Since El Jefe was a large man, it followed that his child would be big.

Maria was quick to survey the new baby and look him over. She too suspected El Jefe was the father and nothing about the baby's appearance informed her otherwise.

Maria made arrangements for the birth certificate. She had fixed it for the child to be named Matvey, Russian for "a gift from God", with only his mother's surname, not in the Cuban tradition of the father's name followed by the mother's name. The father would be listed as unknown, "Desconocido" in Spanish, abbreviated "Descon." This designation would follow him throughout his life; Matvey Valdez Descon, a bastard child born from a despicable act.

Juanita was back at her job fairly soon after delivery, sometimes with the baby at her hip, sometimes with the baby cared for by off-duty maids or in a crib in the laundry.

El Jefe now avoided Juanita. If he happened to be in the same area, he would spin and walk away with a deliberate stride. He asked Maria about the child after he was born, but had said nothing since. His sexual harassment of Juanita stopped cold with the birth of his son.

Often Juanita would inquire about Julio, asking Maria or bus drivers who traveled between the two resorts. There was no response to Juanita's questions to Maria about when Julio would be returning to Girón Beach Club Resort. Maria would never answer with anything more than "I will inquire."

It had been several months since she received any information from her husband or about him when one day a letter from Julio arrived. He had written it around the time she had given birth. It was angry and short. He expressed that he knew all about the sordid past, her change of position, her "affair" with El Jefe, and her bastard child. Juanita wondered, "How could he know?"

She had no way to explain to him what the real circumstances of the past year had been. She had postponed telling him anything hoping, when they were together, she could explain everything and he would understand. She knew he would be so mad that he would want to try to do something drastic. She thought that, in person, she would be able to reason with him and keep him from killing El Jefe. She hoped they could start a new life together, somewhere far away, maybe even in Miami. But now, the hope of a better life with Julio by her side was gone.

Julio's letter said he would make a new life in Cayo Cocolobo. The final line said "You are no longer my wife and I will never see you again." Her heart was broken. It was gut-wrenching sorrow, worse than her morning sickness, worse than El Jefe's violations. Her sadness overwhelmed her.

The hungry baby started crying and her maternal instinct distracted her from her sobbing. She looked down on the innocent, beautiful baby that was hers. Tears flowed down her cheeks and dripped on Matvey. She hated where he came from, but loved this child who was totally dependent on her.

SIX

For Juanita, life had not settled into any kind of routine when all of Cuba was turned upside down. News was hard to come by and rumors spread faster than a hurricane wind. What was evident is that something had happened and there was chaos among the people from Russia.

On December 26, 1991, the Soviet Union collapsed. Countries that were once part of the Union of Soviet Socialist Republics became independent and self-governing. Cubans were unprepared for this. News from the government's sources did not give any advance indication of the possibility that the safety net for Cuba was anything but secure. Cubans put aside their usual aversion to Radio Marti, the U.S. radio broadcast of American propaganda, to get some idea of what was happening.

While Cuba was not part of the Soviet Union, the Soviet government had provided so much support to Cuba in exchange for a close military position to spy on the U.S. during the Cold War. Now, there was no more USSR. What would Cuba do? Food, oil, road and building construction, had all been provided by the Soviets. The number of Soviet citizens in Cuba, as well as tourists from bloc countries, enhanced Cuba's government coffers.

Overnight, guests and workers from Soviet bloc countries were suddenly without a passport. The Soviet investments and supplies stopped. Fuel deliveries and projects stopped. Everything Soviet stopped. Confusion on what would happen without Soviet support put Cuba's future in question.

Maria went to El Jefe's office. She was overwhelmed by the commotion and powerless to bully guests from the Soviet bloc countries. Panicked guests were asking her for help to transport them to the Havana airport. Cabs were arriving and the guests were hurriedly exiting without paying their resort tabs. Cuban currency was suddenly more valuable than rubles.

Some guests were just dazed. Some resumed their walks on the beach and lounging poolside, hoping the news was false and this would be sorted out. But most were panicked and desperate to return home.

When Maria entered El Jefe's office, she found him packing, cleaning his desk and putting things into a zippered duffel. He held his engraved nameplate "Ivan Volkov, General Manager" in his hand. He looked surprised when Maria caught him. He had planned to sneak out without notice.

"Maria!" he said in a friendly and welcoming tone. "There have been changes, changes that mean I am no longer the manager. I must leave and return to Moscow to sort out what will happen to the resort."

Maria was stunned that El Jefe would be leaving. She did not know what this would mean for the resort or for her. But he immediately clarified.

"The partnership of the organization I work for and the Cuban authorities will need to be worked out. I will try to keep you informed, but, right now, so much is unknown. So much is uncertain. But, I will be back."

This was El Jefe's biggest bluff. He didn't have any idea what would happen. He only wanted to get the hell out of Cuba and back to the familiar homeland where he could figure out what to do next. In Cuba he was a man without a country. He didn't know if he could travel on his USSR passport, or even get a flight, but he believed getting to Havana was important and he was in the "Siberia of Cuba" on the south coast, near the Zapata Swamp.

"Maria, while I am away, I am counting on you to keep charge of the resort. I'm sure the Cuban authorities will be here to assist you in a transition." This was another bluff. But he saw his words were being well received by Maria.

He used his diplomatic skills to manipulate her further with compliments on how much he depended on her and admired her ability to assist him for so long. Maria was flattered and her anxiety eased a bit.

"El Jefe, it has been my happiness to help you. You have been such a good boss for the resort." She seemed to forget that he had made her complicit in his abuse of the staff, like his liberties with Juanita, among others. Her secret crush on El Jefe and lack of affection from him had made her resent him, but any attention or compliment always tickled her to her core. Now at a time when he was running away, she rationalized a new fantasy that he would return and be so appreciative of her keeping the resort functioning that he might finally notice her.

It was an ambiguity of love and hate. She had been jealous of his affairs, almost wishing he had noticed her. She would have given herself willingly to his advances. She was a toad, but her Prince Charming was never going to kiss her. If he did, she would still be a toad. Now he was leaving and her only path to his favor was to continue being a faithful subordinate in his absence, and hope for his return and appreciation.

Maria called for a resort vehicle and driver to take El Jefe to the airport. He gave her a gentle hug and kissed the top of her head. Closing the car door, he was gone. Maria stood and watched the car exit the palm-lined drive.

Before long, Fidel Castro began to address the Cuban people. In one of his long-winded speeches, he reassured the citizens that Cuba would prosper without the USSR. His angry speeches targeted the U.S. government for any problems Cubans would face and blamed the capitalist West for the sinister demise of the USSR.

The collapse of the USSR sent Cuba into a period of long-suffering, called the "Periodo Especial," officially the "Special Period in the Time of Peace." Cubans were asked to sacrifice as the government tried to reshape supply chains and priorities. Fuel was in short supply as was the availability of food. Cuba was ill-prepared for such a dramatic, sudden change.

This epic event set Cuba on a new path. Although the embargo had been in place, Cuba had been surviving and making progress with USSR support. Though economic schemes and initiatives were announced and embraced, most failed because the government was big on ideas but short on fulfilment. The beneficial results were envisioned but the practical realities doomed successful implementation. Still, the U.S. and the embargo were convenient scapegoats for any internal failures of the government.

The change at Girón Beach Club Resort was immediate. With the majority of guests coming from Russia, the resort was nearly empty. A few Canadians and some South Americans remained. The staff kept up services and adjusted to the new low room count. But there were more staff than guests. Fresh food ran out quickly and the chefs had to improvise with local sources and more traditional Cuban menus. Because food was becoming scarce, more supplies than usual were being stored to assure availability. The Cuban military partners of the resort kept some minimal supplies coming even in the worst of times. Mostly it was supplying the skeleton staff because so few guests were travelling to Cuba. Each day, when the resort served lunch for the small number of guests, enough food was prepared for the staff to also eat. This practice provided them with one good meal, even when they had little to eat with their families at their homes.

For the next years, the resort floundered. It was often empty and, in the off-season, it shut down entirely. Maria kept the resort running. Her indelicate brutish management maintained the resort through the difficult challenges. By her strong will and ability to make the staff find ways to solve problems, the resort limped along. Even when the resort shut down, the small number of staff was employed, just maybe not doing what their in-season jobs were and at lower income because they did not get tips. But they had something to do and one meal a day, at least. Times were difficult for everyone, even Maria.

SEVEN

Because of the changes that occurred from the collapse of the Soviet Union and the rapid disintegration of the Russian safety net, life in Cuba was very difficult. Cuba was without fuel, funds, and friends. Fidel Castro called upon the patriotism of the people to respond to this drastic situation. Daily lies came from government leaders. The national economy had to be reinvented.

Although sometimes there wasn't much to do, Juanita kept cleaning rooms and did her best to raise her son. Meager wages and reduced government rations were not enough. Even though she was lucky to eat the staff meals supplied by the resort and have the staff housing, she had a child and expenses that were not part of the allowances the government provided.

Matvey grew fast and was a precocious boy. His Russian genes made him tower over his shorter Cuban peers. With dirty blonde hair and eyes like green jewels, he stood out. He was smart and intuitive.

While the resort struggled in the years of the Special Period with a minimal workforce, the staff liked the Russian-Cuban child. The resort was a great place for a young boy to grow up. Matvey had the run of the property and the staff had adopted him as a mascot of sorts. The resort workers tolerated his inquisitive mind. He was literally a fair-haired boy, in all circumstances.

The maintenance crew would let him help with tasks and guided him on repairs. The maids pampered him and played games. In the resort kitchen, the cooks mentored him and gave him cookies and pastries fresh from the oven. The stoic office secretary, now Maria's assistant, even showed him how to use the typewriter when Maria was away. Bellhops would have him help with guest luggage. He learned how to play dominoes to pass the time.

As young Matvey grew from toddler to teen, he became a fixture at the resort. The workers tapped him more and more to assist rather than learn. He was a willing helper.

Although he had full run of the resort, Matvey had a few restrictions. He was not to bother the guests, swim in the pool, or play with any children of the tourists. As he grew, the pampering evolved into work responsibilities with the staff. He was a genuine helper called upon to assist with painting, or landscape maintenance, or bussing tables and washing dishes. He became familiar with nearly every aspect of the resort's operation, except, of course, the administration.

At school, he stood out in stature as well as aptitude. His mother guided him in dance and reinforced English lessons.

Nearby Playa Girón was a small settlement where he had a few friends from school. The town was close enough to ride a resort bicycle to see them.

Growing up in an international resort was a privileged life by Cuban standards, especially in the difficult times. While people who were outside of the gates were struggling to survive, the struggles in the resort were not so much to survive but waiting to thrive again, back to the relatively good life they had enjoyed in the past. Access to foreigners was a great opportunity. Even a few dollars in casual tips in foreign currency were important and exceeded the usual subsidy wages.

Juanita wanted to provide the best for her son. Now he was her light and life. When she looked at him with a mother's love, she saw a boy who she had convinced herself was Julio's. It was only when she saw glimpses of El Jefe in his looks or mannerisms that she had a surge of disgust for the memory of his diabolical, biological father.

Maria would watch Matvey grow up as well, although always at a distance. Maria felt that he should have been her son with El Jefe. For this, she held Juanita in contempt. Juanita had stolen this child from her. But the reality was that Maria did not have time for romantic musings of what could have been, so she kept her distance.

Because there were only a few visitors booked at the resort, Juanita was allowed to change her role from cleaning to mingling with guests in the afternoon and, later, return to dance with guests. When a trio of local musicians were playing, she would join them for a song or two. She was no longer the entertainment, only an extra. No matter, the guests were entertained and that pleased Maria.

The older gentlemen who would sit by the pool enjoying a fat cigar and rum would look over this shapely Cuban with her mesmerizing swaying hips and imagine a chance liaison. Juanita would select one and cajole him into joining her to dance. It was always an awkward dance because the partners she selected were fat middle-aged men.

She would take the selected man's hand and pull him up from his seat. The man's mild protestations did not provide him with an escape from Juanita's persistent invitation to dance with her. She would start slow, showing him how to step to a simple salsa. Before long, the man would succumb to the music and the younger dancer and commit to trying. Most often, the man's dancing was not smooth or even remotely in rhythm. But it was fun for him and the few guests who enjoyed the spectacle. Most of the men in the audience felt lucky it was not them who were called to dance with Juanita.

Sometimes this dancing led to an opportunity for Juanita to be invited to have a drink with a guest and, later, be invited to his room. Coyly, but with subtle suggestions that she could exchange her sexual services for money, she would shyly accept the advances of the older gentlemen. She had been already been made to feel like a whore by El Jefe. If using her physical assets could get money, she could endure a sexual liaison where at least she had some control. Sometimes these older men were generous. Most often, their anticipation of such a tryst with a Latin lover culminated prematurely. Juanita was expert in working them up to a frenzy of expectation by slowly undressing and casting over-the-shoulder glances.

Juanita would motion for the man to unzip her dress. She would cross her arms to hold her loose dress close to hide her breasts and then turn, releasing it to the floor. There in her bra and lace underwear she would unbutton his shirt and massage his shoulders. She would guide him to the bed to sit, her breasts at eye level. Pushing her shoulders back, she would sway her bosom slightly, and allow him to touch her. Then with gentle teasing she would undo his belt, before excusing herself to the bathroom, to make him wait at the bedside.

She would return, saying "I hope you won't think bad of me, but you seem so nice and a special man. I want to be with you." His ego would soar. She would unhook her brassiere and place his hands on her firm breasts. Then she would reach to rub the outside of his crotch and slowly lower his zipper. Usually, before his pants had dropped, he was finished. She would hug him tightly and show sympathy for his premature orgasm. After a little more nude hugging, she would get dressed and gently kiss his cheek.

When her slow-motion tease didn't end the encounter before they joined, she would assist the client to unroll a condom and then endure the act as she had done with El Jefe, but with feigned enthusiasm and quiet murmurs of false enjoyment. In her mind, it was simply a means to supplement her income; she was doing it for her son. Most of these clients were generous with ten or twenty dollars. It was not much for an escort in other countries, but it was a fortune in Cuba's economy.

EIGHT

One day, while cleaning a room, Juanita found a diamond earring under a credenza. She sat on the bedside and stared at the sparkling jewel. It was beautiful and so far beyond the reach of a Cuban worker. Cubans could adorn themselves with paste, but a real diamond was unimaginable. Maybe the Castros or a general's wife or girlfriend had diamonds, but never the working people.

She held the earring cupped in her hands, as if it were a fragile egg. She pondered what she should do with it. It was not unusual for the housekeeping staff to find items left behind by guests. Most items were not valuable. Maids would take them to the front desk, never to be seen again. Either the guest returned to claim the item or the family of the desk clerk enjoyed a windfall prize.

Juanita decided a valuable item like a diamond earring should be delivered to Maria. She did not want to be accused of stealing the jewelry, much less have it discovered in her possession.

Timidly, Juanita took her find, neatly folded into a washcloth, to the resort office and asked to see Maria. When she was allowed to enter Maria's office, she said, "Maria, I found this on the floor of room 212. The guests have already left and I was preparing the room for the new arrivals."

Maria unfolded the washcloth in the palm of her hand and her eyebrow lifted. Pinching it between forefinger and thumb, she held it up to the light streaming through her office window. It sparkled in the sun.

"Wow, this is beautiful. Thank you, Juanita, I'll take care of it."

Then, with indifference, Maria opened her desk drawer and dropped it in a small box full of sparkling jewelry, next to a collection of wrist watches. Maria firmly closed the drawer and locked it. Juanita stood frozen for a moment, until Maria reaffirmed, "Thank you. You may go now." This was a direct dismissal from the new La Jefa, Maria la Gorda.

Seeing the treasure chest Maria horded in her desk, Juanita decided that anything she found in the future would not be returned. She decided that this would be another way to increase her income so she could buy things for her son. She could take the valuables to the local Playa Girón craft market and sell them to one of the jewelry makers to be reused in their trade.

She kept the pesos she made from selling the jewelry in a broken guiro, a percussion instrument made from a gourd, that she hung on her wall as a decoration next to a carved crucifix and framed painting of the Virgin Mother. It was as safe a place as she could think to hide something in a studio apartment that was not really private.

Young Matvey always needed something, shoes, or new shirts or pants. He liked to be in dapper clothes. He seemed to carry himself with a superiority reminiscent of his father. She admired how nice he looked when she could find something in the underground merchandise network. Trafficking of goods was common and, if you had money, you could find what was desired. Matvey's stylish clothing added to his distinction among his contemporaries.

Sometimes Matvey would accompany his mother to the craft market when she traded a few of the found necklaces or earrings. He was more interested in the trinkets and multiple paintings of '57 Chevys parked in front of the Floridita Bodega in Havana that were marketed to the tourists. The paintings were all similar. The same scene was painted in different color schemes, most often shown in the day, but sometimes it was a night scene. Still it was all the same image, representing the tourist's vision of Cuba: a famous bar, a cobblestone street, buildings with ornate iron work and, of course, an old American car.

Sometimes he would see his mother making her secret deals. He asked "Momma, what are you doing?"

She answered honestly, "I am selling things that rich people have lost to someone who can use them to make new pretty things. It gives us a little more money to spend for what we need."

Even at his young age he understood the practicality of selling something for money. "That is good, Momma. Can I sell something if I find it?"

"Sí, sí, Matvey if you find something that is lost, then tell me and we will see."

A new pattern developed to meet the challenges of the Special Period and Maria and Matvey accepted their situation and made the best of it.

At a snail's pace, the economy improved as Venezuela became the new patron for Fidel Castro's Cuba. Economic reforms in the country were tapping into the mystique of Cuba as a forbidden-fruit travel destination. Tourists were returning, not so much from the countries in the Soviet realm, but from Canada, the UK and Germany. Even Americans were visiting by navigating through cracks in the travel restrictions of the U.S. embargo. Some people from the exile community, with family still in Cuba, and people involved in religious missions, educational meetings, or humanitarian endeavors could travel to Cuba as long as they had the appropriate documents from the U.S. Treasury Department and traveled within strict guidelines.

In Cuba, changes in the travel policies that Cubans lived under culminated in the lifting of exit restrictions and resulted in the Mariel boat lift. In 1980, thousands of Cubans made their way to U.S. shores. This proved to be a powerful weapon for the regime to show the U.S. they could overwhelm Florida with economic and political refugees and export criminals and spies hidden in the swarm. The U.S. recognized the peril of not engaging Cuba. Behind the scenes, working with Cuban officials, the U.S. changed its immigration policy towards Cubans, giving them a special status to enter the country. Although Cubans could come to the U.S., Americans still had many restrictions for traveling to Cuba, making it virtually impossible for tourists.

The resort was prospering again. Well, not so much prospering, but doing well enough to employ more staff. Maria had formalized her position as General Manager. The room census was increasing. Supply lines had been reestablished. The Ministry of Tourism had surveyed competition in the Caribbean Basin and arranged updates to amenities and menus to keep pace. The intangible attraction for tourists was the changes in Cuba's natural beauty and vibrant culture. With an aging Castro, Cuba drew guests who wanted to see the island before it changed. It was ironic that the nostalgia tourists were seeking was a factor in changing the very thing they were hoping to experience, "the real Cuba."

Juanita continued working at her job and side-line escort liaisons. She still pined for Julio and sometimes revisited her past memories with melancholy. Her son became her surrogate for Julio. She taught him to dance to acceptable proficiency. Evenings, she and Matvey spent time together practicing the old choreography of the routines she and Julio used to entertain guests.

It was special for Matvey and Juanita to visit the poolside deck to dance to the live band. Their productions always entertained the guests and often was applauded at the conclusion. The audience applause was rewarded with an encore solo dance by Juanita of a vintage routine. In the background Maria would observe tacitly, with jealous admiration, only to depart in frustration.

Dancing at the age of 5, Matvey was a cute performer. At 10, he was skilled enough to be entertaining. As a teen, he grew to be a credible dance partner, growing to dance expertly with his mother.

Juanita was euphoric after dancing with her son in front of an audience. It was heartening for her to be entertaining in front of guests instead of cleaning their toilets or escorting old fat men. For a moment, she would be lost in a past that would never return.

One evening, in the subdued light of approaching nightfall, Juanita was performing with Matvey in a practiced routine. The band was playing the familiar salsa. Matvey was on point with his part. The audience was enjoying the dance. But something was off.

Juanita first missed a few steps and faltered. She fell into Matvey's arms as her legs collapsed underneath her and her body went limp. Matvey lifted her up and carried her to a lounge chair by the pool. The band stopped playing and the emcee called out for a doctor. Juanita had fainted and was slurring her speech, disoriented and making no sense. She even confused Matvey with her long-departed Julio. In a few minutes, she was alert again, although too tired to resume dancing.

The staff nurse at Girón Beach Club Resort had her sip some orange juice and suggested taking her to the hospital. Initially, the diagnosis was exhaustion and dehydration.

The hospital admitted her for observation and recovery. She was in a large ward populated with patients with a variety of maladies, from heart attacks to trauma. The medical personnel were attentive but the ward was busy and not restful, with the constant activity of patient care for so many patients in the same room. After a couple of days, she just wanted to go to her familiar apartment to recuperate. She felt fine, just a bit tired. She returned to Girón Beach Club Resort to rest.

The doctors prescribed some medicines and rest for a week, with slow resumption of her duties. They told her, "You have had a mini-stroke. It is a TIA, a transient ischemic attack. Sometimes this happens when you have a weak blood vessel or blockage in your veins in your brain. It may be nothing and you are not showing any lasting damage. So, just take it easy and maybe change your diet to avoid fatty foods."

Matvey hovered over his mother for the next few weeks, diligent in her care and obsessive about her diet. Gradually he lightened up to give in to his mother's protestations.

"Matvey! I am your mother! You are the child. You are not the doctor, and I am fine!" Slowly, life went back to the normal day-to-day routines and Juanita was able to resume her maid duties and even an occasional tryst with a gentleman.

Most Cubans lived in the society they inherited, peacefully and capably building the best lives they could within the constraints of their circumstance. The Revolution had overturned a corrupt system, wrought with social and economic inequities and promised a better life and fair system.

The challenges of the new system and being victims of international political machinations were beyond what the ordinary Cuban had any control over. Having the USSR's support brought some positive changes during the early days of the new government. Retribution by petty minions and repression of dissent created a compliant social structure. Reforms brought many good things that Cubans had not had, such as education, healthcare, and a more level hierarchy of social status. Those who could not adjust, were fearful of Communist control, or had been part of the abuses of the previous government, fled as refugees to the U.S., leaving behind their assets and privileged lives. Government seizure of property and businesses were a heavy penalty. For many, the prospect of staying in Cuba was far worse than starting over with nothing in a new country.

Cuban society bred innovation and creativity among the people. For those growing up under the revolutionary government, life became normal. The U.S. embargo and local propaganda made for an insular society with little real understanding that life in other countries was not the same as life in Cuba.

While separate underground markets developed and Cubans navigated the strictures of the central government control, they survived and lived honest, normal lives, albeit at a slower pace than other countries. Unlike the turmoil and volatility of other Latin American or Caribbean nations, Fidel Castro brought stability, if not prosperity. The regime was still supported by many die-hard Communists and endured by others who were stoic, complacent, or fatalistic. Cuba was their home and any other possibility was unimaginable.

When Matvey completed high school, he was sent to a compulsory camp to work for the Revolution. These camps, for all young men and women, were scattered throughout the island and designed to teach the value of hard labor and equality. Some were in factories; some were on farms, and many were in the sugar cane fields. The work was hard and the reinforcement of the doctrine of the Revolution was ever present. After completing the service to the government, young adults could resume a life in the jobs that were offered when their qualifications matched the work opportunities.

Some were selected for higher education and would go to university or technical schools. Most joined the workforce in labor or trades. Matvey hoped he could go to university to study international affairs, or perhaps something that would fit with the emerging tourism economy. He was comfortable with foreigners and familiar with the operation of the resort. He had wide experience at Girón Beach Club Resort, working to help in many areas from food service to maintenance and even the cabanas. Yes, tourism would be good and not hard like the labor in the fields at the farm.

Matvey was working at an agricultural project in a camp in the south of the island. It was hard labor to work in the sugarcane fields to do his service. The new experience was fun, even though the work was difficult and dirty. Living in a community of other young people was interesting. Except for school, Matvey didn't have much association with people his own age. In the camp, he was among peers and on his own.

He was doing well and was day-dreaming about being selected for university to pursue a career in tourism. On one particularly hot day, with the sun beating down on his blond head, he was in the field loading a truck when a van from the resort drove up, parking behind one of the co-op's trucks.

The farm supervisor got out of the truck and met the driver of the resort's van. After a brief conversation they both walked toward Matvey. Matvey recognized the van driver and smiled. When the driver did not return the smile, but looked down at the ground, Matvey suspected something was wrong.

The driver said solemnly, "Matvey, it is your mother. She has died. I am so sorry." Matvey was stunned. "What?"

The driver said, "Your mother collapsed at the resort and was taken to the hospital, but there was nothing the doctors could do. It was her brain. I am so sorry," he repeated. Matvey's knees buckled and his legs went out from under him. He sat on the dirt in disbelief.

The driver and camp supervisor helped him up to his feet. In a sympathetic tone, the driver told Matvey, "Maria sent me to get you so you could return to Girón Beach Club Resort to make final arrangements for your mother."

Matvey felt very alone and confused. He loved his mother and he expected that he would see her when his service was over. Now, she was gone. Now he thought of a future when he really would be on his own, and alone without his mother. What would he do without her? His closest family were workers at the resort and not relatives. He had no other family.

When they got in the van for the trip back to Girón, the driver expressed his sympathy again. Matvey thanked him, but said "I really don't want to talk about this. Can we travel in silence?"

The driver nodded, and replied. "I understand. I am sorry for your loss. Everyone loved your mother." Then he kept quiet, focused only on driving.

The route back to Girón climbed up through the mountains. Through some breaks in the trees, he could see for miles. The beautiful vista of rolling hills descending to the ocean was breathtaking. Matvey became emotional when he thought of his mother, wishing she could be there to see this view with him. They had never travelled far from Girón, only the occasional trip to Cienfuegos and one visit to Havana. He remembered when they visited Havana and met Juanita's dance instructors and saw a ballet.

Matvey sat quietly all the way back to Girón. As he stared into space, he resolved that he would survive. He must find a way to go on without her.

NINE

Evelyn gave a side glance to the security guard at the Cuban National Archives. Professor Yolanda Lopez-Ballar was her escort to review documents in the artist registry.

The Professor showed her credentials to the security guard and gestured to Evelyn to walk through the metal detector and allow inspection of her purse and portfolio.

Evelyn Kaye Griffin was in Havana on one of her many trips to the country. As an art history professor at a London university, she was able to travel to Cuba, unrestricted by the U.S. embargo. Her professorship was the culmination of a stellar educational path. From her undergraduate degrees in international studies and art history, she obtained an MFA, followed closely with an art history doctorate in Comparison of Pre- and Post-revolutionary Cuban art. She was a rising star in the world of fine art.

As if her academic credentials were not enough, she was strikingly beautiful. Tall and slender with curly, shoulder-length blonde hair, she could fashion herself to be casual and free-spirited or elegantly sophisticated. She used her physical prowess to charm the artists and dealers in the high-art world. Armed with an engaging personality, she knew when to use her wiles and when to use her wit. Her social status in London was the legacy of an upper-crust family.

By contrast, Yolanda was well-dressed in professional business attire befitting a university professor. Cobbling together her wardrobe from the limited clothing stores in Havana, she made a very presentable appearance. Throughout the Caribbean, professionals take their appearance seriously and are more formally dressed than their U.S. counterparts. Although she was taller than many Cuban women, maybe 5'6", she was half-a-head shorter than Evelyn's 5'10" frame. Her dark curly hair was pulled back into a bun and held with a hand-carved barrette.

She had studied hard in school and made her way from rural Cuba to the capital city of Havana. Her parents were sugarcane workers in a small community east of Havana. The Cuban Revolution provided the opportunity for her to move ahead with higher education. As a student in elementary school in 1959 she was eager to be part of the new racial equality and educational opportunities promised by Fidel Castro. It no longer mattered that she was mulatta, born into the cane field working class. Upon graduating from high school, she travelled to Havana, leaving behind the cane fields to study art history at the university. Though still very close to her family, she was in a different world from her parents.

Happy to have been assigned to chaperone the English professor, it was a perk for Yolanda that would carry some weight with the colleagues in her department. She was a little surprised that she and Evelyn were both about the same age. She expected someone older, and maybe more matronly, like the Queen of England. This was her perception of the British, staid and stuffy.

Evelyn had visited Cuba many times. This visit was primarily to do post-doctoral research on pre- and post-Revolution art and artists. On previous visits she was a tour director for her students and associates who wanted to experience Cuban art and culture. Having the assistance of the professor was essential to getting into the archival records for her research. Many records were lost after the Revolution in an overreaction to devalue and discredit art that had only a decorative purpose. Post-Revolution art needed to be meaningful and have relevance to the human story of the Revolution. Decorative art was seen as trivial, while art glorifying the wealthy was anti-revolutionary and sometimes confiscated.

As the two art historians walked through the marble-floored halls, Evelyn's high heels made loud clacks that resonated through the hall. The marble floors reflected the light glaring through large windows and skylights in the tall ceilings. Simple incandescent bulbs in the vintage chandeliers provided barely enough illumination.

When Evelyn's eyes adjusted to the interior, she noted the space was more like a cathedral than a government building, which was a vestige of the past when Cuba emulated the architecture of the United States. Even the Cuban Capitol in Havana mirrored the architecture of the U.S. Capitol.

On her frequent trips to Old Havana, Evelyn pointed out to her charges that the architecture of the historic city is clearly Spanish, but outside the central city the mix of styles tells the story of the history of Cuba. The influences of Spanish colonialism, North American art deco aesthetics, and the functional, sterile Russian box vernacular are evident throughout Havana. Newer structures, built by investors outside the sphere of influence of the American embargo, are as modern as any major city. She drew attention to the fact that nearly all smaller homes and businesses are in disrepair, evidencing the deteriorating effect of the embargo. Like the economy, buildings were crumbling because it was difficult for individuals to take care of their homes, either from the lack of money or the lack of materials. So, once-lovely homes reveal sad neglect.

Evelyn and the professor descended together down wide granite stairs bordered with ornate metal railings. Illuminated only by chandeliers, the lower floor was dimmer than the entrance. Professor Ballar opened the enormous wood door to one of the archive rooms that housed a collection of confiscated art. She oriented Evelyn to a section that might contain works within her field of interest. Evelyn wasn't allowed to take photos of the works without permission, only notes and visual descriptions under the direct supervision of the professor. Yolanda took her role seriously, attentively shadowing Evelyn's exploration of vintage works. She defended the purposes of confinement of inappropriate art.

Curators entered the room on some pretense to see what the mysterious English art researcher was doing. Each time the curious workers opened the door, creaking hinges would screech and echo though the archive. It was unprecedented to see such an elegantly dressed foreigner, looking more like a fashion model than art history academic, in the restricted areas of the archive. Evelyn took extra effort to be well appointed for her visits to the archive. She wanted to stand out and be noticed, hoping her deportment would gain some deference as a person of importance by the staff.

Evelyn carefully looked through the flat files of canvases and art boards. Some framed works were hung on hinged wire grates which she turned like pages of a huge book. Sometimes she paused, took notes of the subject, artist, date and wrote a description of the work.

Evelyn appreciated the company and the expertise that Yolanda provided. Holding one work in her cotton gloved hands, she remarked, "Isn't this one wonderfully colorful?" It was a portrait of a young couple sitting in an elegant carriage, attended by a host of servants.

Yolanda responded, "The artist's rendering is stiff but it shows excellent draftsmanship. Clearly this work shows the exploitation of the common working people – so many servants virtually enslaved by these rich young people of privilege."

That is exactly what the art revealed, a portrait of wealthy elite and the workers who were serving their elegant life. The gentleman was portrayed attired in an embroidered guayabera and his lady was wearing a flowing white dress and silk shawl. Like the horse connected to the carriage, the workers were painted in deft realism but without expression, as if their souls were absent in the presence of the happy couple, who were shown to be delightfully happy in each other's company, indifferent or unaware of the supporting entourage. It was dated 1951 but might as well have been painted a century before, in colonial times.

Whenever Evelyn pointed out a work of pre-Revolution art the professor revealed her interpretation of why the art was glorifying values that were not consistent with the Revolution. This repeated every time Evelyn presented a work for comment. It became routine.

Evelyn sometimes found a piece of art that represented average people engaged in working scenes. In these instances, Yolanda would concede that the art might be suitable for exhibit or included in the collection of Cuban art, but noted that perhaps the artist was an enemy of the Revolution.

Each time Evelyn visited the archive it was the same experience with Yolanda and the pre-Revolution art incarcerated in the archives. She was pleased the art was being conserved but sad the work would never hang in a gallery.

The post-Revolution archives were different. In this department, the works depict political themes with vivid energy and colors. Even the art showing the hard labors or squalid conditions of workers was seen to have a message that served the communist narrative. Unlike the sequestered pre-Revolution works, this art might see the light of day hanging in a museum.

Evelyn's research on pre- and post-Revolution art was the main reason she was afforded concessions to visit the archives and permitted to travel throughout Cuba. The prestige of having a scholar from England was respected by the conservators and curators. Authorities granted her permission to conduct her research throughout the island.

Cut off from exchange with U.S. institutions, the curators and scholars in art fields enjoyed the interaction with someone from outside Cuba. Since the Revolution, the museums and art galleries had become more insular. Cuban staff wanted connection and respect from professional peers in the world from which they had been excluded.

Being fluent in the proper Castilian version of Spanish, Evelyn was able to engage with the people she met. Her accent gave her an air of pompous authority in conversing with academics. Sometimes her distinct pronunciations were foreign to the Cuban ear, but understandable, even if amusingly formal.

On this trip, Evelyn spent a week in Havana, visiting the archives daily. On each of her trips to Cuba, she stayed at the Hotel Nacional de Cuba. Located on Taganana Hill, the Hotel Nacional is an imposing structure with 8 floors and over 450 rooms and suites. It was built on the edge of the sea in the Vedado district of Havana with views of both the city and the ocean. In fact, its architecture provides nearly all of the rooms with ocean views.

Built in 1930, the hotel's construction reflects a hybrid of styles, including Art Deco, Sevillan, Moorish and Roman. It is a grand relic of the past, an artifact in itself, having housed many famous personalities and royalty from around the world. Pre-Revolution visitors included performers, such as Eartha Kitt, Nat King Cole, and Frank Sinatra, among others. Ernest Hemingway, Marlon Brando, Mickey Mantle, and John Wayne also signed the guest book. In the mid-1940s the mob used the Hotel Nacional and even built a large casino in the hotel that was very popular.

After the Revolution, the hotel experienced a decline. But, when the Soviets pulled out of Cuba, the government realized that the Hotel Nacional would be an asset in bringing tourists to the country. Although the casino was removed, the hotel was restored to its former grandeur. While Evelyn preferred less formal and stuffy accommodations, it was important for her to maintain her aloof superiority with her Cuban peers.

At the conclusion of her week in Havana, Evelyn invited Yolanda to dinner at the Café del Oriente on the Plaza of San Francisco. "I would like to take you out for a nice dinner in appreciation of your kindness and assistance. Can we meet at 7?"

The Café del Oriente is an elegant restaurant that mostly serves foreign tourists and some upper-class Cubans. Yolanda had only been there once, to attend a luncheon for an international cultural meeting funded by UNESCO. It had been a special treat to participate in such an extravagant luncheon with foods, including beef, that she never imagined existed in the "Special Period".

As the two women stepped inside the door, they were greeted by a tuxedoed maître d'. He showed them to a table and pulled out their chairs. A female vocalist accompanied by a virtuoso piano player provided ambiance to fill the room. Ironed table clothes and napkins, polished silver, delicate porcelain place settings, and a vase of fresh flowers were set at the table. A wine steward appeared to ask, "May I offer you ladies wine or perhaps call a cocktail waitress for you?"

Yolanda felt out of her element. She was a brilliant art historian and familiar with art openings and receptions, but fine dining was not in her experience. Evelyn looked at the wine list and suggested a bottle of red, "Would this be agreeable to you?" she asked. Yolanda nodded. Anything was going to be fine, she would go along with whatever and follow Evelyn's lead.

Returning to the table with the selected bottle of wine, the steward went through the ritual of popping the cork and offering a sample to test, deftly swirling the wine as he poured it into sparkling glasses. The women toasted their collaboration and work. Yolanda asked, "Did you get what you needed at the archive?"

"Oh yes, but there is so much more to review. I hope I will be able to come again and resume research on your collections," Evelyn responded, as she sipped her wine and contemplated the menu.

"What will you do now? What are your plans?" Yolanda was genuinely curious about Evelyn's itinerary in Cuba.

"I plan to travel a bit – Jagüey Grande, Cienfuegos, Camagüey, and especially Baracoa, in the east. I am checking into new places to take my art history students to see Cuban art."

Evelyn added, "I would like your help. Do you know of emerging Cuban artists who might be willing to sell their works? I'd like to help Cuban artists by taking some of their work to London or New York to introduce the art community to the remarkable talent you have here."

Yolanda sipped her wine and smiled in approval.

Continuing, Evelyn said, "I will need to make arrangements for legal export. I already do a similar thing for some artists I know in Port au Prince. The Haitian art is very well received and I have collectors for their work waiting for me to bring new works after each trip to the Caribbean. I think that importing art is not prohibited by the U.S. embargo and it should be no problem for England."

Yolanda didn't know what the rules were about exporting Cuban art, but said she would check. "Oh, thank you so much", Evelyn replied, in an exaggerated, pleasant sorority-girl tone. Evelyn was already an expert in exporting paintings, but she wanted to make Yolanda feel her advice was needed.

They continued to have a wonderful dinner and conversation at the Café del Oriente. When the check came, Yolanda glimpsed at the total. It was more than half a year's salary! Evelyn pulled out a small Texas Instruments calculator from her purse and did a conversion from pesos to pounds and then counted out her notes to the nearest round figure.

The maître d' collected the money and Evelyn waved him off, "No change is necessary. Thank you."

The two colleagues walked out to the street where Evelyn would take a cab back to the Hotel Nacional and Yolanda would walk to her apartment in the old city. After a week of professional stand-offishness and formality, Yolanda and Evelyn hugged warmly. "Hasta luego," Evelyn said and Yolanda responded "Hugs, until we meet again."

The next morning, as Evelyn prepared to leave Havana, she had a list of artists waiting for her at the hotel desk. Yolanda had quickly assembled a list of artists in the cities she thought Evelyn would be visiting.

A few days earlier, Evelyn had made arrangements for a rental car and hired a driver who would take her to the more remote areas of the country to search for art and do reconnaissance for tour accommodations in parts of the country she had not taken tours to before. The driver would take her on a ten-day excursion from Havana to Baracoa and back, stopping each night in a different place.

For the past several years, Evelyn led a tour of Cuba for her students and art patrons from the UK to visit galleries and explore the art and architecture of Cuba. She had honed an itinerary to the point that it was a routine schedule. At first it was a hard task fraught with logistical challenges of arranging meals and accommodations and babysitting neophyte travelers in a third world country. Now that the details had been worked out, it was easier.

When traveling to communities outside of Havana, she encouraged her students and tour clients to look for vintage works of art. Her students were her scouts for prospective paintings to purchase. The casas particulares where they would stay were often decorated with portraits and landscapes that predated the Revolution. Many of the homes that had been modified to be a bed and breakfast were formerly well-appointed homes that exiles had abandoned when they fled Cuba in the cacophony of the Revolution. Their art and furnishings were left behind. The new occupants who had assumed the residences conserved the trappings of the original wealthy owners. The art and furnishings remained in these homes and were used in decorating the bed and breakfast accommodations.

When Evelyn learned of the artwork found by her students and tour clients she made careful notes. Then, later, she visited the homes to evaluate the art. She asked the owner if they would consider selling the work and offered a modest sum that seemed a fortune to the cash-strapped Cubans. Because there could be a concern about how the bed and breakfast owner would replace a missing painting, Evelyn brought her portfolio case with her and allowed the owner to select a replacement from the art she had purchased from emerging artists.

In addition to her research, Evelyn wanted to purchase post-Revolution art on this trip, some to sell in galleries, but, more importantly, she wanted to have a selection of works available to replace the vintage art she would take from the historic homes. Evelyn had a pretty good sense of what was saleable in galleries and an encyclopedic knowledge of late 19th and early 20th century Spanish and Italian artists that wealthy Cubans were likely to have in their homes. If these art works were restorable, saleable, and the correct size for exporting, she negotiated a deal.

The driver arrived at the Hotel Nacional in a small mini-van. Parked under the portico, he held a card with her name on it so she would be able to locate him. Actually, the car was so much smaller than a mini-van; it was a micro-van, looking new, but alien to Evelyn's experience. It was like nothing she had seen before in the U.S. or Europe.

She asked the driver, "What kind of car is this?" Ricardo, the driver, beamed as he said that it was a new Chinese van. Evelyn decided there was no point in calling the tour agency to arrange for something else and rationalized that at least this car was new and would have air conditioning. She hoped it would be more reliable than the 1950s clunkers that fumed and sputtered down the roads. Ricardo insisted that she sit in the back seat, which was fine with Evelyn.

They began their journey from the hotel cruising down the Malecón to wind their way to the national highway. Driving through Havana, the historic city had much construction underway. A special initiative used tourism dollars generated in the historic district for repairs and restoration in other parts of Havana. The austere Soviet-era high-rises were vertical hovels, without air conditioning and windows removed for ventilation. Outside the historic district, Havana could not hide twenty years of struggle and neglect, lack of funds and lack of materials due to the U.S. sanctions. The city was crumbling. Once grand structures were mere shells of their former glory. Houses needed repair and paint. Desperate families resorted to using window frames and shutters for fuel to cook. Balusters were broken. Roads were more potholes than asphalt. The Special Period severely stressed the island nation and its people. A decade later, Cuba was crawling back, slowly. Using UNESCO grant funds and money generated from tourism, the Old City was making strides in restoration and bustling with tourists navigating the construction. City squares were clean and manicured.

As Evelyn and her driver drove on the Malecón, they passed lovers strolling the broad sidewalk, young people sitting atop the wide seawall, and a few fishermen. The driver turned at the Plaza of the Revolution, past tributes to the Revolution glorifying the heroes - Fidel Castro and Che Guevara, as well as José Martí, who is beloved to all Cubans.

He drove through the city instead of taking the tunnel under the entrance to the harbor at the fort.

Once the driver was on the outskirts of the urban area of Havana, the landscape transitioned to rural lands, orchards, pastures, and fallow fields. As they traveled through the countryside, traffic was light and the road was better. Smog belched from the old pre-1960 antique cars. Occasionally a modern small tourist bus would pass by with a load of guests on a prearranged cultural exchange tour.

As they drove the highway toward the south, Evelyn saw aggregations of Cubans at bus stops and walking along the verge of the road. People would step into the street, with their thumbs out to beg a ride. Transportation was still limited. There were not many private cars on the road as fuel was scarce and expensive. Tourist cars and tourist buses would never stop to offer a ride to the hitchhikers.

Though things were slowly getting better after the Special Period, hitchhiking was still a routine way to get around. Sometimes empty work trucks stopped and their beds filled with riders. Instead of building materials, these trucks hauled the human capital that was keeping Cuba alive. There were many people waiting for a ride. Some were walking toward their distant destinations. With their journey's end so far away, their only hope was a vehicle that would stop, but still they walked. This was a scene that Evelyn observed on each of her trips. She never got used to it. While it would bother her, she looked away and distracted herself with her own interests. Evelyn was apart from this humanity.

On their way to a hotel at Jagüey Grande, Evelyn asked the driver to stop at a studio of one of the artists Yolanda had listed. The door was open. She knocked on the door frame as she walked into a dimly lit room crowded with stacked canvases. From a back room, she heard "Hola, can I help you?" A small thin man with a dark leathery complexion emerged and met her at the front door. He wore a tattered t-shirt, streaked with paint smears, cut-off shorts and sandals.

Evelyn said, "Buenos dias, Señor, I am Professor Evelyn Griffin, from a university in London England. I would like to see your work. My professor friend in Havana, Dr. Yolanda Ballar, said I should look at your paintings."

The artist smiled and said, "Of course, it is my pleasure. My name is Ernesto and I know Yolanda. It is very nice of her to have told you about me." Then, waving his arm toward the door, he graciously led her to his studio where he had an oil in progress.

Smelling of linseed oil, the room was a clutter of paints surrounding his easel and a collection of containers with brushes of various shapes. He had a canvas in progress and a couple laid to the side, awaiting finishing.

Ernesto then guided her to the back room. He had a surprisingly large inventory of canvases. Clearly, he was talented. He worked across several different styles. His depictions of people were evocative of their daily lives in the mundane burden of living; paintings of farmers working their gardens, children playing, women preparing meals, old people playing dominoes. His landscapes were not merely beautiful scenes, but reflections of how the land was transformed by Cuban resourcefulness in response to the lack of materials and deterioration of time.

Because the back room was lit by a single light bulb hanging from a wire, Evelyn asked him to bring several paintings out into better light. Ernesto took the paintings and spanked them with a rag to beat away the dust and then gently wiped the face. In better light, she could evaluate what might be marketable in galleries in New York or London.

Evelyn looked at the canvases he was bringing to her, thinking that a couple would fit the requirements of size and merchantability. When her visit was concluded, for 100 pounds she had three paintings that would easily fetch several thousand dollars each when hyped in a New York or London gallery. Ernesto was very happy to have the money. She returned to the micro-van with the wrapped paintings and Ricardo packed them in the back of the van.

After staying in Jagüey Grande, they moved on to Santa Clara, the port city of Cienfuegos, and stopped briefly in the historic city of Trinidad. In each city, she stayed in casas particulars that were different from those used on her tours. She paid for Ricardo's accommodations in a separate casa particular affording her the opportunity to look at the art in two homes. She also asked around the city to see the interiors of historic homes that offered rooms for tourists.

In Trinidad, she found only one vintage work by a lesser-known early 20th century Italian artist. She made a good purchase at a reasonable price and did not have to trade a new work for it. Perhaps she would have better luck in Camagüey or Holguin. It was a slow process to find the art. It depended on referrals and a little luck. Still there was so much treasure hanging on the walls of these old homes. Her scheme was profitable, if illegal.

Sometimes news of Evelyn's interest in art spread fast within communities and people would bring paintings to where she was staying. This was problematic because it attracted too much attention and her side business of buying vintage art required discretion. She did not want to attract the interest of cultural antiquities authorities.

Her usual method was to merge the vintage works with a variety of contemporary works and package them for transit to Haiti. Most of the time, she arranged for shipment from Santiago de Cuba to Port au Prince, Haiti. Her contact at a framing store in Haiti would wait to meet the cargo ship. The export documents always listed the contemporary post-Revolution Cuban art and was accurate in description and numbers. The only omissions were dates of the valuable antique pieces. This was an intentional mistake but arguably a technical oversight if ever caught and found in violation of Cuba's export rules.

Once the cargo was in Haiti, the framer, Jean-Pierre Gladstone, would laminate the vintage art work to contemporary Haitian art and fill out the export forms to ship the combined Cuban and Haitian art to a gallery in New York City or London. This scheme had worked a dozen times. The seal of the Haitian authorities on the shipment facilitated export. The contents cleared customs as, often, the concern of inspectors was drugs and agricultural pests, not the legitimacy of art or antiquities. Any package opened by officials revealed only Haitian art and most of the inspectors were probably not art historians or connoisseurs.

Jean-Pierre had met Evelyn while studying in England and they began a fast friendship. After his couple years at the university, he returned to Haiti and established a frame shop business because there was no money in selling his art, and his education was insufficient for a college teaching position.

Years ago, Evelyn had a brief fling with buying and selling Haitian art but found that did not bring high values. Travel in Haiti became too difficult and dangerous. Cuba was a fertile field.

Both Jean-Pierre and Evelyn were careful to pay all duties and make sure the shipment was sealed with the approval of Haitian Customs and Antiquities. The officials at the cultural ministry were so pleased to have Haitian art being exported and artists getting paid for their works. They were helpful to Gladstone and rarely even looked at the art.

The galleries in New York or London would unpackage the shipment, separate the valuable Cuban art from the packaging, culling the Haitian art for sale to secondary markets, and select framing for the new Cuban works. When sufficient inventory was assembled, the gallery would publish a catalog and promote a show of emerging Cuban artists with ample hype about the recognition and benefit to the Cuban artists, who might get some recognition but never share in proper compensation for their talents.

The vintage work was the genuine value in Evelyn's illicit smuggling. She would get a substantial commission from the galleries she worked with. It was a low-profile operation, with little chance of the paintings being discovered as art from Cuba.

Evelyn's expertise was the key to providing art that would sell for from $10,000 to low six figures. More valuable art would attract too much attention in the art world. Her small network of art dealers had ready customers, who were more concerned with having vintage art from known artists than provenance. Everyone involved made a lot of money, except, of course, the Cubans or the original owners who left their paintings behind when they departed Cuba.

TEN

Evelyn returned to Havana to lead another tour with her students and art patrons. The group arrived at José Martí International Airport. She greeted them as they exited the airport and got them loaded onto a tour bus and then settled into a hotel. She and the group visited a gallery of modern art as well as other notable art museums in Havana. As was usual on her tours, she included time in Havana's historic city for the tour participants to explore and enjoy. Then, she repeated her usual tour route from Havana to Baracoa with an overnight stop in Camagüey. Baracoa was promoted as the art capital of Cuba and it was a beautiful place to culminate her tour.

After completing the tour, she made sure her group made it to the airport in Baracoa for their commuter flight back to Havana. She made sure they knew how to get to their flight back to London leaving from the international terminal at the José Marti International Airport, answering their questions about customs and logistics. She always had a sense of relief when she saw the plane take off. Back on her own, it was a long trip back to Havana as she preferred to ride back to Havana in the tour bus. She liked the time alone to decompress and work on her laptop.

Once back in Havana she wanted to visit the national archives and meet with Yolanda again. When she arrived, she broke with her usual protocol and decided to stay in the old city, La Habana Vieja, rather than the Hotel Nacional. She selected a historic hotel close to where the former U.S. embassy had been. Now the former embassy building, located on the Plaza de Las Armas, was a museum of natural history. The plaza courtyard was an impeccably maintained garden.

Street troubadours, wearing well-worn straw hats, wandered the plaza costumed in traditional outfits, playing the guitar, Cuban tres, and claves, and singing *Guantanamera* to every person they saw who looked foreign. A young child, carrying a rusty coffee can for tips, approached the tourists and stared up at them with big brown eyes, waiting for a contribution. The musicians would serenade a tourist until they were successful in getting a tip or spotted a new mark. Their busking was persistent. If someone dropped a coin into the can, the child retrieved it and politely handed it back saying "No metal, please. No metal." This wasn't because the value of a quarter wasn't significant in the exchange rate, but because there was no mechanism for turning coins into useable currency. Only U.S. or Canadian dollars or British pounds were useful.

This public entertainment was successful for the street buskers. The highest paid professional worker might make

$25 a month in salary, but street performers could make a dollar, two or more in just an hour. Splitting a hundred dollars a week between the musicians still resulted in far more than government employment produced. It was a profitable alternative that required knowing only three chords and the lyrics of José Martí's unofficial anthem of the country, *Guantanamera*. Some of the buskers were classically trained musicians who found being a street musician was more lucrative than employment.

Evelyn checked into the Hotel Santa Isabel. She was impressed by the wide staircases and tall mahogany doors that opened to spacious rooms. The amenities provided by the hotel were as elegant as those at the Hotel Nacional.

On the evening of her return to Havana, Yolanda came to the hotel to meet Evelyn. It was a reunion celebration. Yolanda greeted her with such warmth and affection, it was like Evelyn was a long-lost best friend. Though they had only one casual dinner together at the Café del Oriente ten days ago, Yolanda was enthusiastic and affectionate. Evelyn thought for a minute that she might have broken through Yolanda's professional aloofness to be accepted as a genuine friend and colleague.

Yolanda was excited to see Evelyn. "How long will you be here? We must go to the symphony. Do you have time to go to the fort at the harbor? There is a new exhibit opening at the Ministry of Culture. Can you attend?" Pausing for a breath, she continued, "When can you come to see the archive?" A flurry of questions and plans for Evelyn's time were streaming at her faster than she could respond.

Evelyn said, "Let's go to the courtyard bar and sit with a glass of wine and catch up." They seated themselves in the lush tropical landscaping of the hotel's centrally-located marble-tiled courtyard. Three tiers of arched hallways towered above the patio and royal palms in large planters at each corner reached for the clouds. In the open-air courtyard, the sky was a cerulean blue with glowing yellow-orange-tinged clouds drifting by.

Evelyn asked Yolanda if she could visit the archive again for several more days of research. "Of course. We can arrange that," Yolanda agreed. "I have many more things to show you there."

The most important thing for Evelyn was to schedule another visit to the archives to fill in some details of her research. After that, it would be nice to spend some time enjoying Havana with Yolanda. She appreciated the invitations, saying, "Thank you, Yolanda, for inviting me. I feel that it is a more enriching experience when a local person helps guide you through a place rather than being self-directed or on a guided tour." Evelyn would be a participant in the culture rather than an observer.

Evelyn was tired after the long 15-hour ride back from Baracoa. The bus driver had been a dolt, and the conversation was simplistic, but mostly he was quiet. They had little in common and he was not useful to Evelyn in discovering new places for her to search for art.

After a couple glasses of wine, Evelyn found a moment to signal that she was tired and needed to bathe and then sleep. They agreed to meet at the archives in the morning. With a warm hug, Yolanda departed, happy that she had met Evelyn again.

The next few days viewing the collections were more relaxed than her earlier visits. Yolanda was less defensive of the sequestered art and the conversation was enjoyable. Sometimes it drifted from art to life and family. Evelyn learned more about Yolanda's life away from the archives than she shared of her own life.

Researching the art works was still the main focus. For her professional credibility and to maintain her prominence as an expert, it was important for Evelyn to do research and publish. After each visit to the country, she would have new material to lecture about. It was also her cover for frequent trips to Cuba, providing her with the opportunity to mine the treasures of new and old art for her gallery clients and her own financial benefit.

There were times when Yolanda was called away for a few minutes. She trusted Evelyn enough to leave her unattended in the archive. During one of Yolanda's absences, Evelyn discovered one archive cabinet that included drawers containing physical objects. The cabinet was different from the flat art files.

Cuban archaeologists, in partnership with international institutions, did research on the pre-Columbian people in Cuba. They made excavations of Amerindian sites and their findings were catalogued and contained at the university's archives.

Curiosity seduced Evelyn to explore the artifact drawers. She was aware that her respite from supervision was limited, so she checked out the collection quickly, staying alert for footsteps that might signal Yolanda's return.

Inside the cabinet were shelves with shards of pottery, and shells and beads drilled for jewelry. Most interesting were the native Taino sculptures. She mused at the effigies of human figures and the remarkably-intact decorative bowls. She opened a drawer inside the cabinet and was astounded to see a special wood box with a tag labelling it "Crucifix of Fray Bartolomé de las Casas." Inside was a beautiful gold crucifix laying on a faded and frayed satin pillow. She didn't know much about his story, but she did know that Cuban history held him in high regard, as did the Catholic Church.

In the narrative of the Revolution, the friar was first a wealthy landowner in the early colonization of the West Indies as well as a participant in the campaign against the native inhabitants of Cuba. Native peoples had lived on the island for centuries before the arrival of Christopher Columbus and the subsequent European invaders. In the Arawak grouping of Amerindians, Cuban indigenous tribes were reportedly peaceful, whereas the Caribe Indians, found elsewhere in the Caribbean, were reputed to be fierce warriors, who, some believe, were cannibals.

Early on, the Spanish conflicted with the local tribes and brutally dominated their settlements, enslaving the native people. Las Casas tried to convert the indigenous people to Christianity, however, over time, his view of the indigenous peoples changed as he came to know them. He was against enslaving Indians in the Spanish colony and became their champion for fair treatment. This brought him into conflict with Spain's policy, but ultimately, he successfully won freedom for native slaves.

Just prior to the Revolution, archaeologists excavating a destroyed settlement found many objects that led them to believe it was the site of a massacre. Spanish artifacts were scattered among the ruins of the Amerindian site. The most remarkable finds were rosary beads and a gold cross with a few rusted links of a chain. With more questions than answers, the discovery was surrounded in mystery. The site needed more study, but excavation and study were interrupted. In 1959, the location became sequestered when the new government did not want foreigners to research a topic that would draw attention to the Catholic Church. The religious relic was deemed dangerous. Enough Cubans were still lighting candles to the Blessed Virgin that a new miracle crucifix with bona fide Spanish connections could be troublesome. The Church was ineffective in appealing to the authorities for more information and the return of the object. Cuba did not need a new narrative or martyr, so the story of Friar Bartolomé was left alone and the cross was hidden from view, buried in the bowels of the archive's cabinets.

Evelyn heard someone coming down the hall. Clicking footsteps echoed loudly. Then quiet. When the door latch turned, she panicked and slipped the cross into her waistband to hide it. She closed the drawer as quietly as she could, just as a light came on at the other end of the room. The drawer slid in quietly and clicked when she shut it. The sound seemed to echo throughout the room. It wasn't loud, but Evelyn's nerves amplified the actual noise.

The person at the door was not Yolanda, but a curator returning art from conservation work. Evelyn dropped to her knees and flipped her pencil onto the floor, because she was a little farther away from the art files she had been looking at and closer to the gated cultural collection.

Seeing Evelyn on the floor, the curator appeared very curious. "Hola," the curator said and smiled. Evelyn responded, "Hola, how are you."

"Did you lose something?" the curator asked. "Can I help?"

"Oh, I just dropped my pencil and it rolled over here."

"I found it!" as she rose to stand, holding her hand on her waistband to secure and conceal the cross.

"OK, have a nice day. Yolanda said you were continuing your research." And, with that, the curator turned off the other light and left the room. Because of her frequent visits to the archives over the last month, Evelyn was accepted and trusted. There was no question about her activity in the archive.

Evelyn was pleased her ruse had worked and she had escaped discovery. But she was angry with herself for taking the cross. She wanted to put it back quickly and put her momentary lapse of composure behind her. She pulled on the drawer. It didn't budge. Examining it closely she could see that the cross had been in a lockable drawer. It was a fluke that the drawer had opened at all, only because the drawer catch had not been engaged.

"Oh shit!" Evelyn exhaled with exasperation. "Now what will I do? I am smarter than this. I can't believe I got myself into this!"

She always avoided three dimensional objects because they could so easily be discovered in an x-ray of any shipment. Antiquities had complicated protections and rules for import and export. Flat art was so much easier and less risky. This was a mess. Now she was stuck with a religious artifact, one that the Cuban government wanted hidden. It was hidden under her shirt and she still needed to go through security in order to leave the building. She exhaled another heavy sigh of exasperation.

Evelyn was in a pickle. She couldn't return the cross to the locked drawer and she couldn't admit she had been snooping where she was not allowed. That would end her access to the archives, permanently, and probably expel her immediately from the country with admonishment to never return. A prohibition for returning to Cuba would end her lucrative art smuggling sideline.

Moving over to the flat files, Evelyn pulled out a random painting for cover in case anyone else came into the room. Ironically, the painting she pulled out was a religious painting of a monk reading a bible by candlelight. She wanted to collect her thoughts and formulate a plan. She could just hide the cross on top of a shelf and it would be a mystery whenever it was discovered. Or, she could slip it into a trash bin, but that seemed like the situation would wind up a travesty to history if no one found the cross before the bin was emptied.

Evelyn decided she would make the best of her subconscious kleptomania. She would get the cross to a buyer who would keep it secret or maybe even pass it along to the Holy Catholic Church – whatever. The first step would be getting the cross out of the archive. This could be a problem. While she didn't think she would have to go through a metal detector to exit, she might. At the very least, a security guard would greet her and her portfolio case would be inspected at a table. A female guard also might possibly pat her down.

Evelyn came to the doorway of the hall and waved at a security guard, saying, "Excuse me señor, I need to visit the lavatory and no one is here to monitor the archive. Would you please watch the door?" Appearing worried about security was a good gesture for her to demonstrate her trustworthiness.

The officer agreed and told her where the women's lavatory was. Most of the lavatories she had visited in Cuba did not have seats on the commodes or doors on the stalls. But this building had the trappings of the colonial federalist architecture. Evelyn went into a stall and closed the door. The cross was still tightly held by her waistband. She removed it, removed her blouse, and unhooked her bra. With a small scissor she had nicked from an empty desk just beyond the archives' doorway, she slit the bottoms of the cups just over the supporting underwires. Then she slid the ends of the cross into the openings she created. The head of the cross poked up and the bottom laid against her solar plexus. The addition of the cross increased her already busty bosom, but not excessively and, when her bra was loosened, the slack reduced the apparent volume. She buttoned her blouse a bit higher to avoid showing cleavage which would certainly show the head of the cross.

Luckily, she had, in her portfolio case, a cloth tailor's tape that she used to measure art. She thought that wearing it as a necklace might help distract from her blouse, or at least shadow any unusual bumps showing through her garment. When she emerged from the stall, she looked in the mirror over the marble sinks. Not bad, not bad at all. Only a voyeur would notice she was a little lumpy on the top.

She returned to the archive, thanked the officer for watching while she was gone. She returned the painting of the monk to the drawer and waited for Yolanda to return. While she waited, Evelyn put together her step-by-step plan.

First, she would act a little panicked that she had forgotten that she had an important phone call coming to the hotel and she must hurry back not to miss it. Second, she would go to the security station with Yolanda. When she got to the table she would drop her portfolio case, allowing the security guard to gallantly pick it up for her. Then she would wait for the inspection.

As the guard opened the case, she would twist her pump to put pressure on the heel, breaking it off. Holding her blouse to her chest, with the cross lodged in her bra, she would bend over to pick up her shoe and broken heel. Then, in a dramatic over-reaction, she would wail about having to walk barefoot or limp on one high heel while the other foot was shoeless. She would need to make something of a spectacle of herself. In the midst of complaining about the expense of the shoe, how cheaply it was made, and how would she get back to the hotel because she certainly couldn't walk, she would exit the building, barefoot, with her notebook and portfolio case tucked under her arm and shoes held in one hand.

This should be enough distraction to upset the routine. She only needed to avoid a hand pat- down inspection. Even if she got patted down, unless there was a female officer at the table or an overly harassing man, the area around her breasts should be safe from touching. But she worried that close scrutiny by a guard might result in something suspicious being spotted.

She put the plan into action when Yolanda entered the room. Evelyn did not have to feign nervous anxiety. She was operating on adrenaline. Yolanda was accommodating, and hurried with her to the front of the archive building. Just as she envisioned, she dropped the case, broke a heel, and added a little twist to her ankle to exaggerate a little limp. It worked and Yolanda and Evelyn limped quickly to the door to hail a cab.

"Wait, stop!" One guard shouted at them as they pushed on the heavy door to leave the building. Evelyn's heart stopped. The guard said, "Do not leave!" pausing to complete his instruction, "without your heel – maybe you can get it fixed." He held up the 3" spike in his hand and gestured for her to take it with her. Even though her heart was racing, she thought to herself how this kindness was so Cuban of him to offer help; so Cuban to see that something could be repaired.

Evelyn profusely thanked him, almost in tears for the fright she had just suffered and then scurried down the granite steps to catch a cab back to her hotel. As uncomfortable as it was to have the cross poking her midriff, she didn't dare take it out until she was in her hotel room, with the bathroom door closed and locked.

Sitting on the toilet, she examined the crucifix closely, marveling at the details of the object. It was beautiful, about 10 cm high by 7 cm wide, radiating gold, with chamfered edges and minimal engraved details. A gold ring for the chain was soldered to the top at the back.

Evelyn imagined a 16th century priest wearing this cross over his simple robe. It was like touching the past, touching an important piece of history. And the mystery was perplexing. Why would such a valuable object be discarded or lost only to be found half a millennia later? Why would this be impounded and kept from display? For a while she was overwhelmed in the presence of the artifact. Her predicament of having stolen this crucifix of the priest was displaced with her pondering of the history. She sat on the toilet until the reality of the situation returned.

Now she would need to find a way to get this artifact out of Cuba. She would need to hope no one would discover the cross missing until after she was gone. The archive wasn't exactly a bee-hive of activity and the friar's story didn't seem to be a priority for the government. Fencing the object could come later after she was safely back in the UK or New York, or even Haiti.

Restless, she tried to sleep, but her thoughts kept returning to the cross. She had laid it under her mattress, wrapped in one of her silk chemises. Even though it was an unimaginative hiding place, she believed it was safe under her. When she did slip into slumber, she dreamed about a knock at the door and the police pushing their way in to arrest her. She sat up, gasped, and quickly realized it was not real. She tried to return to sleep.

Evelyn awoke to a brilliant dawn with morning light in her face. Yolanda was coming to pick her up so they could go together back to the archives. When Yolanda arrived at the Hotel Santa Isabel, Evelyn asked her to stay and join her for breakfast and enjoy the hotel menu. On the porch overlooking the plaza, daily life was starting, with people walking to their jobs, the street being swept by old ladies, and the police inspecting the park for any homeless vagrants.

The street musicians were assembling on a nearby bench to prepare for another day of busking.

Evelyn said, "Yesterday I learned I must leave Havana. My university wants me to go to Trinidad to look at something for them."

"Oh, might I come along? I love Trinidad and know many people there." Evelyn didn't expect this complication. She did not really plan to go to Trinidad. Instead, she planned to head to Playa Larga or perhaps return to Jagüey Grande, someplace where it would not be so easy for the Havana police to track her. She needed some time to concoct her exit from the country.

Evelyn responded, "That would be wonderful, but I'm afraid I need to do this myself. I don't know how long I will be and would not want to impose on you while I am working. It's not exactly our field of study."

Yolanda persisted. "Oh, but I could help," Yolanda said, almost pleading.

Evelyn had to be more direct. "Again thanks, but no," she said in a firm tone that seemed off-putting to Yolanda. For a moment Yolando was quiet. Evelyn gently took her hand, "Really, I would love to have you along, but this is something I have to do by myself. When I return to Havana, I promise we can have free time to enjoy the amenities of this wonderful city." Of course, this promise was a lie, but she hoped it would eliminate the complication of having Yolanda along when she would be trying to figure out a way to escape Cuba.

Yolanda seemed to accept the rejection and faintly smiled at the prospect of spending time with Evelyn in the future. They parted with hugs and promises to get together when Evelyn returned, whenever that might be.

Evelyn returned to her room and checked to see the crucifix was where she had left it. Before going to breakfast, she had posted a Do Not Disturb sign on her door so that a maid would not enter while she was out. She could not trust anyone. People might be thieves.

She packed and arranged for a cab to take her to the central tourist port. From there she lingered for a few minutes to see if she had been followed. She waited for a cab that looked suitable for her to hire for a trip to Playa Larga. She did not want one of the antique classic American cars, iconic in Havana, but a modern reliable car, with air conditioning.

On the drive, she sat quietly in the back seat, perusing a tourism magazine. An advertisement for Girón Beach Club Resort caught her attention. She thought, "Yes! An out of the way resort would be perfect. She could hide among foreign tourists and not stand out as she did when in a city or small town. When she stayed in the smaller towns, the community of bed and breakfast locations spread gossip fast, eroding her anonymity.

"Driver, I have changed my mind, please take me to the Girón Beach Club Resort. Do you know where that is?" He nodded his head in acknowledgement. "Sí. It is not far from Playa Larga." He turned at the next fork in the road and soon they were at the apron of Girón Beach Club Resort.

Bellmen unloaded her luggage and she tipped the driver. She approached the desk, saying, "I have no reservation, but my travel plans have changed. I hope you have a room." As a large resort, still working their way back to full occupancy, there was no question that a room would be available.

The desk clerk replied, "Let me check." She casually leafed through a reservation booklet as if there might be a question, and then smiled, "Why yes. We can fit you in. What kind of room would you like? Ocean view or garden?"

Evelyn replied, "A nice room; one with a phone."

"Of course, we will make it ready for you." The clerk called housekeeping to freshen the room and a bellman waited to take her to her room.

When Evelyn reached her room, she noted that the air conditioner had just been turned on and the room was faintly musty, but it was clean overall. While the room was not as luxurious as the Hotel Nacional or Hotel Santa Isabel in Havana, it was large enough and the bed was comfortable when she flopped down on it.

When she opened the curtains on the double wood and glass doors, she could see that her view was looking out over the Caribbean. The green landscape bordered a strip of sand beach, looking tan against the water's edge. The view extended to turquoise waters with a streak of deep blue offshore at the edge of the reef. It was beautiful and just like the advertisement in the tourist magazine. With the doors open to the south breeze, the mustiness evaporated and the fresh ocean fragrance washed through her room. From what she could see, there were not many people at the resort. This was going to work for her.

ELEVEN

Evelyn spent the day in her room, occasionally wandering out to her balcony to stand at the rail overlooking the Caribbean Sea. If she wasn't so overwhelmed by the circumstance of having the cross, she could enjoy the view. Always in motion, it wasn't her habit to really relax and just do nothing. This was the burden of her active mind. She needed to stay ahead of what could upset her schemes of art trade, art tours, and art history academia. The complications of her life were of her own making. The cross only added to the weight she bore.

She turned on the TV and scrolled through the channel listings. Resorts had TV that the ordinary Cuban populace didn't have. Some satellite channels were blocked but there was the BBC and some feeds from Latin countries and even a movies channel. She flipped through the offerings and stumbled on a Caribbean music channel that looked interesting and was a distraction. The station was showing music videos made in various Caribbean countries. There was a wide variety of styles. Some of the videos were authentic to the location; calypso, reggae, Latin, salsa. Others clearly emulated U.S. "gangsta" culture, showing luxury cars and scantily clad women dancing to hip-hop tunes or reggaeton. These videos were somewhat amusing. The cars were not late models and showed signs of rough island use. The cars were only the best the video producers could find on the island where the video was shot. Some videos were from the UK and Netherlands, but even these had an island vibe. This was the Caribbean reflection of MTV.

Evelyn found herself entertained by the music videos. Watching one particular video of a group of rap-wanabes, she got an idea. The entertainers were weighed down with excessive gold jewelry, chains with outrageous medallions that hung from their necks. This would be the ticket to get the cross out of Cuba and to the U.S. No reasonable customs official would ever assume the cross was real gold. Or, if it was thought to be real, it wouldn't be suspected as an antique relic, only one of many decorations around a guy's neck. All she would need was a suitable mule.

She called Gladstone in Haiti, taking several attempts to make the international connection. She asked him, "Do you know someone with a passport who can travel to Cuba and have no problem entering the U.S.? Preferably a young black man. He must be completely clean of drugs, paraphernalia and prohibited items." She believed this was a good plan, working out the details in her head.

Evelyn would plan to meet the courier at the Havana airport after he had cleared customs. She would arrange a room for him, as well as for herself, in Havana. She would instruct him on how to deal with U.S. Customs. The next morning, she and the courier would fly to Miami on one of the special charter flights that routinely flew between the two cities. In Miami, they both would go through customs. She hoped that U.S. Customs and Immigration would look at the young black man, weighed with chains and the cross, through a lens of prejudice and stereotype.

The purpose for his visit would be to attend a hip-hop concert. He would have to be coached to remain calm and be rehearsed with answers to questions he might be asked. Customs and Immigration could make it difficult for him but, in the end, there was no chance they would think the genuine antiquity in the mass of chains was real gold. She would then collect the cross, go to an ATM for cash, pay him and then purchase a return flight for him back to Haiti or the Dominican Republic.

With this plan worked out in her head, she only had to wait to hear from Gladstone. It might take a few days for him to find a suitable candidate for her. In the meantime, she tried to relax, blend in with the crowd on holiday at an all-inclusive resort, and enjoy the resort, not for her own gratification, but in an effort to be just another foreigner in Cuba.

A couple days passed and she did not hear from Gladstone. Relaxing was driving her crazy with boredom, interrupted with anxiety. She convinced herself that she would have to wait and hope that the cross was not discovered to be missing at the archives. She decided to go to the poolside for the evening's entertainment. Before leaving her room, she checked to be sure the cross was safely hidden.

She sat alone at a high-top table near the back of the audience. Surveying the crowd, she could assess the customers. Most looked like they were from Europe or Canada, maybe a few were from South America. There were middle-aged couples dressed in casual island wear, young people on honeymoons, old women travelling together, and mixed groups from the U.S. on special tours under a cultural People-to-People license. Only the most uninhibited couples made it to the dance floor to show their newly learned Latin dance skills. Everyone seemed to be enjoying themselves.

Evelyn spotted Matvey. He was a svelte specimen of youthful masculinity, with striking green eyes and a wave of dirty blond hair. He was tall, standing out and over the other men, and well dressed. She saw him approach the dance floor. He tapped the shoulder of an older man dancing with his partner so he could cut in and dance with the older woman.

"Por favor, may I dance with this beautiful woman?" A little surprised, the gentleman acquiesced. Matvey started slowly with a back-and-forth salsa step. The lady followed. When they reached a rhythm together, Matvey led his dance mate into more complicated moves. After a few minutes. Matvey took her hand and placed it back into the palm of her husband. Some in the audience applauded.

Matvey saw Evelyn seated alone at the high-top and approached her. "Are you here with someone? May I join you?" He was seated before she could answer to decline. "I hate to see a lady drinking alone on such a beautiful evening. You should be enjoying this with company." Matvey was suave beyond his years, partly from the mentoring by his mother but mostly from the trial-and-error education of seducing lonely matrons.

Evelyn was not like the overweight, aged women Matvey usually targeted. She was only a few years his senior, beautiful and fit, stylishly dressed and not ogling him with reserved desire. Matvey asked the waitress for a mojito. Knowing about Matvey's exploits with women, the bartender was accustomed to mixing his drink on the light side and the ones he ordered for the women heavy with liquor.

Like his late mother, he was an escort to the lonely who were searching for lost thrills and casual romance. His scheme was a bit different. While the tips for his service were important, his main intent was to take a piece of jewelry. After exhausting the woman in a romantic tryst, she slept and he pretended to sleep. Then, he would find a suitable piece of jewelry and slip it into his shoe, careful not to awaken his client. He only took one piece, usually an earring, or maybe a broach. Matvey selected what he thought he could broker with the local jewelry maker. The woman would likely think it was lost and accept that she would not be able to find it before she left the resort. If she did think it was stolen, she would be restrained from complaining, else reveal the embarrassment of her indiscretion.

While the partners he had were not youthful or particularly attractive, they were appreciative and enthusiastic after they got over the embarrassment of being in a casual tryst. The excitement typically sent them to happy slumber. Though the sex was not great for him, he got satisfaction from his performance. Sometimes the ladies even gave Matvey money as a gratuity. He deposited the women's "lost" jewelry in the same percussion instrument that his mother used to hide her finds.

For young Matvey and the sophisticated, worldly, art history professor, there was little in common beyond superficial conversation. After chatting about dance, music, and life in Cuba, there was only dancing and drinking and physical attraction. Evelyn's life, both the legitimate academia and secret art trafficking, were beyond Matvey's experience. She had no intention of sharing either story with a young lothario. Still, she enjoyed the company after being self-quarantined for several days.

After a pause in their trivial conversation, Matvey reached for Evelyn's hand and shepherded her to the dance floor again. She complied without hesitation. Dancing and the live music were as intoxicating as the drinks. They looked good together dancing. Both were tall and attractive, a good fit.

The night came to an end. Evelyn was a little unsteady on her feet, but far from drunk. She was happy and carefree, liberated from the worry and concern about the cross and shipping her art.

In a gentlemanly gesture, Matvey escorted her to her room. After saying goodbye, he turned to leave. Uncharacteristically, Evelyn hugged his neck and invited him in. She abandoned her sophisticated propriety and gave into promiscuous eroticism.

It was a torrent of passion as they both undressed, dropping their clothes along their way to the king-sized bed. They both were gripped with carnal desire. Matvey felt lust that he never had with the older women he dutifully serviced to get their jewelry. With Evelyn, it was genuine arousal. They fell together onto the bedspread and spent an hour in rushed copulation, followed by gentle foreplay and romantic intimacy.

Similar to Matvey's senior marks, Evelyn was exhausted after their hot lovemaking, sedated by the alcohol, and tired from the dancing. She pulled the covers over her nakedness and fell into a deep slumber. Matvey's stamina and youth prevailed to keep him awake. Lying by this beautiful, elegant woman, he stroked her hair and rubbed her soft skin. She was out.

Matvey pondered if he should spend the night and have morning pleasures with Evelyn, or dress and leave. He truly cared about Evelyn's feelings. While he thought about what he should do he could not resist his routine pattern of assessing what treasures his partner had in her possession. He had no plans of taking anything, but his curiosity led him to his old habits.

He turned off the lights and searched her purse and quietly opened dresser drawers. Evelyn had some nice jewelry, but not much. Then he saw the corner of a towel sticking out from between the mattress and box spring. He felt something lumpy through the well-worn foam mattress that had not been replaced since the Soviet-era. He lifted the corner of the mattress gently so not to awaken Evelyn. He pulled out the hand towel. As he unfolded the towel he discovered the cross.

In the moonlight shining through the thin curtains, he could not make out the writing inscribed on the relic, but it was gold, shimmering, and weighty for its size. He sat on a chair admiring its beauty and wondering why she had hidden such a valuable object in her room rather than securing it in the resort safe.

He decided he would stay with Evelyn until morning. He wrapped the cross back in the hand towel and lifted the corner of the bed. Evelyn stirred and brushed her hair from her eyes, to smile at Matvey. Then she saw he had the cross.

Evelyn went berserk. She surged with anger and screamed at him, throwing the bedside lamp. It missed him, as Matvey ducked. "Shhh, shh. Please be quiet, let me explain."

She yelled "You bastard, you fuck me, then steal my things! God damn you!"

Matvey continued to try to calm her. "Please, you don't understand! I was coming to bed and found this at the corner," holding the cross partially unwrapped, shining in the moonlight.

Evelyn was inconsolable, angry, crying, hurt, and feeling victimized. "Get out! Get out!" She pulled a resort bathrobe around her. Her rage returned and she berated Matvey again. As he opened the door, she screamed at him again. He closed the door and rushed back into the room.

"You must be quiet! I can explain. We can work this out! I really care about you." Evelyn kept yelling hysterically.

Matvey grabbed her and covered her mouth with his hand. He was strong but Evelyn struggled to escape his grasp. She was feeling faint. Still naked under the bathrobe, she stepped on the robe as she twisted and fell to the floor, hitting her head on a night table. Blood started flowing from her forehead. There was a lot of blood.

Matvey kneeled at her side and called her name, "Evelyn, Evelyn. Please, Evelyn." She was limp in his arms.

She was pale and appeared not to be breathing. The blood was dripping onto the floor. He had never seen a dead person before. He cried. "Oh, my God, I have killed her." He fell back into the chair, his head in his blood-covered hands. "I did not mean to. I only wanted her to be quiet and let me explain," he whispered to himself.

Minutes passed and he gazed over at the beautiful woman he was infatuated with just a few hours before. Now, she lay motionless on the floor.

Matvey thought, "I must leave. I need to remove anything that ties me to this room and clean up the room. People will assume she was drunk, slipped and hit her head on the table." Matvey washed his face and hands. Streaks of blood swirled in the sink and down the drain. He carefully dressed and poured most of bottle of rum down the sink, placing it by her side.

He was about to leave the room, looking it over one last time, when the larceny in his heart overwhelmed his head, and he grabbed the cross. He stuck it in his belt, under his shirt. Opening the door slowly, he checked to see if anyone was around. It was 4 o'clock in the morning; it was unlikely that he would be observed leaving the room.

Matvey returned to his room. Hyperventilating over the events of the evening, his thoughts returned to the fact that he had the cross. In the light he could see its full magnificence. The inscription of the back of the gold cross was "Bartolomé de las Casas".

Matvey was astounded. Could it be real? He had learned about the Saint when he was in school. In Cuban history, the man was both a pariah and a hero. He had been a wealthy land owner and a slave owner. His attitude toward enslaving Amerindians changed in time and he was a champion for fair treatment of native people during the period of colonization. Unfortunately, his concern for native tribes was at the expense of Africans, whom he advocated be used to replace enslaved Indians. He had a wide reach in the Caribbean, from Cuba to Hispaniola, Guatemala and Venezuela.

Not promoted in the Revolution narrative was the friar's religious importance, or his becoming a Bishop of Chiapas in the Catholic Church and being sainted as "The Protector of the Indians." He had fought for recognition that the natives were fully human. If this was the cross of the Saint, it was old, really old, from the 16th century. It was also beautiful, but most important to Matvey, it was gold, a lot of gold and would be worth a lot of money.

He gently rubbed the cross, thinking this would be his salvation from poverty. Greed outweighed his conscience.

Now he would need to hide it. Not under his bed. He knew there really was no safe place in his apartment. So, he went outside his room and dug a small hole in a flower pot and buried the cross in its hand towel covering. Carefully dusting the dirt to disguise any disturbance, he placed a small rock over the location so he could tell if anyone messed with his treasure.

He laid back on his bed and dozed off, exhausted emotionally from the evening.

TWELVE

A maid used her master key to open Evelyn's room. She saw only a woman's legs and feet lying on the floor. There was blood, lots of blood. She ran to the office to tell Maria that the lady in room 312 was dead. The ambulance was called immediately and Maria called for the resort nurse.

When the ambulance arrived at the resort, the EMTs were directed to Evelyn's room by the resort security guard. Emergency personnel carefully loaded Evelyn onto a gurney. Her room was up two flights of stairs so they had to struggle with the gurney to get it down the stairways without disturbing the patient. They wheeled her to the emergency vehicle, in front of a crowd watching the excitement, lined up like they were viewing a parade.

The staff had no idea if she was dead or alive, just that she was being removed. Guests and staff were being held back by the police who had responded to the emergency call. As the ambulance departed, a local investigator arrived with the police commissioner for the province. It was a big deal for a foreign tourist to be a victim of crime and of even more concern that a foreigner was hurt in a violent incident. Although Playa Girón is in Matanzas Province, the investigation was being conducted by the Cienfuegos Province police. A case as sensitive as an assault on a foreign tourist at a resort destination needed the attention of the police that were closer to Girón Beach Club Resort than the 2 1/2-hour trip from the central station in Matanzas.

Detective Inspector Carlos Costa was assigned to the case. He had earned the reputation of being a diligent investigator, leaving no stones unturned. The police chief for the Matanzas district specifically asked for him to conduct the investigation, knowing he would be thorough.

Maria met the police investigator and the chief of police after the ambulance left with Evelyn. The inspector introduced himself. "I am Inspector Carlos Costa, a criminal detective with the National Revolutionary Police District for Cienfuegos Province." He turned to face the man who was accompanying him. "May I introduce the PNR Police Chief for our district, Major Gutierrez." The Chief nodded to Maria and stretched out his arm to shake her hand.

"This is very troubling. Be assured we will find out who did this terrible crime. Please cooperate with Señor Costa." Major Gutierrez then politely stepped away.

The two police officers asked for directions to the location of the violent incident. Maria led them to Evelyn's room. Two junior officers were already there, protecting the site. The chief stood outside, looking concerned and officious.

Inspector Costa went in and instructed Maria to wait outside. The first officers on the scene had already spoken with the maid. They directed Inspector Costa to the maid who discovered the body. She began telling him what she had told the other officers. Soon the investigator would learn about Matvey being seen at Evelyn's room.

Maria did not like the police at the resort. This intrusion was upsetting to the guests and a distraction for the staff. She hoped they would be done soon and the resort could get back to normal.

Inspector Costa was in Evelyn's room for a long time. He was taking photographs and fingerprinting objects in the room. He took an inventory of the room's contents. After he was finished, he called for an officer to help bag up items, directing the officer to wear gloves when handling anything. He asked another officer to get a cart to remove Evelyn's luggage and the art works that appeared to be boxed for shipment.

Inspector Costa mentioned to Maria, "I would like to speak with your staff. Who found the woman? Can you arrange for me to meet the workers?"

He started his questioning of the staff with Maria, asking about who the victim was, her passport, what Maria knew about her, and any associations or interactions during her stay. Maria did not know much about Evelyn, who was something of a mystery. She relayed the details of her stay and had the secretary retrieve Evelyn's passport from the office safe.

She told Inspector Costa, "She kept to herself mostly. She ate alone. I don't think she knew any other guests, but she was pleasant enough to me. Occasionally she would come to the

110

poolside to listen to the band or maybe have a drink." Maria didn't mention that she had seen Evelyn dancing with Matvey.

When his interview with Maria was concluded, she took Inspector Costa to ask questions of the staff, asking them to cooperate with Señor Costa. Carlos spoke first to the housekeeping staff. Maria overheard one of the maids mentioning she had seen Matvey at Evelyn's room late at night. The bartenders mentioned Matvey and Evelyn were dancing and looked like they were having a good time. The desk clerk had no information beyond the details of her check-in. Other staff members contributed little to create a picture of the lady.

While the police questioned the staff, Maria returned to her office and pondered the possibility that Matvey may have been involved. She wondered whether someone had come in to Evelyn's room from the open balcony. She didn't want to believe Matvey could do something like this.

A heavy pall fell over the resort. This was not the idyllic tropical holiday the visitors anticipated when they booked their vacations. Guests were disturbed by seeing the police and ambulance. They had been asked to stay in their rooms and many were frightened. Not knowing anything led some to concoct their own explanations, rooted in scenarios of their imagination, knitted together with the brief glimpses of the chaos. A few already had anxiety about being in a state so impugned by America's spin on the evils of the Castro regime. The violent incident only added to these visitors' worry about their own safety in a third-world country.

After spending hours clearing the scene at the resort, the police and inspector left. Now Maria could get the staff to clean the room. She went in and was shocked to see the pool of blood on the floor next to the bed and nightstand. All of the towels and linens were scattered. The sliding glass door to the balcony was open and the curtains were blowing in the wind.

Maria clapped her hands. "Someone, please, clean this mess up!" Two housekeepers who were standing nearby, watching the police, scurried to the room. They were surprised to see the copious blood that stained the bed and floor. It was foul job to clean it all up.

Maria told the maids, "I want no talking about this to others," although she knew it was useless for her to try to quash rumors with the staff. There would be rumblings despite La Jefa Maria la Gorda's instructions. Although rumors were spreading through the staff, she emphasized that the staff were forbidden to discuss the events with the guests. Maria's bullying could tamp down the flames, but she couldn't extinguish the fire.

Once the police were gone and the mess cleaned up, Maria began to relax and resume her daily routine managing the resort. When Maria had total control again, the guests were allowed to resume their vacation activities. All were nervous to some degree. Maria presented a calm demeanor, as if the events and lock down were normal. When pressed for information, she would downplay the situation, saying that a guest had a serious heart attack and was transported to hospital.

In an effort to distract the guests from the day's excitement, for the evening meal she arranged an even more opulent buffet, including lobster, a delicacy available locally that was never offered to guests under normal circumstances. The emcee for the evening's entertainment announced an apology for the disruption during the day. Bartenders and wait staff kept the mojitos flowing.

The next day it seemed Girón Beach Club Resort was back to the usual routine. Guests were swimming in the pool, sitting under umbrellas at the beach or playing chess with the giant-sized patio pieces. Soon this group of guests would depart, with an exciting story to entertain their friends. None would ever know the real account of actual events.

The ambulance took Evelyn to a hospital about 40 kilometers north, in the community of Aguada de Pasajeros. When the ambulance pulled into the emergency entrance of the Consultorio Médico, the medical center staff quickly took over from the ambulance technicians. On the ride to the hospital, the EMTs stabilized Evelyn, started an IV and cleaned her wound. By the time she was admitted to the hospital a large bump had emerged on her forehead.

Evelyn was unconscious. In a coma, it was likely she had a concussion. The nurses prepared her for a bed in a ward, removing her bloodied bathrobe and dressing her in a hospital gown. A physician's assistant stitched her forehead. A doctor came, checked her eye dilation for response to light and scheduled an x-ray.

Detective Inspector Carlos Costa arrived at the hospital a few hours after Evelyn. He asked to speak with her, but found she was still unconscious and unresponsive. There would be more tests and waiting. The head nurse said she would call him when Evelyn regained consciousness. Carlos asked to speak with the doctor.

The physician came to the desk and, after introductions, Carlos asked if they could speak privately. "We believe this lady may have been a victim of a violent assault. It is early in our investigation, but we would ask for you to perform a test for sexual activity." The doctor said, "We will take care of that, but we are more concerned about her head injuries. It may be hours or days, or never, for her to recover from the trauma she suffered. We do not have all the facilities of a larger hospital, but we will do our best for her."

Carlos thanked the doctor for her assistance and said he looked forward to being apprised of Evelyn's condition. "I really hope to speak with her about what happened." With a sarcastic smile, he continued, "As you know, the safety of our foreign visitors is a high priority for the Ministry of Tourism and the Ministry of Interior."

Inspector Costa returned to his office in Cienfuegos to look through the materials collected at the resort. Evelyn's luggage and personal effects were not unusual, including money and some jewelry. Because the money and jewelry did not seem to be disturbed, the inspector assumed the assault had not been a robbery. The crate of artwork contained a number of contemporary paintings and a few that looked older. Her laptop computer was locked. She had a few files and a notepad with scribblings about art. Her camera had digital images of different kinds of artwork. Nothing really stood out as out of the ordinary.

In Evelyn's purse he found a slip of paper with contact information for Professor Yolanda Lopez-Ballar. He phoned the number and left a message that he wanted to speak with the Professor about Evelyn Faye Griffin.

When Yolanda got the message, she was panicked. She called Inspector Carlos immediately.

"Detective Inspector Costa, this is Yolanda Lopez-Ballar. I am a friend of Evelyn. Is she alright? Where is she?"

Carlos answered in a sympathetic tone, "She is in a hospital in Aguada de Pasajeros. She suffered an injury at the resort in Girón. She is in stable condition and in the good hands of a doctor."

"Girón! I thought she was in Trinidad doing research. What was she doing in Girón?"

Carlos said, "We are just beginning our investigation and I was hoping you could help provide some information on Evelyn. For now, we know very little."

Yolanda relayed that Evelyn is a professor at a British university. "She is in Cuba to do research at the national archives. She also brings students to Cuba from the UK and other countries to study art and culture." Continuing, Yolanda said she would come to Aguada de Pasajeros to see Evelyn and meet with Detective Inspector Costa in person.

"Thank you, that would be helpful. Please let me know when you arrive and I will arrange for transportation to the police station in Cienfuegos. The case is under our jurisdiction."

Yolanda began to arrange for transportation to Aguada de Pasajeros. She could take a taxi, but it would cost more than she could afford. This was not an expense her university department would authorize, so she would have to take a bus even though it would not be as quick as she would like. The next bus from Havana to Aguada de Pasajeros was not until the next morning. It was crowded with people traveling to Cienfuegos. For most of the 3-hour trip, she was standing, being bumped and jostled each time the bus stopped to allow passengers to depart while more passengers crammed in.

When Yolanda arrived at the hospital, she asked to see Evelyn. The nurse brought her to Evelyn's bedside in the ward. Evelyn was still unconscious. Yolanda held her hand and kissed her cheek. "I will pray for you." Yolanda was emotional, holding back tears from seeing her friend so debilitated. When she asked the nurse for the prognosis, the nurse shook her head and then looked up, indicating it was up to God. Yolanda was despondent. She sat in the waiting room trying to be calm.

Once Yolanda regained her composure, she called the Inspector from the hospital phone. "Inspector Costa, this is Yolanda Lopez-Ballar. I am at the hospital and just visited Evelyn."

Costa asked what Evelyn's condition was.

"I am not a medical doctor, but she is still unconscious and the nurse did not know for how long, or if..." Yolanda choked.

Costa said he would send an officer to collect her. Late in the day a police car arrived to transport Yolanda to Cienfuegos.

At the province central station, the officer who picked Yolanda up at the hospital escorted her to Costa's desk. They went to an interview room that was usually used for interrogation. It was an intimidating space, being small and austere. Costa had Evelyn's crate of art brought in.

Inspector Costa did not reveal any more information about the incident at Girón. He only recited the facts about

Evelyn being found in her room with injuries and her transport to Aguada de Pasajeros. He was anxious to speak with Evelyn when she recovered. He tried to be positive.

He opened the crate and asked Yolanda about the artwork. She leafed through the paintings, noting what she knew of the contemporary artists and their works. When she came to the old works, Yolanda said she was not an expert, but knew they were colonial and vintage. She said, "The new work by Cuban artists can be exported without restriction, but works like these need to have certification by the Ministry of Culture and Antiquities before they can leave Cuba."

Costa asked, "What is your relationship with the Professor?" Now it felt like an interrogation to Yolanda.

"I only met her a few weeks ago. The university asked me to help her research the archives. She is a professional colleague, nothing more. But we became casual friends. I don't think she knows anyone well in Cuba, only the contacts for her tours."

Then, Yolanda began asking the questions. "What was Evelyn doing in Girón when she told me her plans were to go to Trinidad? She and I were supposed to meet when she returned to Havana. I did not hear from her since she left Havana a week ago."

Costa shrugged, "There are many questions that we can't answer until we speak with her. Thank you for your help. I hope your friend will recover soon. You are a good friend to come to her aid. I'm sure she will appreciate this."

Yolanda was taken back to Aguada de Pasajeros by the same police officer who brought her to the station. She needed to find a place to stay. She quickly found a room in a casa particular near the hospital. Since the government's new push for economic tourism, people were allowed to open their homes to tourists as bed and breakfast accommodations, if the rooms met the standards established by the government. Yolanda's room was very nice, having been remodeled to meet the government's requirements.

When Yolanda returned to Evelyn's bedside, there was some improvement. Evelyn was in a deep fog, mumbling unintelligible phrases. Yolanda tried to comfort her and spoke to her. "Evelyn, Evelyn, my dear. This is Yolanda. I am here."

It took a few minutes before Evelyn began to slowly turn her head back and forth and blink her eyes.

Evelyn mumbled, "Yolanda?" Pausing, she then repeated, "Yolanda? Where am I? I am sorry."

After a long pause, she spoke again.

"Where am I?" She kept repeating the phrase "I'm sorry….so sorry …. I did not mean to take it. Sorry…." Then, she was asleep again.

Yolanda said, "No worries, just get better. You need to rest. There is no problem, I'm sorry this happened to you." Yolanda had no idea what Evelyn was talking about. She was saying she was sorry, but she was the victim!

The nurse was happy to see that Evelyn was mumbling. It was a good sign that Evelyn was coming out of her stupor. The nurse told Yolanda to go and come back tomorrow. "Your friend will be fine. She knows you are here."

When Yolanda returned the next day, she was surprised to see Inspector Costa in the waiting room. He said, "Your friend is doing much better today. We need to wait while the doctor is seeing her. She has some more tests."

They waited together in an awkward silence until the nurse called for Inspector Costa. Yolanda would have to wait longer.

The Inspector went to Evelyn's bedside and said, "I am with the police. I need to ask you about what happened to you at the resort."

Evelyn could not remember. With her eyes half-closed, she spoke slowly, somewhat slurred in her speech, "I only remember dancing with a young man at the resort. I think we had some drinks, while the band was playing."

"OK. OK, slowly. Do you remember how your head was injured?" Evelyn had a headache and reached to touch the painful area. "Ow...this hurts!" gently touching the bandaged bump on her head. Carlos took her hand and laid it back at her side.

"It's OK. We can talk more later. You have a friend here to see you." He then asked the nurse to bring in Yolanda.

Yolanda was happy to see that Evelyn had her eyes open. She was not the glamourous idol that had impressed Yolanda at the archives, but now just a plain, feeble woman who was suffering. Yolanda said, "I am here now to help you. I am so glad you are better. I was so worried." Tears formed in her eyes and she wiped them with a tissue. "How are you feeling?" She knew immediately that it was a stupid question.

Evelyn formed a thin smile. "I am feeling terrible. I did not mean to cause you any troubles. You have been a friend I don't deserve. I am sorry."

"For what? You were involved in an incident. The police are investigating if you were attacked or if you had an accident."

Evelyn paused and closed her eyes to process the conversation. She realized, "I should not say any more until I know what is going on."

She said, "I am tired now. I think I should sleep. Please don't worry." Then she closed her eyes. She didn't have to feign sleep; the pain medication and her injury made sleep come easy.

Yolanda stayed another day sitting at Evelyn's bedside before returning to Havana. She planned to return to Aguada de Pasajeros in a week. Perhaps she could help care for Evelyn then. For now, Evelyn was safe and getting better; there was little Yolanda could do for her.

The inspector returned to Evelyn's bedside a day after Yolanda left and asked more questions. Evelyn didn't quite know how to respond to his questions, but as the pain medications were wearing off and she was beginning to be more clear-headed, she was a little more cautious about revealing anything more to the police. Evelyn did not remember anything about the fateful night, but she had a good memory of dancing and a bad feeling about Matvey.

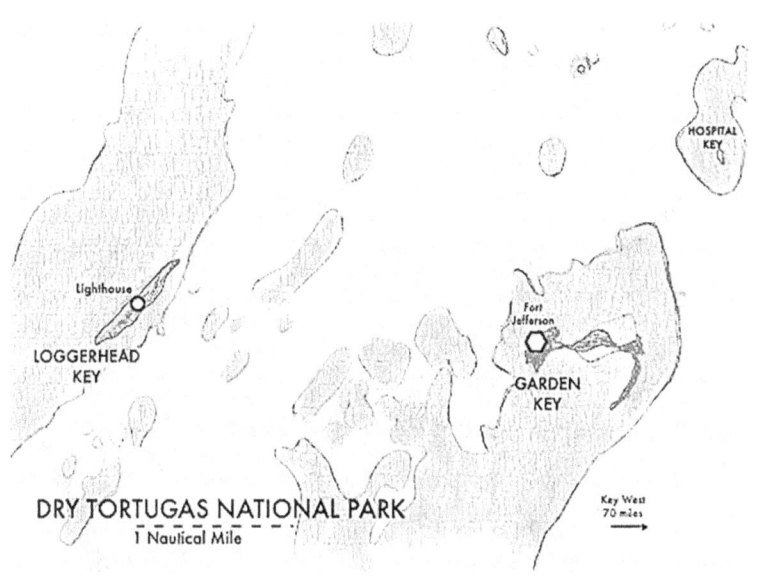

DRY TORTUGAS NATIONAL PARK
1 Nautical Mile

Lighthouse

LOGGERHEAD
KEY

Fort
Jefferson

GARDEN
KEY

HOSPITAL
KEY

Key West
70 miles

THIRTEEN

Sondra Faye "Sunny" Carter walked the Loggerhead Key beach every morning to catch the sunrise illuminating the sky over Fort Jefferson, about 3 miles to the east. As an artist in residence for the National Park Service the island was all hers at dawn. Boats were not allowed to anchor overnight at Loggerhead Key. They were restricted to specified anchorages lying off the fort on Garden Key. She was grateful that she was selected from all the applicants for the opportunity to spend a couple months on Loggerhead Key in Dry Tortugas National Park as a visiting artist.

Sunny was as bright and warm as her nickname. A talented artist, she felt a generous empathy for people and nature. Her art reflected her awe of the natural world and beauty of the landscapes. Whether painting with vivid colors or drawing in black and white she aimed to share what she saw with others and hoped they too would value her subjects. Her lack of concern with the business of art didn't provide financial success, but she made enough money to pay her bills. She was humbled to even be earning a living as a full-time artist. Fortunately, Chris, her spouse, was more grounded in the practical aspects of life and helped keep their finances on track. Sunny was simply a hippie, born 20 years too late.

Dry Tortugas National Park is a place of history and mystery, shipwrecks, sunken Spanish treasure, pristine coral reefs, and special nesting and migratory bird life. Sunny was thrilled to have been selected through the competitive process to be the park's artist in residence. What an exciting opportunity to spend time doing art on a remote sub-tropical isle! It would be an adventure, not without a little trepidation of living alone for a couple months. From her every-day, safe, studio life, she approached this sabbatical with enthusiasm. The excitement of the opportunity superseded any apprehension.

In preparation for her stay, she needed to become familiar with the history of the Dry Tortugas. She was expected to engage with the few visitors who might venture to Loggerhead Key, providing interpretation of the ecology and history. She studied materials supplied by the Park Service before she arrived and, once she was on site, she was rehearsed by a park ranger during her orientation.

She learned that the national park is administered by the National Park Service and includes the Dry Tortugas bank, which are the last islands in the Florida Keys archipelago, located seventy miles west of Key West. The Spanish named the islands Las Tortugas, for the abundance of nesting sea turtles. At some point a cartographer added "dry", an apt descriptive name as no freshwater is available. It was hard for Sunny to believe that native people had not set foot on the Dry Tortugas, given their amazing distribution throughout the Caribbean. But experts believe no indigenous Amerindians ever settled on the islands and who was she to argue.

While researching her future home for the summer, she learned about the huge fort built on the largest island, Garden Key, to protect the Straits of Florida. Started in 1846, and under construction for thirty years, it was obsolete before it was finished. The U.S. Civil War interrupted the construction. The supply of bricks had to switch from southern orange Georgia clay to New York red clay, giving the fort its distinctive appearance of the deep red cap on orangish walls. She learned that the fort is the largest brick building in the U.S.

Sunny found it interesting that troops were garrisoned at the fort, even serving as a prison during the Civil War and afterwards. One of the prisoners was Samuel Mudd, the doctor who set John Wilkes Booth's leg. Of course, she already knew that John Wilkes Booth assassinated President Abraham Lincoln. She speculated that, with limited food and water and frequent outbreaks of yellow fever, the fort and surrounding islands were no paradise for the soldiers, workers, and prisoners, while, in contrast, today the area is a popular recreation and fishing site.

To better guide mariners, a lighthouse larger than the one built at the fort was constructed on Loggerhead Key in 1858. This lighthouse towers 150 feet above sea level. The original oil lamp was kept by keepers living on the island. In 1987, the U.S. Coast Guard automated the light so it operates on generator electricity and back up batteries. The light can be seen from 20 miles at sea. Attendants are no longer necessary, so the abandoned lighthouse keeper's quarters are now available to researchers and guest artists, creating the opportunity for Sunny and others to have an artist retreat.

Sunny brought with her to the island a virtual library of field guides for birds, coastal plants, marine life and reptiles and amphibians. She was a good naturalist, but by no means an expert on the natural history of the Florida Keys. She filled her limit on luggage with art supplies, bringing minimal clothing. It was more important to have the materials for her art than a fashionable wardrobe.

Although she isn't a park ranger, she helps keep an eye on activities on Loggerhead Key and cautions folks about the rules. With a marine VHF radio and a park supplied 2-way radio she can call the staff at the fort for assistance if she needs it. From Loggerhead Key, the fort on Garden Key is easily visible on the horizon.

Most of the time she is alone on Loggerhead Key. While Sunny loves the solitude, there is a little comfort in knowing there are other people living at Fort Jefferson, the massive red brick structure that seems so out of place in the Caribbean-like islands and waters of the Dry Tortugas. The six-sided structure is a bricklayers work of art. Whenever she visits Garden Key and walks through the fort, she marvels at the arched hallways, circular stairwells with granite steps, and the gun emplacements with huge cannons.

The National Park Service maintains a small rotating staff at the fort to manage the steady stream of visitors coming on their own boat or hired sea plane tours and a daily ferry from Key West. She gets bi-weekly provisions from a shopping list that she gives to the park staff. Staff resupplies her when the rotating shift of rangers changes and they are bringing new supplies to the Park.

When tourists visit the fort, park rangers explain that the fort was obsolete before it was completed because, with the invention of the rifled cannon, these more modern weapons could spin a projectile with enough force to penetrate the 8-foot-thick walls. No longer used for military protection, the fort then became a coal station that refueled steamer ships as well as a harbor for military vessels patrolling the Straits of Florida between the Keys and Cuba. In 1935, it became a national monument and was redesignated as a national park in 1992.

Visitors can walk most of the circumference of the fort on a brick wall that creates a moat, but the west moat wall has been breached in some places, particularly where it is exposed to the open ocean. Snorkeling the near-shore reef is one of the major draws of visitors to the island. Cruising sailors wait out bad weather in the protected harbor and fishermen stay overnight on their go-fast open fisherman boats.

To Sunny, night is special. The historic lighthouse nearly 40 feet above the fort walls shines through the night, sparkling on the water. Without artificial city lights, on a new moon, the sky is enveloped in darkness and the stars shine in a brilliant spectacle. Clear skies reveal the Milky Way in glorious splendor. Only the flashing of the Loggerhead lighthouse beacon every few seconds intrudes on the darkness. Sunny looks forward each day to lying on the dock, watching the man-made satellites pass in their orbits and making a wish when she sees a shooting star. The solitude of this temporary life on a tropical isle is blissful.

Morning is her quiet time, before visitors come to the island to snorkel the near shore reefs or the historic shipwreck site. In 1907 a Norwegian windjammer, launched in 1875, sank in the shallow water off Loggerhead Key. Its 79-meter skeleton is still discernable. Not many people visit the wreck because they need to come on their own boat and anchor offshore. No tours are offered to this island, unlike Fort Jefferson where there is regular ferry and sea plane service.

As the artist in residence, she has a few tasks to complete each day. She is alone on the island while she attends to her few responsibilities as the island caretaker for a summer term of about 10 weeks. She checks the function of the tall lighthouse and makes sure the posted Closed Area signs alerting people to the off-limit areas of the island are maintained. She also checks the security of the doors to the historic lighthouse and a National Park Service maintenance shed. These chores are easily done in her daily regime.

Each morning, Sunny walks the entire circumference of the island, about 3 miles. On this morning and many more just like it, the sunrise revealed "Bible-book skies." The corpuscular rays of yellow light turned to the color intensity of the golden hour. The low angle of sub-tropical morning sunlight produced a rich palette of pastels, with yellow-tinged clouds and violet streaks across the azure sky.

As she walks around the island, the beach is usually fresh, after the night. Any traces of human footprints, hers and the infrequent visitors, are erased by the wind and waves. She might find the tracks of sea turtles coming ashore to dig a nest and lay eggs. Sunny carries a small sack of flag markers and records the sites in a log to aid the park biologist who is monitoring turtle nesting. The character of the tracks reveals the species. Most often it is green turtles, sometimes loggerhead turtles, but occasionally the giant leatherback nests on Loggerhead Key.

As Sunny rounded the beach, returning from her morning walk, she was surprised to see a small inflatable dinghy pulled up on the eastern shore. It was tied to the dock. Sunny didn't see anyone, but she assumed the boaters were walking up the path to the lighthouse. She hurried to catch up with them.

A family of two young adults with their towheaded kids were at the lighthouse, picking up a coconut. They were all tanned, with sun-bleached hair, from living several months aboard their boat. The young girl appeared to be five or six, while her brother was older by a year or two.

Sunny waved and called out, "Hi! Welcome to Loggerhead Key!" They smiled and returned the gesture. When she got closer, she said, "I'm Sunny, the artist in residence here. I just walked the beach to look for sea turtle nests." Kneeling, she spoke directly to the two children. "Do you want me to show you?"

Pat and Judy explained that they were on an extended cruise on their sailboat. It was anchored at the fort. Pat added, "We came over in our dinghy to see the lighthouse. We're headed to the Marquesas for a few days, then on to Key West. We might stay there for a couple weeks before moving on – maybe to the Bahamas."

Hearing Sunny's offer, the girl's face lit up with excitement and her older brother nodded. Sunny looked to the parents. Judy agreed, saying, "That would be great! What do you think Pat? Do we have time?"

Pat said, "Yes. We can snorkel on the wreck a little later."

Sunny led them on the path to the west shore of the key, chatting about the lighthouse and history of the island. Sunny was the family's dedicated and enthusiastic guide.

When they emerged from the dense casuarina forest, Pat and Judy and their children discovered the beautiful unspoiled beach that Sunny witnessed every day. Waves passed over the shallow coral reef to gently break on the off-white sand. For a moment, the family stood in silence, looking out to the horizon. Breaking their trance, a congregation of shorebirds fluttered by, landing at the water's edge to play tag with the waves on the beach.

Sunny said, "Now, let's go find the turtle nests." The family followed. Explaining as she walked, Sunny told them that she helped the Park biologists keep track of turtle nesting by walking the beach every morning to see who had visited over the night.

Linda, the little girl, asked, "How do you know that a turtle was here?" Mike, her brother, replied before Sunny could, saying, "She looks for the tracks in the sand."

Sunny confirmed what Mike said. "I can tell who visited by looking at the tracks."

Being a visual artist, Sunny used a stick to explain with a drawing. She started making lines in the sand to illustrate her story.

"The green turtle tracks are like this." She drew lines that were opposite divots in the sand. "The green turtle makes symmetrical tracks. Do you know what that means?" She took a minute to illustrate, saying, "Like a bulldozer track. But the tracks left by the loggerhead turtle are comma-shaped swirls, like they are rowing up the beach in the sand." Sunny made a pattern of alternating left and right commas.

"We also occasionally get leatherbacks. They are much bigger, the largest sea turtles. They leave large tracks. The smallest turtles are the rare Ridley turtles. We don't get many of either of these species. But, this year, so far, we have had 100 loggerhead nests and nearly 400 green turtle nests!"

Pat and Judy were pleased to see this kind of interaction for their children. It was the kind of experience they would never get in a classroom.

Sunny took them to a nest she had flagged on this morning's survey. Seeing the flag, the kids ran up to the tracks and then waited patiently for Sunny. Pointing to the flag, Sunny explained, "This is a marker I put on this nest so the park biologist would know about it. Can you tell what kind of turtle laid her eggs here?"

Both children simultaneously shouted, "Green!" Mike asked, "Where is the nest? I don't see a hole."

Sunny explained the process, beginning with "The mother sea turtle emerges from the ocean, dragging herself across the sand with her flippers, leaving the distinctive pattern of tracks, like these. Then, when she gets to the edge of the dune, she digs a hole and deposits 80 to a hundred or more round eggs into the cavity. The nest must not be too high above sea level, but high enough up on the beach so the incoming tide doesn't flood it.

"She breathes hard in her labors. To answer your question, Mike, she uses her rear webbed feet to scoop sand to refill the hole, covering her eggs completely. Then, she returns to her natural element, the sea, and swims away into the night."

The kids were wide-eyed with the story. "Guess what happens then!" she asked the family.

Sunny continued, "Well, about 2 months later, always at night, the baby turtle hatchlings boil up from the nest hole, swimming up through the sand, to emerge on the beach. Then, guided by the shimmering light of the moon reflecting on the water, they orient themselves to scramble to the sea. Few survive, but those that make the journey from hatching to breeding adult will return to the same beach to repeat the process, creating the next generation of sea turtles. It will be years before the turtle returns. How about that?"

Sunny considered how much more she should share. It was better to leave an audience wanting more rather than being overwhelmed with too much.

Then, Judy, amazed by this remarkable cycle of life, said, "How many natural perils the turtles must face to survive! First, there's the chance of hatching, then the little baby turtles have to make their way up from a 2 ft deep hole to the surface, then they have to crawl along the beach until they reach the water."

As they walked to the next nest, close by, Sunny explained, "After they hatch and get to the surface, the baby

130

turtles have even more challenges before they get to the sea. Ghost crabs or gulls can ambush them on their way to the safety of the waves. But, even after getting into the water, the hatchlings must run a gauntlet of predatory fish that can catch them before they find cover in the floating rafts of sargassum seaweed. Their life cycle is like a lottery, with many chances but only a few winners."

Concluding her story, she finished by saying, "Growing to adulthood is not easy either, because sharks can attack them. Then, as if the natural threats weren't enough, there is human predation, beach development, disorienting beach lighting, and getting entangled in our marine debris and plastics. Turtles can confuse plastics with natural jellyfish food and if they eat the bags, they can starve.

"But, you know, even with all of these difficulties, we still see turtles continuing the life cycle by coming up the beach to lay their eggs."

Linda said, "We often see sea turtles swimming in front of our boat, before they get scared and swim away. It's so cool! We look for them all the time."

Sunny had a heartfelt passion for the turtles and hoped she recruited the kids to care too. "Will you be a turtle protector?" she asked. They enthusiastically agreed.

"Great! Now I need to get back to the lighthouse. I have to get back to my painting and you have a shipwreck to explore!"

Pat and Judy thanked Sunny for the time and sharing with the kids. "It's things like this that affirms our decision to take a year to sail and home school our kids during an adventure that we hope they will remember all of their lives."

As Sunny helped push their inflatable dinghy back into the water, she gave the kids each a seashell, with a little painted smiley face. "Thank you for visiting my island. This is a souvenir to remember Loggerhead Key." Sunny watched as the family motored away. Then, as much as she enjoyed the company, she was anxious to get back to her art.

Daily life of "living a dream" on the island constantly distracts her from her main purpose for being there - creating art inspired by the location. Many artists had come before and executed beautiful works. Some pieces were abstract, reflecting the colors of the land and sea. Some of the artists focused on plein air painting of the scenery. Her work is more illustrative, creating representational drawings and paintings of island plants and wildlife. Past artist alumni included writers, poets, and sculptors.

For her art, Sunny first selects a subject, then she sketches the rough position with a few faint lines for reference, and begins applying layers of transparent acrylic paint to build the image, adding detail until she is satisfied that she has created an accurate depiction. When her internship is over, she will exhibit her works at the Key West Artist Studios and Gallery, a wonderful local fine art venue.

After the first week on the island, Sunny settled into a routine: morning sunrise walk, simple breakfast, painting. At midday she swam, rinsed off in the outdoor shower, and then spent the afternoon painting. After dinner she took an evening walk, and if the weather was nice, laid on the dock watching the stars while listening to an iPod playlist. Usually, she went to bed early, just after the sun set and it was fully dark. She lost track of days of the week, only recalibrating when she met visitors who came to Loggerhead Key for a day trip. She liked meeting people, but resented the interruption of her art time. Still, the human interaction was refreshing and she could share her enthusiasm for the deserted island with intrepid day explorers.

During her daily explorations she became familiar with specific features and observed daily changes. She noticed plants going from buds to blooms, submerged logs buried in beach sand disappearing and emerging in shifting sands, and the greening of the landscape after thunderstorms only to wither again in the hot sun. Sometimes, she would sit at the beach edge and just watch – shorebirds, ghost crabs, schools of fish silhouetted in breaking waves. When sand gnats awakened her from her daydream, she returned to the keeper's house to resume painting.

Five weeks into her stay on Loggerhead, Park Ranger Robert "Bob" Nelson knocked at the keepers house door and walked in. Sunny was startled from her painting trance.

"Oh my! Hello Bob, you surprised me. I'm sorry, I was lost in my painting." She pointed to a canvas propped on her easel.

Bob replied, "Very nice." Looking around her makeshift studio, he could see a dozen or more works, adding, "Looks like you've been busy. I've come over to go over some emergency procedures to prep the lighthouse in case of a storm."

Sunny looked a little puzzled as Bob explained, "There is a small tropical disturbance brewing around the Virgin Islands." Showing her a slick fax paper weather map of the Caribbean, he continued, "One possible track might take it

133

south of Cuba or there's a chance it could come to the Lower Keys."

While Sunny looked closely at the weather map, Bob said, "I don't think it's anything to worry about now, but we'll certainly be keeping an eye on it. I thought I should give you a heads up, in person."

Bob went over a few things to help her know how to prepare for a storm and what the evacuation plan would be. Sunny was nonplussed, always believing that things would turn out fine. Bob left and she quickly returned to painting, anxious to detail the part she had been working on.

As a few days passed it seemed that the disturbance would dissipate over the mountainous regions of Hispaniola or eastern Cuba. That would mean all of the Keys might get a little stormy weather, but it would not be much worse than the frequent squalls or a northern front. Sunny was a little relieved to hear these reports from Bob, since she had no experience with hurricanes.

Late one night a few days following his visit, the park 2-way radio crackled on and Bob called. He told her, "It looks like we are going to get a tropical storm after all. The storm picked up speed and intensity as it tracked west following the opposing Gulf Stream current in the Florida Straits. The Park Service is evacuating all personnel to Key West."

Now, Sunny was truly frightened and abruptly wide awake. Bob instructed her to pack a small bag of essentials and to stand by for the park boat to come in the morning.

Sunny had no idea how she would get to the boat, much less survive a seventy-mile trip to the safety of Key West. Early in the morning, even before day break, she was ready with a change of clothes, a few toiletries, her camera, and binoculars in a day pack. She could see that seas had built overnight and the normal surf was a torrent of breakers. The sky to the east was a foreboding darkness and squall lines were beginning to break over the Tortugas.

She called on the Park radio for Bob. "Ranger 1, Ranger 1, this is Sunny on Loggerhead. Over."

No answer. Sunny thought, "Not to worry. Sometimes it takes a minute for the Park to respond."

Trying again, "Ranger 1, Ranger 1, this is Sunny on Loggerhead. Over. Please answer."

Still no response. Was the radio broken? Sunny was a little panicked. She adjusted the volume and squelch. Again: "Ranger 1, Ranger 1, Bob Nelson. Any Park staff, this is Sunny on Loggerhead. Can you hear me? Over." This time her voice had an urgent tone.

The park channel only buzzed with static. She remembered the VHF radio she had. Fishermen and sailors used the marine VHF to communicate. Using channel 16, the hailing frequency, she called, "This is an artist in Dry Tortugas. Can anyone hear me? Over."

In a few seconds the VHF barked "Person calling on channel 16, please repeat."

Relieved that she had a response she quickly answered, "I am at the lighthouse on Loggerhead Key, trying to contact the Fort Jefferson staff. My park radio doesn't work, over."

A brisk reply came in a thick twang accent, "This is the shrimper *Cajun Spice*. No surprise, little lady, we saw the transmission tower crumple down, so they're probably without a radio."

She thought, "Little lady. Really?" But, she didn't have time to take offense. She continued, "The park was supposed to pick me up this morning. Can you relay a message?

"Little lady, little lady. We are about 25 miles north. It's blowin' like hell. We saw the Park boat leave a little earlier. Honey, if you can't get them what makes you think we can? We're heading to Florida Bay to ride this one…" The radio went silent. Sunny looked at the screen and saw it flashing "No Battery." Then it went dark.

Dammit! She didn't use the VHF and never charged the battery. She would have to plug in the charger and hope to get the shrimper back to relay a message to somebody who could rescue her.

Where was the park boat? She waited for a squall to pass and ran down to the pier. Waves were pummeling the shore, breaking over the dock. She scanned the horizon. The fort was obscured by oncoming rain. She ran back to the safety of the keeper's house. The lighthouse's beacon shone out to a darkened sky. She could almost see the wind blowing the thick humid mist. Fortunately, in the keeper's house she still had power from the generator located in a shed at the lighthouse. The lights were on and the windows were shuttered and locked as Bob had instructed.

She plugged in the VHF radio to recharge the batteries. She would just have to wait. She felt totally alone and scared. She thought it couldn't get worse and then it did. The lights went out. The circuit coming from the lighthouse made a loud clunk. Now back-up batteries in the keeper's house were the only power. Only a small light and the park 2-way radio were connected to the DC current system. Again, she thought it couldn't get worse. Then, it did. The wind was howling more now. It was raining harder, too. It was only 5 PM and already it was as dark as night. It was doubly dark in the boarded-up keeper's house.

She rationalized that she was safe in a dwelling that had been built strong in the 1920s and weathered many storms before. This one was only supposed to be a tropical storm, not a hurricane. She would be safe and this storm would pass.

The night stretched on and on. She had no VHF radio and the only light was from the little lamp at the radio station and her flashlight. She couldn't read. Art was out of the question. She found a blanket and went to the central hall to sit and listen to her iPod. She started a playlist of music related to the Keys. Ironically, many of the songs were about hurricanes. One in particular was an ear-worm song about water spouts, high seas, and surviving storms.

It was a comforting thought that, after this was over, she would be in a better place. She would be back at home with Chris and their cats. Sure, it was cold. Sure, they had tornadoes, but there were no hurricanes.

Tomorrow will be a new day. This will be over soon. Exhausted, she fell asleep as the iPod battery expired and the music stopped.

When she woke in the morning, bright sunlight was illuminating the slats in the shutters. She rubbed her eyes and combed her auburn curls back with her fingers. Approaching the door, she pushed it open against a pile of palm frond debris. The sky was clearing. Winds were brisk and humid. The island, her island, was beaten up. Bushes were stripped of leaves, leaving only a skeleton frame of branches. The majestic coconut palms were pruned with broken fronds hanging like a ragged skirt. The tall Australian pines were toppled like pick-up sticks revealing an island view that was previously obscured.

The fort was visible again on the horizon. At a distance it looked no different. It had been there for over a century and withstood storms before. It was probably damaged, like her island, but the fort was still standing guard to the Gulf. Sunny could see two sailboats making their way out of the channel and a shrimper offshore heading north. She whispered to herself, "The storm must be over. The park staff will arrive soon to get me." Now, after she survived, there really wasn't a reason to evacuate her. The only real impact was the defrosting refrigerator and food that would soon be lost.

The storm was devastating. She could see that the power line from the emergency generator shed to the keeper's house had been severed by a fallen tree. Fortunately, the breakers tripped when the line was cut so she wouldn't get electrocuted. The generator in the shed was okay and, because it was still running, the diesel exhaust was fouling the air when she was downwind.

She hadn't heard the rumble of the generator during the storm's fury, but now was pleased to see that there was still power to the lighthouse, even though the power to the house was cut. She could climb the 225 steps to the top and recharge the VHF radio in the outlets at the lamp room. It was a climb she had made before, for the view and exercise. Now it was an exercise for her survival.

It wasn't long before USCG helicopters were flying over the fort and making a pass over Loggerhead Key as well. She could see out of a small window halfway up the lighthouse tower, but she had no way to signal them visually or radio for assistance. She saw them land at the fort.

One of the helicopters took off shortly after landing. The other left an hour later and headed east to Key West. Later she saw another helicopter and a low flying large-propellor search and rescue aircraft circling the fort and disappearing into the distance.

The day passed and the sun sank in the west. She had had no contact from the Park; nothing on the now-charged VHF radio. She would spend another night at the lighthouse alone in the dark.

FOURTEEN

Alvero Camilo Marin-Zayas was proud of his boat. He had worked hard over many years to bring the old wood sport fisherman boat back to stylish glory.

Before the Revolution, when he was 14, Alvero had been working in Havana as a first mate, taking rich men fishing off the coast of Havana. They were mostly wealthy Americans who were intrigued by Hemingway's early 1950s novel, *The Old Man and the Sea*. The gamblers visiting Havana wanted to catch a marlin or sailfish, so they chartered the boss's boat to troll the deep water off Havana. At night they would frequent the casinos and bars and, by day, fish the Gulf Stream.

The waters off Havana are deep. Only a mile off the fabled Malecón, the ocean floor is over 1000 feet below the keel. Pelagic fish cruise by on their migratory routes. Lucky and skilled anglers might catch a tuna, king mackerel or trophy fish like a marlin. The captain could always guarantee a barracuda, an excellent fighter but not a preferred food fish due to the reputation for dangerous cyanotoxin in the large specimens. Eating toxic fish can be very serious or even deadly.

Young Alvero would tend to the clients, rigging their trolling lines, baiting hooks and serving beverages. He was an affable teenager and was tipped well by the customers, especially those customers who caught a big fish and were feeling good from drinking beer. He was learning much about operating the boat, fishing and catering to the customers.

The captain operated the boat from a tall tuna tower, scouting for man-o-war birds and gulls. That signaled that there were bait fish. Where there were bait fish, there would be dolphins – not the bottlenose dolphin mammals, but dolphin fish, also called dorado or mahi-mahi. When the bait fish was spotted, the captain yelled to young Alvero to prepare the trolling lines and get the clients ready.

Alvero learned a lot from the captain, like how to fish and how to run the boat. It was his own affable nature that made him endearing to the clients, even through language differences. His broad smile and sixth sense of willingness to step in when he saw the need was natural. The captain recognized his abilities and felt good to have this young Cuban as his first mate.

One of the clients was Rodolfo Diego, an important security official in the Batista government. He was a regular customer who enjoyed the fishing. Often, some Americans joined him for a day trip. They were boisterous, drinking and joking, and teasing one another. But at times they were serious and quiet, involved in whispered conversation. Alvero was careful not to intrude but suspected they were talking about political unrest. Times were getting tense in Cuba then.

Rodolfo and Alvero enjoyed an unlikely friendship. Alvero was a young novice from a working-class family and Rodolfo a well-to-do government official, who was almost old enough to be his father. Fishing was a common bond. Rodolfo credited his fishing success to Alvero's mentoring. It was good that they could associate without the prevailing class constraints that divided Cuba's population.

The fishing charters came to an abrupt halt on January 1, 1959 when the Revolution succeeded in overturning the Batista regime. The captain of the fishing vessel Alvero had been working on fled to Florida with his boat and a full capacity of passengers. Some were escaping for their lives to avoid retribution for their excesses; others escaped out of fear of change. The next years were a whirlwind of reinvention of the Cuban political and economic system.

Still in Cuba, Alvero was connected to the sea working as a stevedore on the docks. It was not fishing. The work was onshore and not at sea, but it was work. One day he was surprised to see Rodolfo Diego come to the dock to meet a Russian ship. He was in a tailored uniform of the Revolutionary Army with a contingent of lieutenants. Alvero stood back. He had luggage to unload. He wanted to avoid being seen.

"Alvero! My young friend, it is so good to see you!" Rodolfo shouted, with genuine enthusiasm. This newly-minted general broke away from his entourage and strode toward Alvero who was frozen in his shoes, not knowing what to expect. Rodolfo hugged him warmly, and patted his back.

"I miss going fishing with you, but I have been busy in the new government." He added, "I was always part of the revolution and hated to be placed in the Batista regime. It was my honor to help the Comandante in any way. Now, I am a General!"

Alvero recalled the Americans he had seen on the boat. He figured that they must have been the CIA working to cover their bases by being invested in both sides of the conflict. Who knew what was the truth with so much propaganda flying. The reality now was that Rodolfo was not purged for his activities with Batista, but rewarded for his service as an undercover operative in a high place.

"Let's go fishing again. I will need you to bait my hook." General Diego broke into a wide grin and returned to his duty meeting the Russians.

So began the long special relationship between the General and Alvero. They continued to meet up to go fishing off Varadero and even to the Malecón. Alvero trained as a captain and was given charge of a sport fishing boat, confiscated from a capitalist bourgeoisie, to operate for the government at Varadero. By 1963 he was established enough to think about getting married. Life was good. He was fishing again, with Russian clients, and had a new wife, who was deeply invested in the Communist Party. The General, along with an aide, would give Alvero advance notice when he came to fish on the boat. When the General called, all of Alvero's plans were put aside in order to schedule the boat for him.

When the General came aboard, and they were motoring out the harbor past the fort at the entrance, Alvero could see the mood of Rodolfo change from the tough, macho leader to a happy fisherman. They would revert to their relationship of the past, the first mate helper and the hopeful angler. It was refreshing for both. There was much joy in the General's eyes when he fought and landed a fish. Even a small 15-pound inedible tunny fish brought a wide smile across his face.

"Rodolfo, keep a tight line. I think you have a big one on." On this day, Alvero suspected the quick hard hit on the line was a barracuda. "Slow, easy."

Rodolfo reeled, pumping back and forth on the rod, leaning in his slatted-back fighting chair. He fought the fish, obviously well-hooked, for 15 minutes. It had not tired. The fish was still fighting to keep his place in the sea as much as Rodolfo was battling to remove him from it. Twenty minutes and not a single jump but the fish was running from left to right. Rodolfo was tiring, but so was the fish. Nearly thirty minutes passed and the line slacked. It was still weighted, but there was no resistance except dead weight. Alvero grabbed the line to pull up what was on the hook. He turned and smiled at Rodolfo.

"Congratulations, Rodolfo! It looks like you are now the old man … and the sea has won!"

Laughing heartily, Alvero pulled up the head of a large barracuda hooked on the line, missing the rest of the body. Like in Hemingway's story, the shark had stolen Rodolfo's hard-fought prize. They both laughed, opened Cristal beers, and toasted Hemingway, the sea, the fish, even the shark!

It was good to have such a friend. And, in the new Cuba, it was good to have a powerful friend.

The devotion of Alvero's wife, Amalia, to the Revolution and local communist organization often conflicted with his upbringing. Alvero was not a devoted Catholic but he had been raised in the teachings of the church and schooled by nuns who drove home their lessons with a stiff wooden yardstick. Sometimes opposites attract. Alvero and Amalia were in young love, with a daughter and a mostly happy family life. To keep peace at home, the two young lovers avoided discussions of the government. Politics didn't matter much to Alvero. When problems emerged from the government, he shrugged them off as something he had no power to control. Amalia vigorously defended and excused any failings of the new system. For family peace, it was best to avoid conflict.

Operating the small charter fishing boat for the government was a lucky break. Most people had jobs that were not related to their passion. They could only choose from limited opportunities the government laid out for them. Alvero was in his element, and when on the boat, he was in charge of his own life. Alvero grew strong and fat over the years.

When the Cuban government lifted restrictions on people leaving Cuba, Alvero did not think about leaving Cuba and going to the U.S. But he was happy to help purge the nation of the people who did not want to live there. He asked for permission to take passengers to Key West on the promise he would return to Cuba.

On his first trip to the U.S., it didn't take long for him to be overwhelmed with Cubans wanting to leave on his boat. He tried to limit the number, but finally relented and took many more than he should have on board for the crossing.

Each person showed up at the dock with suitcases and other belongings. He had to set an ultimatum, telling his passengers, "Your possessions or you, but not both." Scavengers at the dock quickly made off with the discarded luggage.

What Alvero didn't expect when he decided to take Cubans to Florida was that he would be swept up in the immigration confusion at the docks in Key West. It was his boat, or actually the Cuban government's, but he was rounded up along with the people who had come to the U.S. to stay. Even though he didn't want to stay in the U.S. he was taken to a processing facility called "Krome". He didn't know where it was, only that it was a warehouse for people who were all desperate to get to their relatives in Miami. He thought he might have a cousin in Hialeah, but he had no contact information, only a name. He wasn't even sure he had ever met his cousin, but that seemed to be no problem as Cuban families had strong bonds, even if distant and unseen.

He met with immigration officers and told his story over and over, explaining he was not trying to immigrate. He was worried about his boat, which was unlike the other derelict and decaying vessels that transported people leaving Cuba. His boat was a nice, if small, old sport fisherman. Alvero kept the woodwork varnished and took pride in polishing the vintage craft to be attractive to his customers.

It was a 30-ft Lyman sleeper with a small cuddy cabin. The Lyman was built in Michigan and had a distinctive lapstrake hull. The original owner likely had placed a special custom order in the 1950s and arranged to have it shipped to Cuba. It was powered by two gasoline engines and could speed across calm waters. When the owner fled Cuba, or was expelled or perhaps worse, the boat fell under the supervision of the General.

The vessel was perfect for tooling about in Havana Harbor and useful to go offshore when the weather was suitable. Unlike offshore fishing boats, like Hemingway's prized *Pilar*, the Lyman was more of a lake boat. It was well-built and seaworthy, but not designed for rough weather. With only a small hardtop connected to a windshield, it provided little protection from spray or rain.

Alvero was given the boat to run as a charter, so long as he would be able to take the General fishing whenever he called. Sometimes it was on very short notice and Alvero would have to cancel a tour with a foreign visitor. But it did not matter, because the foreign visitor was there but once and the General was Alvero's long-time patron, and more importantly, his friend.

Now, the U.S. Coast Guard had impounded his craft. Alvero was livid to be caught up in the retention of refugees. He was merely the conveyance for refugees and had no plans to immigrate to the U.S. He was being herded with the other Cubans and his boat was gone. All he could think about was, "Where was the boat now? Is it safe? How will I get back to Cuba?" He worried it over and over in his mind, like an ear-worm that he couldn't shake.

He had heard the U.S. Coast Guard sunk unseaworthy vessels after taking passengers on board their ships. His knew his boat was seaworthy. After all, he had made it to the dock to disembark his refugee passengers. He hoped, he prayed, that the officials wouldn't scuttle his pride and joy.

He told any official-looking person he met who would listen, "Where is my boat? I want to take it back to Cuba. I must go back! I only brought people here to help them." He continued to say that all he wanted to do was drop off the refugees and return to Cuba. He did not have any interest in seeking asylum in the U.S.

It was the same at each interview. An officer would take the statement, say they would look into it, and then the next time it was the same again, telling his story and pleading to be returned to Key West and his boat. Weeks passed before he finally was called to an interview where he met someone he did not recognize. It was his cousin, Manuel Gonzalez, from Hialeah. He was quickly released into his cousin's custody. On the drive to Hialeah, they compared notes on family and got acquainted. He could stay with Manuel until he could return to Key West to search for his boat.

It took another couple of weeks for Manuel to get time off from his two jobs to arrange to take Alvero to Key West. All along the long drive through the Keys, Alvero was overwhelmed with worry about what had happened to his boat. It was nearly two months since he had seen her. Although he now had American papers, including a green card, as well as a cash stipend, he had little else. And, his boat was gone. Also, he had no way to contact his family or the General.

When Manuel and Alvero arrived in Key West, they visited the Coast Guard station and the immigration office, inquiring about the whereabouts of his boat. Usually, the language barrier was an obstacle for the U.S. personnel and they dismissed the questions as the rant of a crazy Cuban.

Often, the officials deferred the problem to someone else, asking Alvero to "come back tomorrow" to speak to another person who could help. In desperation, he could only think, "Mañana, mañana."

After several days of the run-around Manuel couldn't stay any longer. He had to return to his work in Hialeah. That meant that Alvero would need to be on his own in Key West or wait for another time when his cousin had time off from work and could travel from Hialeah to the Keys.

Manuel remembered that he had a distant cousin who worked in Key West. Manuel and Alvero looked him up and arranged for Alvero to stay in the Keys to continue pursuing getting his boat back. Manuel gave Alvero all the cash he had and wished him luck. "I will pray for you that you find your boat. And, if we have contact with our family in Cuba, we will tell them what has happened so they can tell your wife."

While he was staying in the Keys, Alvero worked in the same restaurant as Manuel's cousin, washing dishes and clearing tables. It was honest work, but well below the prestige of a sea captain.

Alvero spent his free time walking the storage areas of Key West and Stock Island. Finally, one day, he saw his boat behind a fence, in an impound lot, destined to be auctioned off. It was on blocks in a yard crowded with an assortment of boats and cars, containers and equipment. His spirits soared that it was not at the bottom of the ocean and at least he could see her, dirty but intact.

Seeing his boat, Alvero reinvigorated his resolve to get her back. He pushed and rattled at the gate until a guard came. He tried to explain to the guard that one of the boats

149

was his prized possession. The guard stated in a harsh tone that he was required to call the authorities. But Alvero was unmovable as he pressed his case again and again. Finally, there was some progress. Fortunately, his captain's certificate was framed and mounted on the cabin bulkhead, confirming his claim to the boat. Although, in reality, the boat belonged to the Cuban government and he was merely the steward, he could claim to be the owner since there was no one to say anything contrary. Eventually, after weeks of pressing the officials, the boat was removed from the auction schedule, and Alvero was instructed to get a Florida registration for it before he could take possession.

With only the cash Manuel had given him and a few dollars from his restaurant job, he didn't know how he could accomplish this. Nonetheless, he had to do it to retrieve his boat. Another month passed and finally he had his registration from the registration department in Tallahassee, the state capital. He cobbled together every cent and begged a local boatyard to move his *La Luna* to their yard for repairs. He offered to work at the boatyard in exchange for storage fees and do-it-yourself yard privileges.

Seeing how well and hard Alvero worked on the boat repair jobs he was given, the boatyard management hired him on for pay. It was better pay than the restaurant and he could save money by living in a storeroom at the boatyard and showering at a nearby marina. Every day, after his paid job at the yard ended, he worked on fixing his own boat, using salvaged materials left over in the yard.

More months passed. What must his wife think? What would the Cuban officials who gave him permission to take passengers to Key West think? Would he be in trouble? He missed his daughter and wife. While many Cubans were overjoyed to be making a new life in the U.S. or escaping punishment for their criminal past in Cuba, he was an accidental immigrant who desperately wanted to go home to his family and his country.

Finally, his boat was finished and launched. Alvero passed the test to get his USCG captain's license. When he took a slip at the Garrison Bight Marina, he hand-painted a sign on cardboard "Fish with a Cuban Fishing Guide like Ernest Hemingway, $100 USD, plus gas." As soon as he could, he moved to live aboard his boat, in an austere lifestyle. He was careful not to encrust his boat with personal possessions that might interfere with his charters.

Alvero's Lyman did not look like the other large charter sportfishing boats that had new and sleek tuna towers and outriggers for trolling. His boat was a beautifully restored wood boat with varnished mahogany seats and a slatted wood fighting chair. The polished stainless-steel railings glistened in the bright sun.

It still had *La Luna* painted on the stern, with Havana as the home port. It was good promotion for the boat to say Havana, until a Florida Marine Patrol officer gruffly told him he was in America now and he needed to change the port of call to Key West or somewhere else in the United States. Alvero was very careful not to provoke any problems so he complied without complaint.

His business took off and soon, with tips and full charters, he was able to pay his slip rent and moved from living on the boat into a small room near the marina. The other charter captains accepted him as a peer and didn't resent him as competition. They considered his clientele small fish compared to the money they could make by fishing offshore. He stayed busy, often with Cuban clients. He did not take more than three people out fishing at a time. Sometimes he took his clients to the flats, sometimes to go bottom fishing on the reef, or trolling offshore. More often than not he returned with fish. When clients didn't want to take all of the fish they caught, he sold them through the back door to the restaurant where he used to work.

Alvero was a natural entrepreneur, adapting to capitalist business fast and well. He was saving a lot. Since his business was conducted in cash, he had wads of money hidden in the recesses of his boat. Soon, he would be able to return to Havana and face whatever consequences his long absence entailed.

Alvero watched for a good weather window to make his trip across the Straits of Florida. Planning for the worst, he prepped with extra fuel and water. When it was time to cast off his dock lines, he motored out of the channel in darkness and passed the Sand Key lighthouse as the dawn broke in the east. Then, turning to the west, he ran out past the U.S. territorial limit before setting a course for Havana harbor.

It was an uneventful trip until he was in sight of Cuba. His heart raced as a Cuban Defense Ministry vessel approached him several miles north of the entrance to Havana Harbor. An announcement broadcast out over their loud speaker hailer, "Atención - esta es la guardia costera cubana. Le ordenamos que apague su motor, prepárese para ser abordado."

Then, in broken English, "Attention, this is the Cuban Defense Force. Stop your engines and prepare to be boarded."

He understood immediately and took the boat out of gear and turned off his engines.

The military cruiser was intimidating, with a large gun manned by a uniformed sailor on the foredeck. Alvero had seen these patrol boats before, but was never concerned as he was a familiar sight when he was fishing out of Havana. He knew many of the military captains and they would exchange waves as they passed. Now, he was a foreign U.S. boat entering Cuba. He was humbled.

The patrol boat pulled alongside. Alvero quickly reached for bumpers to keep the cruiser from scratching the hull he had painted to perfection. This made the officers a bit nervous as they stepped from their deck to his gunwales. One kept his hand on his side arm.

The senior officer asked, "Do you speak Spanish?" Alvero chuckled to himself. Had he been away so long that he lost his Cuban looks? "Sí, hablo Español. Soy Cubano!"

The officers conducted a professional inquisition, "What is your name? Where are you from? Why are you here?" Questions came faster than Alvero could answer, and, besides, his story was complicated.

He said, "One moment please. Let me answer!" Alvero continued, "Do you know who I am? I am a friend of General Rodolfo Diego. He gave permission to me to take Marielitos to Florida. I was captured by the U.S. Coast Guard and it has taken me a year to get back home. So, please don't fuck with me! Call the General!"

The officers did not quite know how to react. They did not want to get on the wrong side of a general, but they also knew they would be in trouble if they did not perform their due diligence to enforce the rules. So, they punted and called for a superior to decide. *La Luna* was taken in tow to the Defense Force dock.

Alvero was glad they backed off from their aggressive interrogation. He and the defense force officials all waited in silence. Soon, the General appeared and greeted Alvero cautiously. He sat on the boat and asked to understand Alvero's story. By the time they finished their conversation, it was like old times. The ordeal Alvero had endured was amusing to the General and he arranged for Alvero and the boat to be welcomed back.

When the General departed, he said, "Alvero, my old friend, we will go fishing again soon. You can bait my hook again." The soldiers at the dock and their superior officers witnessed this exchange, giving Alvero relief from any future interference by the military police.

Now Alvero could return to his wife and see his daughter. When he got to his house, they were stunned to see him. In tears, his daughter ran to him, grabbing him tightly and not letting go. His wife was not as readily welcoming. She was happy to see him and loved him deeply, but angry that he had been gone for such a long time. She had assumed he had left with the Marielitos, abandoning them both or he was dead. She had hated him for a year for that.

During the time he was gone, she became even more devoted to the Revolution and unforgiving of the traitors who had abandoned their homeland and rejected the Revolution.

When Alvero tried to embrace his wife, she pulled back, saying, "I am so happy to have you back, but why did it take so long?"

Alvero told her the truth, with a little embellishment, hoping to gain some sympathy. "It was very difficult. I was captured by the Americans. They tangled me up with the people I was taking to the United States. They took my boat and held me in a jail. Then I had to find my boat again and get it back from the government officials. It needed work to make it seaworthy and I had to work to make money to fix it. It was hard and there was no way to contact you. I am sorry it took a long time. I missed you terribly. I thought of you and our baby girl every day."

Amalia didn't know how to respond; she was conflicted between her love for Alvero and her feelings about being abandoned for a long time. She was angry and disgusted with the Cubans who had left, believing them to be traitors to the country. These refugees that kept her husband away from her by leaving Cuba were just like the first exiles - deserters.

"You were tied up with los gusanos… the worms, who would abandon our country and the Revolution! You should know that when you are with the worms, that you are with their mierda!"

Alvero was a little hurt by this, "I was not with them, I was only taking them away. General Rodolfo provided his permission to do it. I think Cuba is better to have them gone."

Amalia calmed down a little, but she was still intense with disgust for the refugees who had betrayed the revolution by leaving, and upset that Alvero was involved in their exit. "Alvero, I am happy that you are back with me and your daughter, but you must not help these people again, even if the General approves. They are worms!"

It took all night to ease her qualms. They would share a bed for the first time in a year and renew their passion. But something had changed in both of them.

Alvero would rebuild his life and, using his American papers, go between Cuba and Key West. Alvero's status as a legal resident of the U.S. gave him special privileges that came in handy. His American resident status allowed him admittance to the U.S. His Cuban passport gave him admittance to Cuba to visit family. It was a wrinkle in U.S. policy that Alvero was able to use in order to have a place in both worlds.

In 1993 the Cuban government opened opportunities for private businesses, and Alvero decided he should own his boat. The next time the General came to fish, he asked him if he could have *La Luna* for his own. After 30 years of fishing together, the general said "Of course. I've always thought of her as your mistress."

In Key West, Alvero made money with fishing charters, enabling him to bring goods back to Havana where he could live the life he wanted with his family, at ease with the fishing charters he had for foreigners and the protection he enjoyed with the General.

FIFTEEN

Maria banged on Matvey's door. "Open, open, this is important!"

Matvey woke abruptly. Still in his clothes he was startled by the loud knocking. He cracked the door and saw it was Maria. He was still shaken, knowing he had just killed Evelyn and stolen the biggest thing he had ever taken in his gigolo exploitations.

Maria pushed her way into his apartment and closed the door. She said breathlessly, "The police are on their way! An ambulance has taken away one of our guests. They talked to a maid and she said she saw you leave the room. They will be looking for you! You must go! You must go – NOW!"

It surprised Matvey that Maria was there to warn him. She had barely spoken to him all his life. He knew how much his mother despised Maria and he had no love for her either. He was confused that she was warning him about the police.

She handed him the keys to the resort truck. "Take this and drive to the town square and then find your own way to hide somewhere safe. Maybe you have family that can help you. This is as much as I can do. Go!"

Matvey thought for a moment. "But, I cannot drive a car," he said as he handed the keys back to her.

Maria responded in exasperation, "Then walk or take one of the resort bicycles – just go before the police come!"

He had no idea that Maria cared about him. In Maria's mind, Matvey was her son born by another, albeit undeserving, mother. She could not bear to see him taken by the police and was sick at the thought of this beautiful boy, Ivan's son, being prosecuted and imprisoned. He could not have done anything wrong.

She left quickly, looking up and down the hall to see if anyone had seen her. It was as much as she could do and perhaps more than she should have.

After Maria left to go meet the police, Matvey quickly retrieved the cross from the flower pot. He found a small metal box where his mother kept the letters from Julio and old photographs. He paused to look at the photos. His mother and father were so young, his age. They looked happy. He thought, "How beautiful my mother was? I wish she had told me about my father and why he went away."

After 20 years Matvey was still unaware of his Russian ancestry and in denial about his physical attributes. All this was too much to ponder and there was no time. He snapped back to the urgency of getting away and emptied the box's contents into a dresser drawer, placing his collection of jewelry and the cross into the security of the metal box.

Matvey hurriedly packed a small backpack with a few clothes and his passport. The metal box, with his trove of stolen jewelry, watches, and now the crucifix, took most of the space in the pack, so he barely fit in a change of clothes. He grabbed the money he and his mother had hidden in the guira gourd that was hanging on the wall with the other percussion instruments and scurried out to the bike rack. He rode on a nature trail from the resort to connect with the main road to Playa Larga.

The road was not frequently travelled except when tour buses were going from the small coastal community at the head of the Bay of Pigs. He could hear cars coming for quite a distance, so every time he suspected a vehicle was coming, he would leave the road and lay low in the shrubbery on the roadside. After he was about 10 kilometers away from the resort, and past the intersection with La Caleta de Fidel Castro on one side and the road to Los Hondones on the other side, he waited in the forest until dark.

As the sun set, the waxing moon illuminated the roadway. Night travel would be even safer. He could see the glow of headlights even before he could hear the cars on the road. Even fewer cars would travel at night so he had the road to himself for the 6-kilometer ride to Playa Larga.

He waited to approach Playa Larga until midmorning, trying to be inconspicuous. He sat at the edge of the bay near a spring that vented water from the aquifer to flow into the bay. He knew the settlement well. It was a place he went to, to escape the confines of the resort. In the past, he swam at the beach and sat under a palm tree, sipping a Cristal beer while watching the ocean. For now, he figured he could stay in one of the open beach cabana shelters and eat from the community garden.

He remembered seeing sportfishing boats come into the harbor during his previous visits. Offshore fishermen in large yachts used Playa Larga as a retreat from bad weather or just as a stop to give the fishermen on the charter a chance to visit Cuba. They came to the restaurant at the spring to have rum, smoke cigars, and tell boisterous lies to one another. Matvey thought he might stow away on one of these boats and go to the Cayman Islands. But he realized it wasn't really practical since there were few places to hide on these sport fishing boats and the boats were monitored by the marine police when they entered and left Cuba.

He would need to find another way out. There was no place to hide in Cuba and the police were certain to find him. Playa Larga was too close to Girón and the police might begin looking for him here. He didn't know much about the north side of the island, beyond a few visits to Havana. He thought hiding in the big city would be better than this place where some people knew him. He decided he needed to get to Havana.

Matvey found a tattered straw hat on the roadside and put it on his head to hide his blond hair. But he could not hide his height. He stood with other people waiting for a bus or thumbing a ride toward Havana. When he saw a military vehicle or police car coming, he sat on the ground. While waiting for a ride, he began talking with a few fellow travelers. One guy told him about how he would one day go to the United States. He would take a boat with a trafficker, or bribe people on a foreign yacht. He would leave the country, one day, when he saved enough money.

Matvey reasoned that this might be the way for him to get away and start a new life. He asked the guy about places where boats were and was told Marina Hemingway is where the rich people come in their yachts to visit Cuba.

A truck stopped and more than a dozen people, including Matvey, climbed on the flatbed enroute to Havana.

Matvey didn't know that Evelyn did not die, that she only passed out and was comatose. He was only thinking about not being arrested for murder. He would never know that she would recover and that her troubles would catch up with her when the contents of her room were surveyed by the crime investigators. She was a victim of one crime but the perpetrator of another. To Matvey, she was dead and he was her murderer.

Matvey found his way to the Marina Hemingway and saw the entire property was surrounded by a chain metal fence. There was a guard station at the road entrance with two security guards. The sign said "Bienvenidos a Marina Hemingway Yacht Club – Gateway to Cuba". Matvey thought, it should say "Exit to America and Freedom!" Matvey casually walked along the fence looking for an opening. At one end there was some vegetation where the fence met the ocean. He thought, "Simple, just get in the water and swim around to find a place to get inside." Matvey decided to walk around the neighborhood outside the marina until after dark.

In one of the yards nearby he saw a clothesline with clothes hanging to dry. Matvey saw the opportunity to replenish his wardrobe so he took a shirt and pants. He stowed his t-shirt and pants in his daypack, wrapping them around his metal strong box.

That night, he slipped into the water near the marina, holding his pack over his head. He tired quickly and found it was easier to swim on his back with the pack on his chest. Slipping under the fence, he entered the marina canal and swam past a few boats tied to the marina's extensive concrete seawalls. The boats tied to the seawall had their names and their ports of call painted on their stern: Georgetown CI; Key West, FL; Nassau, BA; Toronto, CA. Any of these places would be suitable to seek refuge. The U.S. was his foremost desire, but anywhere would be good, anywhere but Cuba.

Matvey heard voices, loud laughing and conversation. It was late and, from the sounds, the people seemed drunk. The boat people were at the yacht club, heading to the boat dock returning from a night out in Havana. He quietly dog-paddled to the back side of one of the boats. He was under the sheer of the stern and out of sight. Fortunately, the water was deep enough for their boat but shallow enough for him to stand.

The boaters got on their boat and went inside. Now their voices were muffled through the hull. A stream of water flowed over his head. They had turned on their air conditioner and the cooling water pump was spurting through an outlet directly over his head. His strongbox and pack were submerged.

After a few minutes, Matvey decided it was safe to move on to one of the vacant canals at the far end of the marina. In this marina, there was much more capacity for boats than there were yachts. Some parts of the marina were falling into disrepair due to the lack of use and empty boat slips. Matvey found a collapsed seawall leaving an eroded cavity under the concrete cap. The area above was roped off to prevent people from tripping. This would be a perfect place to wait for a boat he might stow away on.

He was planning to stay hidden at Marina Hemingway in his sea-wall cave, screened behind the red mangroves, until he could figure out a way to leave Cuba on a boat. He watched the marina and the routine of the guards, biding his time in the day and scavenging for food at night, careful to avoid the night security guards. The guards posed little threat since they were complacent and stayed in their small air-conditioned guard shack. Sometimes he could see them sleeping.

When the marina was a little busier with tourist visitors, Matvey could hide among them and use the lavatory facility. Since he did not appear to be Cuban, he didn't attract the attention of the marina workers or security. They all assumed he was either a tourist or visiting yachtsman. Only his worn-out black leather shoes could give him away.

Matvey noticed that a few boats were docked but had no visitors. One was older and looked abandoned. He slipped aboard to look inside. There was a rusty lock on the companionway doors. It was easy to pull the hasp from the rotten wood frame of the companionway and go inside. It was musty but so much drier than his seawall hide-out. And he found canned food. This would be where he could wait. Nobody was going to use this old boat, not with an engine that was in pieces on the cabin floor.

Matvey retrieved his strong box and change of clothes from his seawall cave hideaway and moved aboard, careful to position the lock back to appear secure. It was a restful night. Awakening with sun streaming into the main cabin, he was in a better place to watch and wait. He was hiding on the derelict boat for nearly a week, only going out late at night when he felt the guards were in their cubicle.

One night, late, while exiting the boat, he saw a flashlight scan the seawall. It was coming from the other side of the canal, toward him. He was already out of the cabin and on the deck, so he scrambled to the bow laying low on the faded teak surface. He could hear two guards talking.

"I think I saw something, on the old boat," one exclaimed. Then two flashlight beams were scanning the boat. The guards walked around the end of the canal and headed to the boat. Matvey lifted a small dinghy turned upside down on the foredeck just enough to squeeze himself under the hull. He didn't fit. His body lifted the dinghy so he had to support its weight while not moving.

Matvey could see the lights moving around the seawall and bathing the deck of the boat. He felt the boat shift as one of the guards stepped aboard. Matvey hoped the screws pushed into the rotten wood would hold. They would release if the guard pulled on the lock, but might stay if he only shook the lock. If they opened the door, it would be obvious that someone was secretly living aboard. He heard the guard rattle the lock. It thunked against the companionway door as he let it go.

Just then, a raucous screeching noise and whoosh of air from above caught the attention of the guards. A large great blue heron was roosting in the rigging on the spreaders. As the bird departed a jet stream of excrement shot out past the guard in the cockpit and landed on the water with a splat.

Their lights flashed on the wings as it flew away. Both of the guards laughed.

The guard in the cockpit said "Hey man, that is not funny. It could have shit on me!" The bird had been patient during the intrusion on the boat, but the thunking of the lock startled it. The guards laughed a bit, determining that what they saw was a bird and not an intruder. The boat rocked as they stepped off the boat and, then, they were gone.

Matvey resolved to be more careful. He stayed under the dinghy until the security guards were long gone. Matvey returned to the cabin to forgo his nightly stroll scrounging for anything he might use or eat.

Boats came and went while Matvey was hiding out, biding his time. Many of the boats were from Canada because Canada wasn't part of the embargo restrictions that the U.S. imposed. When boats arrived, customs officials and medical personnel came to clear the passengers, allowing the visitors to cruise Cuban waters. Matvey watched from the shadows of his sailboat hideout. Most of the boats were cruising sailboats, coming to Marina Hemingway as a first stop on their circumnavigation of the island. Matvey had seen boats like these at the port in Cienfuegos but had never thought much about them. He wondered if he might befriend one of the owners and ask to be taken to Florida. He would have to be patient to find a good prospect.

A small power boat entered the marina. It was old, not like the foreign sailboats and large power yachts that frequented the marina and docked close to the office. This boat was on the same canal as Matvey's hideaway home, tied up to the seawall, away from the office and guard house. An old fat man was on the boat, cleaning and fussing with lines and buckets. The boat had varnished mahogany trim and a salty look. Matvey watched for hours through the small portlight on his boat. He thought that boat must be an antique. On the stern he could see the name *La Luna* painted in gold letters and Key West painted underneath. It was a pretty boat, but Matvey did not like having a close neighbor.

One night he observed a family with packed bags sneak into the marina, getting onboard the old boat, *La Luna*. Matvey immediately thought trafficking – Cubans making their escape. The mother and father dragged their 3-year-old boy to the boat and tossed their luggage to the heavy-set captain. They were in a hurry.

Matvey grabbed his pack with the strong box and ran to the boat, jumping on board. "Take me with you!" he yelled. The captain shook his head "No!" The family said "You cannot come with us. We are only going fishing."

Matvey argued, "You do not need luggage to go fishing. You are leaving Cuba. I must go with you. Take me or I will alert the police that this is trafficking!" Matvey had them.

"Fine," said the captain, "but you must pay!" Matvey reached into his pocket and pushed a handful of crumpled paper money into the captain's shirt pocket.

Fearing discovery by the commotion Matvey was causing, the captain said, "Bueno, but I want no trouble! Shut up or the guards will come! We must go … now!"

The plan was to drop the family at Boca Grande Key near Key West. The captain then would radio to friends in Key West to pick them up so he could avoid immigration and the family could sneak into the U.S. unnoticed.

The captain cast off and motored into the darkness on a moonless night, into a windy and rainy sea. It was a perfect night to avoid discovery by the Cuban Coast Guard, but horribly rough to make the 90-mile crossing to the Florida Keys.

SIXTEEN

As they motored out of Marina Hemingway, Captain Alvero switched off the running lights. Darkness swallowed the boat. Only a dim glow illuminated a compass at the helm. The child hugged the captain's legs as he stood at the wheel. His mother hugged the captain and whispered, "Thank you for saving us. I love you always for this." Then she pulled the boy from the captain's leg and, together as a family, they huddled in the port corner of the small open cabin, across from the wheel.

When the boat emerged from the breakwater, a sea swell rolled the boat from side to side. It wasn't an extreme yaw, but rocky enough that Matvey needed to hold on to a rail.

Soon they passed a sea buoy. Alvero had been focused on steering toward its blinking light. A few lights gleamed on the southern horizon and a hazy glow reflected in the skies to the east. It was the lights from Havana illuminating low clouds and the thick humid air.

The gas engines rumbled a constant drone. They were not going fast, maybe 6 knots, certainly no more than 10. The skies were dark with no moon. Occasionally stars could be seen through breaks in the clouds, until the gap closed and blackness reclaimed the sea and sky. Typical of squall lines, rain came in sheets and winds increased, broken by respites of calmer winds and seas.

Two hours after leaving Cuba they were in international waters on their way. They had evaded discovery by the Cuban defense patrol boats. There had been no conversation. The tension between Matvey and the Captain precluded any questions from either.

The captain glanced at Matvey and looked him up and down. It was dark, but Matvey could see his furled brows on a scowling face. Alvero barked, "Can you steer this boat?"

Matvey reacted immediately without even thinking. "Yes, of course! How hard can it be?" His young machismo self-confidence was speaking for him.

"We will see how you do. I need a few minutes to check the charts." Alvero responded with skepticism. He was pained to need any help, especially from this stowaway. He coached Matvey on how to adjust course to anticipate the waves.

Matvey was not a natural at this but he was determined to prove himself capable. After a few minutes, Alvero ducked inside the small cuddy cabin and held a flashlight over a well-worn paper chart. On a calm day, in the light, he could make the run to Key West easily by steering 0 degrees north, with a little compensation for wind and the Gulf Stream. At night in foul weather, this was going to take some calculation. Alvero checked the VHF radio for traffic. He heard only static. He did not expect any transmissions, but he wanted assurance that another boat was out in this weather.

Alvero returned and grabbed the wheel back from Matvey, shouldering him back to the place where he had been leaning.

The old Lyman boat was built 50 years ago from mahogany over an oak frame. It was in very good shape, mostly because Alvero had access to materials when he was in Florida. In Cuba caring for an old wood boat like his was a challenge. The resourcefulness of the Cuban workers was essential in a place without materials and parts. Alvero was proud of his boat but knew in his heart that his old, small, 30-foot boat was a pleasure craft built for fair weather not a sea going vessel designed for serious conditions.

The tropical weather system that had been building did not dissipate with interaction with the island's mountains. Instead, the system was strengthening and moving west, counter to the Gulf Stream. The Gulf Stream current is a river in the ocean, flowing counter-clockwise around the Gulf of Mexico, through the straits between Florida and Cuba, then up the east coast of the U.S. to flow across the north Atlantic to the UK. When the winds are with the Stream it can be flat calm and glassy with long periods between gentle rolling swells. With wind opposite the Stream, the waves build into tumultuous haystacks.

Alvero hoped the bands of weather would be all they faced over the next 10 hours. He searched the distant horizon seeing the flashes of lightning illuminating the bands of clouds. He could tell that the storm was probably 60 or 70 miles off. It would be close but he hoped for the best and turned his attention to steering the course he had plotted.

Each squall line seemed worse than the last. The conditions were subsiding less between each band of strong wind and rain. Seas were piling up and their progress was slowing. Making less speed over the ocean floor was troubling. Not only were they facing handling the weather, but they were also using more fuel than planned. Alvero was constantly monitoring his gauges; check engine oil and temperature, fuel; check compass heading and seas ahead; adjust for waves, repeat. This was the pattern for hours.

Matvey was feeling the mal de mer, trying to imagine that this would be over soon. He had no idea of how long it would take to get to Florida. The family was huddled together with the boy asleep after exhausting himself from crying. Matvey wished he could sleep but fear gripped his gut as much as the seasickness.

Conditions continued to deteriorate and it became a challenge to keep the boat on a heading to Key West. Alvero yelled at Matvey to take the wheel again and steer directly into the waves. As Matvey moved to take the helm, just then a large wave pushed the boat hard to the side and he lost his balance. He grabbed his prized day pack carrying his stolen treasures. Alvero yelled again, "I need you to pay attention! Now!"

Alvero set a course into the wind and waves which were now screaming from the northeast before handing the helm to Matvey. The small waves rocked the boat, the large waves broke over the bow and flooded over the windshield. They were all soaked and cold.

Alvero seemed to be in the cuddy cabin forever looking at the now soaked chart. He emerged and took the wheel back from Matvey and made ready to steer a new course to run mostly with the wind and waves instead of against them. This was a dangerous move. Alvero would have to pilot the Lyman carefully or risk broaching when the boat was broadside to the heavy waves. He maintained his course into the wind and tried to get a sense of rhythm to the chaotic wave pattern. When he saw an opening, he pivoted carefully to surf into the new course.

Now the priority was not getting to Key West but to the Marquesas. These islands are an atoll-shaped grouping about 30 miles west of Key West. They are the last group of Keys before the Dry Tortugas. Alvero reasoned that if they could get to the Marquesas, they might be able to shelter in the lee of the islands until the storm passed. At least on this tack, the seas were a bit easier since they were not going against the grain. The engines could make more speed as the boat was pushed by the waves and wind.

What Alvero did not count on was being caught in a counter current of the Gulf Stream. This phenomenon occurs when the Gulf Stream breaks into an eddy and swirls back to the west instead of the east-north tract. The Gulf Stream can flow at a speed of 4 knots. Alvero's boat was now making 6 to 7 knots running before the storm according to the speedometer and the counter current was adding another 3 miles each hour. With no navigation aids, Alvero was navigating on intuition and guts, bringing every bit of seamanship experience to pull them through.

Alvero went back to his routine: check engine oil and temperature, fuel gauge, compass heading, seas ahead, adjust for waves, repeat. Then, squint to search the horizon for any sign of another vessel. By his guess they were more than halfway across the Straits. Alvero rationalized that soon they would have daylight to see the Marquesas. He mentally calculated his speed, course and distance in comparison to his visual memory of the chart. The fuel supply weighed heavily on his mind.

The weather continued to get worse, constantly beating them from behind. Shivering, Matvey clung to his bag and wished he had more than an old life vest to shield him from the piercing rain. When lightning lit up the sea, he got a flash of the sea condition. He saw mountainous waves streaked with white foam, and spray blowing off the tops of breaking waves. It was more terrifying to see the ocean than to be oblivious in the darkness.

The mother of the boy was heaving uncontrollably. After the bile, she had nothing more to bring up. Still, she held tight to her son, surrounded by her husband's arms. They were one mass huddled together still on the port side opposite the helm. In this corner, they were more out of the wind and biting rain.

Alvero continued piloting the craft through the unrelenting assault of the storm. How much worse could this get? How long could they last? How long would this ordeal last? The father was praying out loud. Matvey wished he had a God to call upon to extract him from this nightmare.

Matvey felt the metal box holding the cross in his pack. As he rubbed its outline for good luck, he fantasized that its gold would bring him riches when he survived. He just had to endure. In a moment of fatalism, he thought perhaps this is punishment for murdering the woman at the resort and stealing a holy object. It was a fleeting day dream, as a large wave hit the bow of the boat, stopping forward progress. The bow buried into it. The boat shuddered and spurted, and then like a fighter who had been knocked down, slowly rose back up, to crawl forward and resume the battle against the sea.

Dawn came with a faint glow. The darkness moved into a gray twilight. Now they could all see the cauldron they were in. A torrent of breaking waves and skirts of wind rippling the surface and ripping the sea foam from the waves. Alvero told Matvey to keep an eye on the horizon to the north to see any glint of land. This assignment was a welcome distraction. Matvey thought he might save the day by his will alone to spot land and safety. For hours he strained to see anything more than an endless swirling sea and rain.

It did not seem possible but the wind and weather was worse. Alvero slowed the engines to conserve fuel, powering with just enough to maintain steerage, following whatever course the ocean allowed. The new plan is to survive and hope for rescue. By his estimates, they should have already hit the Marquesas. They must have missed his destination.

It was a miracle of seamanship that Alvero had kept a day-fishing boat afloat for this long through such a rough storm. Daylight began to give into gloom. Soon they were in darkness again as the clouds and rain thickened. For a moment, Alvero checked on the family in the corner. They were all alive, but exhausted. Matvey was acclimated to his cold, wet condition, in a precursor to shock. The hardy

Captain was at the helm, weary, but tough and operating on a strong will.

In the faded light Matvey looked ahead and saw a glimmer of light flash on the horizon. At first, he thought he was hallucinating, but then he saw it again. He shouted to the captain, "There is a light over there! Maybe a ship that can save us?"

Alvero pursed his eyes and looked in the direction Matvey pointed. Indeed, it was a light. He didn't know what. Maybe it was the marker for Rebecca Shoals or maybe a territorial marker off the Marquesas. No matter. He powered ahead with resurging energy and attention to making it to the light source. This course was a rougher ride, crashing through breaking waves and healing to waves pushing on the side of the boat. It was getting closer, but was still so far off. Rain squalls obscured it for minutes, but both the captain and Matvey were bolstered when they sighted it again.

Alvero thought now they might make it. Two long hours later they were approaching a lighthouse. A flat island was ahead and another was off the starboard quarter. The waves were building to amazing heights, cresting and breaking. The turbulent water gave no clue to the depth, but the water must be shallower for the breakers to build so steep.

Just as things were seeming to turn in their favor, one of the engines sputtered and went silent. The helm turned hard so the boat was broadside to the giant waves. To regain control, Alvero struggled to right the course and increase the rpm of his other engine. A wave lifted the boat and dropped it. A horrible cracking sound boomed above the howling winds and reverberated through the hull. The family was jolted from their nest. Alvero hung to the wheel and dropped to his knees. Matvey was ripped from his hold on the rail and slid back to the transom. He tried to climb back to his perch, fighting the angle of the slippery deck. He made it back. The family was on their feet hanging onto each other and the boat.

The engine roared as Alvero increased the throttle, but the boat didn't move until another breaker lifted and pushed it with another crunch and a bang. They had hit a reef and the boat was being dismantled from the keel up. The second engine sputtered and seized. Now the old Lyman was broadside to the breaking surf.

Another wave came and flooded the boat. The suitcases popped up from the cabin. The chart broke apart and fluttered off in the wind.

Another breaker broke the family huddle. In an instant, the man was over the side, head first, grasping for something to hold on to. Then, he disappeared with the waves. They could hear him shout as he washed away. Alvero stumbled to grab the mother and child but fell flat on the deck, sliding into the hull.

Another wave lifted the boat and crashed it down on the coral. For an instant the boat was solid and grounded. The captain raised up, his forehead bleeding, blood streaming into his eye. He wiped his eye and reached out for the woman and child. Another wave rocked the boat, and the woman and child were washed overboard.

Alvero yelled to Matvey, "Get a line and throw them the life ring! Do it now!" He tried to climb the deck over to Matvey and the ring, but he slid back as another wave tossed the boat. The boat was off the reef and sinking fast. It bumped the bottom again.

Matvey saw the mother in the water pushing her child up to the surface. The boy's eyes were wide with fear and panic. His eyes fixed on Matvey. They were caught in a gaze that looked into one another's soul. Stalled, Matvey hung to his rail and with his free hand tried to unfasten the life ring attached to the gunwale. He looked back and the mother was gone but the child was bobbing on the water. Matvey was frozen with fear for his own safety, still tightly holding his treasure.

The captain yelled, "Throw the ring! You bastard. Damn you to hell. Throw the…" Another wave hit and the boat turned over. Matvey found himself under the hull. He surfaced after the waves turned him in summersaults underwater. He was a rag doll scraping against the coral bottom.

When he surfaced, he had his backpack and the rope attached to the life ring. The upside-down boat hull, holed and broken, was being pushed farther away from him by each breaking wave. It all happened so quickly and yet it was an eternity unfolding in slow motion. No one else was in sight. Not the family. Not the Captain. Matvey was alone in the ocean.

Matvey could see the light flashing in the distance. Holding the ring he swam and surfed toward the island with each breaking wave. Fortunately, the waves were pushing in the direction he needed to go. Perhaps it was a mile to the shore. He didn't know, but his instinct was to survive and move toward the light. Choking on sea water and eyes stinging from the salt water, he used every bit of determination to hold on to his bag and the ring. He looked back and the boat hull was gone. There was no one else in sight. Surely, the old captain was lost with the family.

It was the twilight just before dawn when he woke on a sand beach, stunned and confused. He was half buried in the coarse sand. The wind was still blowing. He could hear waves crashing on the opposite shore. He was on the lee of the island. He had washed ashore, but he had no idea where he was or how he climbed from the ocean. He was dehydrated and wanted water. Stumbling to get up, his strong legs buckled. The life ring was still wrapped tightly on his wrist. He didn't notice until he tried to walk away and the line now buried in the sand pulled him back.

It took a few minutes for him to regain some sense of his situation. He sat on the dune and decided to return to the water's edge to rinse the layer of sand from his clothes and bag. The sun was shining and low clouds were blowing by fast. The storm must be breaking up and over.

His head was still foggy. He was wobbly, feeling the motion of the ocean. Looking around, he could see the lighthouse towering above the few standing Australian pines and coconut palms. A roof of a small house was just visible at the bottom of the lighthouse. Matvey thought he must do something with his strong box. Probably there would be American soldiers at the lighthouse and he did not want to be discovered with the collection of stolen jewelry and, especially, the cross of Bartolomé de las Casas.

Looking up and down the island he could see the ravages of the storm. The plants were stripped of their leaves. Debris accumulated into wrack lines above the dunes. A sea buoy was stranded high up on the beach.

Matvey walked along the edge of the dune. The soft sand was difficult to walk on, so he moved up to walk on the higher ground that provided better footing. He came to a monument not far from the water. He saw a bronze plate inscribed with a dedication. The monument commemorated a scientist, Alfred Goldsboro Mayor.

The patinated bronze plaque was inscribed:

ALFRED GOLDSBORO MAYOR
WHO STUDIED THE BIOLOGY OF MANY SEAS AND HERE FOUNDED A LABORATORY FOR RESEARCH FOR THE CARNEGIE INSTITUTION DIRECTING IT FOR XVII YEARS WITH CONSPICUOUS SUCCESS, BRILLIANT VERSATILE COURAGEOUS UTTERLY FORGETFUL OF SELF. HE WAS A BELOVED LEADER OF ALL THOSE WHO WORKED WITH HIM AND WHO ERECT THIS TO HIS MEMORY. BORN MDCCCLXVIII, DIED MCMXXII.

It didn't matter to Matvey what or who the marker commemorated. He thought, "This out of the way monument is the perfect place to hide my box. The jewelry and cross will make me rich in America. I can have the life I've always heard about. I'll bury my box like a pirate buries his treasure chest. Someday I'll retrieve it, once I know what is going on and how I can become a legal refugee."

It was not important that he didn't have an exact plan; he knew he was in the United States because the monument was in English. Nobody could find his treasure and steal it for themselves if it was safe underground. He could find his box again because the marker was so old. It withstood this storm and many more storms before this one. He thought this is a good plan and started digging with his hands.

He tired quickly from excavating a hole. When it was about an arm's length deep, he wrapped the box in a t-shirt from his day pack. Then he decided he needed the shirt, but didn't need the bag, so he retrieved his shirt and placed the metal box in the polyester backpack. Then he started re-filling the hole with the sand he had removed. He was about half finished when he sensed that he wasn't alone. Paranoid that someone was watching him, he stood on the concrete base of the monument and scanned the beach and island to see if anyone else was there. Maybe it was a soldier? He saw no one and returned to quickly finish filling the hole. He was almost done when he was startled.

"Hello! Hello! What are you doing? Where did you come from? How did you get here?"

Matvey looked up to see the figure of a woman, silhouetted and glowing in the glare of the early morning sun. The bright sun was directly behind her head and he squinted to focus. She was walking toward the opposite side of monument.

He was so afraid that he had been caught in the internment of his treasure chest that he lost his balance, falling back from his knees and landing on his side. Matvey took a moment to reply, staring at this woman who seemed to appear out of nothing.

He answered in Spanish, "Yo soy Cubano." Switching to English, he continued, "I am wrecked from the storm."

"Oh my God, are there any others with you? You look terrible. You're all scratched and bleeding." She came toward him and helped him sit up. Now he could see that she was real and not an angel. She was beautiful. In a natural sense she <u>was</u> an angel.

Thinking as quickly as his dulled mind could, "There are no others from the boat. I fear they have drowned in the sea." Matvey knew they died with the ship and were washed away. "We came from Cuba on a small boat. There were three others with me and the captain."

It took a minute for the tragedy to sink in. She choked at the thought of the tragedy and felt sorrow for the lost souls that didn't survive the horrible storm. She was moved, but now more concerned with helping the living survivor. "I am an artist. I'm stranded here too! I will help you get back to the lighthouse where we can get some water and treat your wounds."

SEVENTEEN

Sunny was a crutch under Matvey's arm on their walk back to the keeper's house. Matvey wasn't an invalid, but his legs were wobbly. She found Matvey could speak English, albeit with distinct accent and unusual syntax. Her Spanish was very limited. On the way Sunny told him that she was there alone as an artist in residence at the lighthouse. She had survived the storm too. He was in the Dry Tortugas, a national park in the United States. The storm had knocked out her power, but the house was OK and she had enough supplies.

She opened the door and gestured for Matvey to sit at a table. Sunny said, "I will get the first aid kit. But first, I'll pour you some water." She went to the water dispenser and the 5-gallon jug atop the stand bubbled and gurgled as she filled a glass. "Here, drink it slowly. We have more and you can have all you want." Then she went to the cabinet for the first aid supplies.

Sunny helped Matvey remove his shirt, revealing a well-formed young body, sandy, scratched, and bleeding. She took a washcloth from the drawer and used a bowl for the water. Sunny wasn't a nurse but she figured she should first wash the dirt from the abrasions on his leg and shoulder. She gently wiped his shoulders and chest with a damp towel to remove the sand and salt from his tanned skin.

Matvey started to respond to what he perceived as a sensual gesture, when Sunny abruptly backed away and looked at him with a disapproving frown.

"No Mister! Don't even think about it! Besides, you're injured. Let's just keep this friendly." Matvey hadn't been rebuffed by any woman before and took it as a lesson.

Matvey winced as the washcloth rubbed his skin. She might as well have been using sandpaper. It was painful only because the coral had rubbed him raw when he was tumbled under the boat.

"Well, that's the first step, now for some antiseptic. This will sting," she explained.

She poured hydrogen peroxide over the wounds. The scrapes bubbled and fizzed as the blood oxidized. Sunny patted the wounds with a dry towel and then applied antibiotic cream with a gauze pad. She cobbled together enough patch bandages to cover the worst scrapes and secured the dressing with a gauze wrap. Hanging in the closet, there were a few long-sleeved fishing shirts left by Park staff or previous artists. She found one to fit Matvey. Covering his bare chest was a little less distracting.

Matvey was still and quiet during the treatment. After Sunny had him patched up, and he drank nearly a half-gallon of water, he felt better and realized he was hungry. It had been 2 days since he had had anything to eat.

Sunny said, "You must have been through a lot. When I saw footprints on the beach, I started searching for you. Were you looking for the others on the boat?" Matvey nodded. He had no idea if he had walked on the beach. He only knew he woke up on the sandy shore.

"It is terrible that the others with you are lost. Maybe the Coast Guard will find them alive. There is always hope." Saying that snapped Sunny's memory that she needed to be concerned about her own rescue.

Sunny knew the park 2-way radio at the fort was probably out of commission but she tried it first. Both the 2-way and VHF radios were recharged from the back-up battery system.

"This is Sunny on Loggerhead Key calling for any park staff. Please reply. Over."

The radio was silent. She adjusted the volume to maximum and fiddled with the squelch knob.

No reply.

Then she tried with the marine VHF radio on Channel 16, the hailing channel. Again, she broadcast "This is Sunny on Loggerhead Key calling for any park staff. Please reply. Over."

This time she got an answer. "Sunny, this is Joe at Fort Jeff. Go to 72."

Once both radios were on Channel 72, Joe said, "Fort Jefferson on Channel 72. Sunny, are you okay?"

She was relieved to hear a voice, even if it was someone she didn't know. She responded, "Yes, I am fine. Without power, but the lighthouse generator is working still. And I have a backup battery system."

Joe replied, "We are relieved to hear this. There are three Park staff at the fort. There's a good bit of damage here. We have several wrecked boats that washed ashore. About 16 boaters sheltered with us at the fort. We are still trying to account for missing persons. Over."

Sunny replied "Ranger 1, Bob Nelson, said you were sending the Park boat to evacuate me before the storm. But no one came and I haven't heard anything since. Is he, err, and the others okay? Over."

Joe said, "We assume they made it to Key West. They had to give up getting you at Loggerhead since conditions were unsafe for them to land the tender on the island. Did you get their message? Over."

"No, but I made it! I need to report a boat that was lost at sea during the storm. 5 POB. Repeat, 5 persons on board. One has survived and is weak, but he is ok. He is with me at the keeper's house. We are OK. Over."

Joe replied, "Stand by. I have U.S. Coast Guard on the other radio."

In a few minutes, Joe called, "Loggerhead Key Light, Loggerhead Key Light. This is NPS Fort Jefferson. Over."

Sunny replied "Loggerhead here. Go ahead Fort Jeff. Joe?"

"The USCG confirmed the park boat made it to Key West safely, but the city is flooded and pretty messed up. The Coast Guard is flying search and rescue now and will not have a copter to pick you up until later. Are you ok to wait. Do you have any emergency? Over."

"No, no emergency. We're fine. We have food and water and there is minimal damage to the facilities. No urgency. Over."

Joe replied "OK, stand by. I will contact you with any update or ETA for rescue. Please advise information on lost boat. Over."

She asked Matvey for details about the boat and passengers and relayed it to Joe.

"The survivor says the boat was about 10-meters, a wood fishing boat. Two men, one woman and child still missing. He thinks the boat broke up on a reef, probably north of Loggerhead. Over."

"I copy. I will pass this along to USCG. They are very busy, but the Navy is helping by flying search missions. It was a hell of a storm. I'll get back to you ASAP. If seas calm down, we can come get you, but we only have the little aluminum Jon boat. Over."

"No problem, we can wait. Don't worry, I am fine to wait here as long as necessary. Over and out."

Matvey understood most of the conversation, but listening to the radio garble wasn't as understandable as face-to-face conversation.

Now they would both wait. Sunny asked, "How about something to eat? I have a freezer full of food that is thawing fast, so we can have a feast."

She made a fire in the fire pit and retrieved some fish from the freezer, along with a pot of canned beans and rice. She made a dinner for breakfast. She even made coffee in the percolator pot.

Matvey was starving. The meal was delicious. But then anything would have been delicious.

Now that they were waiting for instructions and information from the Park, they could talk. Sunny asked, "When did you leave Cuba? Did you know how bad the weather report was?"

Matvey didn't exactly know, but he said; "I think two nights ago. We were on the boat for a night and a day until dark. I have lost my memory of the time."

Sunny was amazed that anyone could be at sea in a hurricane, especially in a small boat. She thought, these people must be desperate to try to escape Cuba in a storm. She felt sorry for them, not only for his lost shipmates, but for all the refugees that braved the Florida Straits to get to the United States.

A plane passed overhead and they paused to look. It was a big Navy plane. It flew low over the lighthouse and turned to the north. Maybe they were looking for the boat Matvey was on.

It was the middle of the day and the sun was heating up the island. The humidity was heavy and the winds had subsided to merely a strong breeze. In the shade and out of the breeze, it was tolerable, except for mosquitos, that apparently had weathered the storm well.

Slapping a mosquito, Sunny suggested they move inside. While they were bringing the utensils from making and eating their meal, she asked, "Why were you digging at the monument?"

Matvey had an answer. He'd been thinking of how to explain what she caught him doing.

187

He explained, "I was so hungry. I was looking for turtle eggs to eat. I thought I saw tracks on the beach and maybe there was a nest."

Sunny told him that turtles would never make a nest as high on the shore as the monument. "Turtles make their nest closer to the water. They crawl out and stop at the edge of the dune, never on the higher land. You were digging for nothing. You wouldn't find an egg even if you dug all the way to China."

Matvey was relieved to get the explanation. He wasn't concerned about the information, only that she accepted his lie. He didn't understand the China idiom, but that didn't matter. He wanted the topic closed.

He changed the conversation to ask about why she was alone at the lighthouse? "Where are the soldiers? In Cuba there are military stationed to guard our lighthouses."

He recalled a trip to the national park near Guanahacabibes on the western end of the island. There were many armed guards at the Faro Roncali lighthouse.

Sunny chuckled politely. "Here we have the lighthouse automated and don't need keepers or armed guards. I'm here as a guest artist, temporarily, to do art inspired by this beautiful location." She said sadly, "But now it is so damaged. The trees, the wildlife, the dunes - destroyed by the hurricane." She almost choked up. "I don't know how it will ever recover."

Hurricane? This was the first Matvey had heard the storm he was in called a hurricane. "I did not know it was a hurricane. When we left Cuba, it was only a strong storm."

Sunny said, "Yes. Just a few days ago, the forecast was for only squalls and no development because of the track over Cuba's mountains, but it changed course and became a hurricane, fast. It is amazing you made it through, at sea."

Matvey bowed his head and nodded. He felt something between guilt and gratitude.

They conversed for a couple hours. Occasionally an aircraft would fly by and they would rush outside to see what it was. Flights were searching for lost boats. Rescue teams were called to haul stranded sailors up into the USCG helicopters.

Matvey was spent. He politely asked if he could go inside the house to sleep. "Of course, I know you must be exhausted! Lie down in the bunk next to the window."

While Matvey was sleeping, there had been a little radio traffic during the afternoon and evening, but no news regarding getting picked up. The U.S. Coast Guard had broadcast a notice over VHF channel 16, "Pon Pon. Pon Pon. All mariners keep a sharp eye for survivors of the storm and report all information to U.S. Coast Guard Key West. For more information, switch to channel 22 Alpha, the official communications frequency." Then, Channel 22 repeated the announcement and listed boats that were reported missing or had broadcast a May Day, including the latitude and longitude of their last known positions. One report was a 30-foot wood fishing boat with 4 persons on board, missing a mile south of Loggerhead Key. She thought, "That must be the boat Matvey was on!"

When Matvey woke, it was dark outside. He noticed that light was bleeding in through a hallway from the other side of the house. The bottom floor had two rooms, divided by the stairway. Sunny was in the kitchen, sitting at a table with a Coleman lantern burning brightly. He asked Sunny, "How long have I been asleep? What time is it?"

She replied, "It's close to midnight. Would you like something to eat? I didn't want to wake you. You obviously need rest to recover."

Matvey nodded and Sunny placed a plate of cobbled together provisions from the freezer; frozen peaches once meant for a pie, peas and a fried ham steak heated on a camp stove. She asked if he would like noodles too, showing him a package of ramen. Matvey said maybe later.

It was fortunate that the camp stove worked. With the gas lantern and the Coleman stove they had light and a way to cook.

While Matvey was eating, the radio crackled to life. "Loggerhead Key Light, Loggerhead Key Light, this is NPS Fort Jeff, do you copy?"

Sunny answered immediately, "This is Loggerhead Key Light. Over."

Joe updated her on the status of the fort and casualties. He told her that there were 16 people from the boats that had anchored at the fort. Nine wanted to be transported to Key West. Seven would stay to work on retrieving their beached boats and await salvage. The three NPS staff would remain until later.

In the morning, they could come in a small skiff that they recovered from one of the wrecked boats to bring them to Garden Key to be transported to Key West with the others. Joe told her to be ready at sunrise and he would confirm at 6 AM. Two National Park concession contractor seaplanes that normally brought tourists to and from the island would arrive by 10 to take the people to Key West. Joe cautioned her that it would be difficult to find a place to stay in Key West since the town was cleaning up after the storm. She could stay at the NPS maintenance shop if she couldn't find anything else.

Just before he signed off, he added, "Pack light, space on the planes will be tight."

Sunny hadn't told Joe that her survivor was a Cuban refugee. She figured that was not relevant. He was a person, surviving the storm, and his immigration status was a minor detail.

The skiff arrived at Loggerhead as planned. The sunrise over the fort was a beautiful yellow-gold sky dotted with small puffy cumulus clouds. The morning light was reflecting in the glass-smooth, mirror water. The morning coolness was comfortable after a day of heat and humidity. Sunny wondered how could something so vile and violent as a hurricane turn into such splendid calm so quickly.

She had packed a small case with some of her art, and a few changes of clothes and other essentials. Matvey of course had nothing except his spare T-shirt and his passport in a plastic bag. They climbed aboard the skiff and were off to the fort. Sunny looked back at Loggerhead and the light, the downed trees and broken pier. She knew she had to return, not only to collect her things, but to do what she could to help nature recover.

At the fort, Sunny introduced Joe to Matvey and fessed up that Matvey had arrived from Cuba. By the "wet foot, dry foot" policy that had been implemented in 1995, Cubans caught at sea were returned to Cuba. Those who made it to American soil were welcomed under the Cuban Adjustment

Act. Joe said he would inform Immigration and Customs Enforcement to meet the seaplane and process Matvey. Sunny relayed the information to Matvey and offered to go with him to Immigration.

They loaded onto the seaplane and taxied to the runway channel. Taking off, the engines roared and the plane gained speed, planing on the water until they lifted off. They circled the fort. As they gained altitude, the damages that were so overwhelming to see in person on the ground, were diminished by distance. The fort and islands looked like the beautiful tropical paradise of the postcard aerials. Flying over the Marquesas, the shape of the atoll-like configuration was evident. The water displayed the same beautiful colors, the sandy beaches looked pristine. From the altitude, it was as if nothing had ever happened.

As the plane descended on the approach to landing in Key West the view was vastly different. Nature's fury was unleashed on the island and, even from the air, the destruction was evident. There were damaged structures, flooded streets, broken utility poles, and sunken boats – boats on the land and rafts of sunken boats stacked against the shore in a horrible jumble. Emergency vehicle lights of red, yellow, and blue twinkled in the city like Christmas lights. Loggerhead and Fort Jeff did not seem so badly damaged in comparison.

Sunny looked at the wrecked boats and shuddered at the thought that the family that had visited her might not have escaped the wrath of the hurricane. They left a week before the hurricane, but she remembered their plan was to visit the Marquesas for a few days before moving on to Key West and beyond. To her core, she hoped they traveled beyond the reach of the storm. She was upset that she would not know their fate and tense with worry, thinking about the children Linda and Mike.

Matvey's eyes were wide in amazement. Sunny's eyes were wet with tears.

They landed and taxied to the tarmac of the airport to disembark.

EIGHTEEN

When the seaplane landed in the harbor and motored to the seaplane base in Key West, an Immigration van was waiting with two officers. They had a description of Matvey, who stood out from the other passengers. They took him by an arm to the van. Sunny ran up saying "I am his representative and I'll go with you." The officers asked who she was and accepted that she could come along. The island was in survival mode and Immigration had plenty to deal with, including their own damaged facilities.

The Immigration and Customs Enforcement office was running on emergency generators. The streets were still draining from the storm flood. Matvey was led to an interview room to meet with an immigration officer. He faced a long session of questioning about details of his life in Cuba and arrival on American soil. The interviewer completed the application and asked Matvey to sign it. Then he was placed in a detention cell with two other immigrants awaiting processing. Both men were from Haiti and fairly well dressed. Matvey was wet, dirty, and ragged from the voyage and days in the Dry Tortugas. He wanted a shower and clean clothes.

Matvey was with the ICE officers for several hours. While Sunny waited for him, she made a couple of cell phone calls. Cell service was sketchy because of the storm damage, but with persistence, she got connected to Chris in Indiana. Chris didn't answer so Sunny left a message. "I'm OK; I survived the storm. I just got to Key West. Cell service is bad. I have a lot of arrangements to make so I'll try to call again later. I love you and miss you!"

Then she called her friend, Shelley Abram, in New York, who split her time between Long Island, Provence, France, and the Lower Keys and was a patron of Sunny's work. Shelley helped Sunny get the NPS artist in residence spot. More than a patron, Shelley was a friend.

Shelley had been worried about her and, once Sunny got through to her, was relieved to hear she had survived the ordeal. After telling her an abbreviated summary of the past few days and her present predicament Sunny asked, "Would it be possible for me to stay at your place, until I can work things out?"

Shelley replied, "Of course, my dear. My caretaker has already told me that everything is OK, except for damages to the landscaping. Some trees are down and the garage was flooded, so the only working vehicle is Henry's truck. The emergency generators are powering the houses." Sunny was relieved that Henry was alright and happy that she would have a place to stay.

Shelley told Sunny she would not be down to her compound until later, when the weather was cooler and the dreadful hurricane season was over. Her live-in caretaker, Henry Forbes, could arrange for Sunny to stay in the guest house or one of the small cottages on her estate. Shelley insisted Sunny take refuge there until things were settled.

Happy to know she had a place to stay until she could make plans, Sunny continued to wait for news about Matvey. Periodically, she checked with people in the immigration office about the status of Matvey's processing and the procedure for clearing immigration. An ICE worker told her that, usually, Cuban nationals reaching the U.S. were sent to the Krome North Service Processing Center in Miami-Dade County until their story could be verified and arrangements made for their temporary residence, with family or friends.

Another ICE worker that she pestered for news told her that the hurricane was hampering the usual immigration process and asked for her patience, explaining that there was no place to keep the detainees in Key West. He explained the Monroe County Sheriff's Department jail was the normal place for temporary housing of immigrants pending transport to Krome. The county jail was nearly flooded and prisoners there were being relocated to higher floors. Things were so bad at the jail that a judge signed a special order to release non-violent offenders awaiting trial. The county jail was not an option.

Sunny learned that transport to Krome wouldn't be possible until the Overseas Highway was cleared and passable. There was no prediction on how long it would take to open the road, but it might be days. A special charter flight to move detainees north to Miami seemed excessive. The ICE office was calling superiors for directions on what to do with the pending cases.

Finally, after hours of waiting, the immigration officer asked Sunny to step into an interview booth. He grilled her about her relationship to Matvey, what she was doing at Loggerhead Key, her NPS "job", and personal info like her residence, date of birth, passport number, etc. He asked if she had helped Matvey get to Florida.

Sunny explained how she found Matvey on the beach on Loggerhead Key. She reiterated his story about being in a small boat, caught in the storm. She explained in much detail as much as she knew and insisted that none of the circumstances she and Matvey currently found themselves in was planned.

The officer said, "We have a little problem with your friend. Normally we would hold him here and transport him and others to the Krome North Service Processing Center for processing. But as you can see, we are without power here. Our ability to provide food and housing for detainees has been wrecked by the storm. We can't predict when we can get a transport to Krome and we do not want to dump a refugee on the Sheriff's department for them to hold for us when they have their hands full.

"If you will take custody with the responsibility for this guy making his immigration hearing, and keep an eye on him so he does not flee or disappear, we can process him here for a temporary visa and contact you when he can get into the queue for the provisions that the U.S. makes for Cuban refugees."

Sunny wanted to help Matvey. She didn't want him to have to stay in a jail cell, especially since there was no telling how long ICE would have to hold him. She told the official that she would have to check with her patron to be sure it would be okay for Matvey to come stay where she would be staying. She asked for a half hour to check and make plans.

Leaving the room, Sunny called Shelley Abram again. "Shelley, could I ask another favor? Please let me know if it is too much to ask. I don't want to impose on our friendship and your generosity. Please be honest if this is too much to ask …"

Shelley interrupted, "What is it dear? When have I ever not let you know what I think?"

Continuing, Sunny explained, "The man who washed up on Loggerhead Key after his boat shipwrecked, he is a young Cuban and seems nice. He has no one here in the U.S. to take him in. He'll be stuck in Immigration custody until the storm repairs are further along. I don't know when that will be, so…"

Shelley answered before Sunny could finish her request. "Yes, he can stay. Ask Henry to put him up in the crew cabin. Is this your new beau?" This was a gentle tease as she knew Sunny was in a committed relationship. Sunny could see the smirk on Shelley's face over the phone.

"Oh, thank you so much! If he is released to me, I'll assure you he will be no trouble. I think he will be able to help Henry clean up the gardens after the storm." Sunny was so relieved and thanked Shelley over and over. "Hugs, goodbye," Shelley said.

When Sunny hung up, she asked if she could see the Immigration Officer about Matvey again. Sunny told the officer that she would vouch for Matvey and provide him a temporary place to stay at the Cassiopea Estate on Cayo Blanco where she was going to stay. She continued, "The caretaker will transport us and he won't leave the property." The officer paused and went in another room to speak with a supervisor.

"We can release Mr. Matvey Valdes-Descon to your custody. You will have to sign the paperwork assuring he will return for further processing. He will have temporary admittance to the U.S. He shall take no employment and not travel outside of Monroe or Miami-Dade County."

The officer explained, "It's kind of like parole. Any violation will revoke his visa and jeopardize his application for permanent residency and a green card. He's lucky not only to survive, but to make it to land. If he had been intercepted at sea, we'd see him returned to Cuba."

After completing the paperwork and a stern instruction to Matvey, the two of them were released. They waited outside for Henry to pick them up.

Matvey was a bit smelly and his clothes were tattered and dirty so he sat in the bed of the pickup for the drive up to Cayo Blanco. Along the way they could see the devastation wrought by the storm. It was lucky that the hurricane did not hit Key West directly, but as a strong storm, it was more than enough to cause havoc throughout the Lower Keys.

Cassiopea was an island on an island. A natural jungle surrounded by development, Shelley's estate was a tropical coppice forest filled with rare native trees and shrubs. She had worked hard to restore the habitat on her property. When the Abrams purchased the place in the early 70s, it was a run-down homestead dating back to early Keys settlers. Shelley saw the inherent value in the place and set to restore and strengthen the historic structures and develop a native garden. Her reward was a yard full of blooms, butterflies, migratory birds and white-crowned pigeons. It was a wonderful place to spend the winter.

Sunny was impressed with the oasis Shelley and her late husband had made at Cassiopea. It was sad to see the damage from the storm. Sunny almost cried, but even with the wrecked forest, it was beautiful nature and would be beautiful again. The scrubby native coppice forest would recover in time, sprouting again from the stumps and roots after the insult of the storm.

Henry had cleared the drive by chain-sawing branches from toppled trees. Some larger mahoganys and gumbo limbos had fallen into the road. Fortunately, the cabins and main house were not damaged. The biggest loss was the vintage Mercedes that had been flooded to its headlights.

Henry Forbes had been at the property as a trusted steward for nearly thirty years. He started working as a helper and became pseudo-family to the Abrams. Together they learned the plants and wildlife of the Keys. Henry was from the Bahamian community in Key West and sought information on cultural and medicinal uses for native plants from elders in the community. Henry could trace his lineage back generations to the Turks and Caicos Islands, part of the Bahamas when the Forbes Company owned plantations in the early 1800s.

Henry was devoted to his roots in the Bahamian community. His people were the descendants of the Bahamians who came to Key West as capable workers, even before Henry Flagler's railroad needed laborers. They were experienced with working in the Keys and mangroves. In the past, before the railroad, long before bridges to the mainland, Key West was as connected to the Bahamas by the sea as it was to Florida. The Bahamians settled in a part of Key West, segregated from the white community. Following rapid growth in the town, their settlement was engulfed by development. Yet the culture and history endured, as an enclave ever threatened by gentrification and commercialization.

After Henry got Sunny settled in the guest house and Matvey in a small cabin, he brought some clothes for Matvey. They were almost the same size. Matvey was grateful to finally have a shower. Henry told Matvey and Sunny they should come to the main house for dinner when they were ready. He said, "I'll prepare a dinner of grouper, plantains, and peas and rice. And johnny cake. You probably are starving after all this." The meal was an appetizing treat for the two survivors who had not had much to eat for days.

In the days following their arrival at Cassiopea, Sunny worked on her laptop, using the solar-powered electricity at the compound. While many in the lower Keys were without power, she was blessed to have lights and a fan. Shelley wanted the place to be self-sufficient and made investments in the latest technology. Generators provided electricity when the sun wasn't shining. It was a tropical paradise and authentic, not like the excessive palaces rich folks would build on their postage stamp-sized lots.

Matvey filled his days helping Henry with the cleanup. They labored hard to right fallen trees that could be pruned and saved. Others were cut and chipped for mulch and trail surfacing. The water features were cleared of debris and re-filled. Repairs were made to broken shutters and roofs were patched. Matvey and Henry worked to restore the main house's gutters that collected water for the cistern. It was hard and hot work. Matvey tapped into the mentoring he had from the maintenance crew at Girón. Cassiopea was taking shape again. With the fast-growing coppice, the estate would be green again soon. Henry was impressed with Matvey and appreciated the strength of the young man.

In a few weeks the Keys were getting back to something more like normal. The roads were cleared and power restored. Trash trucks were still collecting piles of debris on a daily basis. Heavy equipment was still working on removing boats and over-turned shipping containers. Sunny made several trips to the upper Keys that were less affected by the storm to purchase clothes to replace those that she had left on Loggerhead Key. She visited with the NPS office in Key West to see when she could get back to the lighthouse to retrieve her belongings. She really was most concerned about getting her artwork. She had produced a number of pieces, enough for the show she was obliged to present as a requirement of her sabbatical in the Dry Tortugas.

The National Park Service was making progress at Garden Key. The fort was safe enough for visitors to return, but few boats were visiting. The daily ferry to the Dry Tortugas had suspended service for a month. The seaplane service was operating again at a reduced schedule of one flight per day. She would have to catch a ride on the seaplane and, once at the fort, the Park Service would get her over to Loggerhead Key to get her belongings and art. She planned to stay on

Loggerhead for a night or two to clean up the mess she had left. It was likely that the freezer was a soup of putrefied food. She winced at the thought.

She decided that she would return to her home in Bloomington after she retrieved her materials. It seemed like an eternity since she had been home. She missed her comfortable life and studio. She missed Chris, who had been taking care of the cats and house in her absence. She could get back to completing works for the show. She had new ideas for updating the art pieces to include her impressions of the storm. Getting back to Loggerhead would allow her to take photos and make reference sketches of the changes the storm had made to the island.

The dilemma was how to fulfill her obligation to keep track of Matvey. She visited the ICE office in Key West to ask how she could return to Indiana when Matvey was limited to staying in South Florida. She told them how he had settled into staying at the Cassiopea estate and that he was a model guest. ICE said they would arrange another interview and expedite his permit to stay in the U.S. If he passed muster, and there was little chance he wouldn't, he could get his residency and green card. He would only need to find work or show some means of support.

Sunny thought about this on the drive back to the estate. She asked Henry for advice and suggestions. He smiled and told her he was thinking of asking Mrs. Abram if he could have Matvey continue at the estate for a while as a temporary worker. He had been a big help with the cleanup and repairs. Henry said, "He can help finish the repair work and take on a new project to build a rock-walled garden patio and pergola.

This could take months. It'll be much faster with a young man's strong back!"

Sunny was thrilled with the possibility that Matvey could stay at Cassiopea. That meant she could return home and Matvey would be safe and accommodated until she returned for her exhibit at the Key West Artist Studios and Gallery. Sunny did not want to ask Shelley for yet another favor so she asked Henry if he would ask and he said he would. A day later he had an answer.

After she grilled Henry about how Matvey had been working out as a guest and volunteer helper, Shelley was agreeable. Henry told Shelley, "I can't imagine a better fit for Matvey. He knows how to work and what needs to be done. But this young man is likely destined for something else. I don't think he's looking for a career at Cassiopea."

That fit with Shelley's disposition. She told Henry that Matvey could be hired if he could legally work. She wanted no part of anything that was not legal. When Henry relayed this news to Sunny, she was ecstatic. She could now inform ICE that he had a job offer and a place to stay. In a week, Matvey was legal, on his way to being an American citizen, or at least a resident.

Matvey and Henry had formed a strong friendship in the brief month they had been working together. They would drink a beer after a hard day, enjoying each other's company and sharing stories of their lives. On weekends, they would go fishing, sometimes near the pilings at the estate's dock, sometimes launching Henry's pride and joy, a 26-foot Parker sport fisherman. They were forming a fast friendship built upon their diverse backgrounds.

Sunny started planning her return to Loggerhead. Matvey desperately wanted to go with her. So much so, he became a pest. It was the first time Sunny lost patience with him. "No! The National Park Service will only arrange for me to go. This is final and I do not want to discuss this any further."

She made her trip back to Dry Tortugas. On the plane she flew over Key West, then Boca Grande Key and the Marquesas. Tourists on the plane were thrilled with the excursion, seeing the clear waters, reefs and palette of blues and greens of the water. From 3000 feet, the aftermath of the storm was absent. Only when they landed and beached the seaplane at the fort was the pain inflicted upon the islands evident. Long Key was washed over and only stubs of plants were poking through the white sand. Bush Key was scoured clean. The formerly tall buttonwoods where the magnificent frigatebirds roosted were mere spindles.

The fort looked the same from the outside, but in the central parade ground, trees were toppled and a large pile of brush was pushed up. Another part of the seawall that created a moat around the fort had been breached.

The NPS archaeological team from Tallahassee was on site doing assessments. Survey transits were set up. Stakes were planted in the ground noting features that needed to be addressed.

Park Ranger Bob Nelson met Sunny at the entrance and warmly hugged her. He apologized for the snafu about not evacuating her. He was unaware that she did not get his message. He was distressed that the park staff could not pick her up to bring her to the security of the fort for the storm.

He was greatly relieved to see that she had weathered the hurricane and admired her courage.

Ranger Bob assured Sunny, "The park is in pretty good shape, actually, all things considered. The Park Service will apply for disaster recovery funds, so maybe we can get some of the long-standing maintenance backlog funded."

Sunny was pleased to hear this. "I hope it will include Loggerhead too."

Bob added, "Yes, it's all a part of the Park. As you know, this place is special and popular. We partially reopened quickly, just a couple weeks after the storm. But, you know, fishermen were out here just a few days after the hurricane hit." Shaking his head in disbelief, he continued, "While we were still working on emergencies, they were catching fish like nothing happened."

She told him about the shipwrecked Cuban and stressful navigation of Immigration and Customs Enforcement on his behalf. As much as she enjoyed catching up with Bob, she knew she had things to do on Loggerhead and asked when she could get over to the island.

Soon they were off in the Park's patrol skiff for the 2 1/2-mile trip to Loggerhead. The landing dock was now only delineated by pilings. The boardwalk was missing, so they landed on the beach. Bob put out an anchor to secure the boat and walked with Sunny to the lighthouse. No real maintenance work had been done at the lighthouse, only a rapid assessment and stabilization. When they unlocked the door to the keeper's house and stepped inside, it was like she had never left. Someone had cleaned up the mess she left when she and Matvey quickly departed. Even the freezer was clean and back on a restored power grid. A few people working to do assessments and make repairs on the fort had stayed at the lighthouse and they inherited the task of cleaning. Sunny was pleased that she did not have to face the task she dreaded, cleaning the freezer.

Bob made sure she was OK and departed, giving Sunny a park radio. "Call if you need anything and let us know when you are ready to go. Keep in mind the Park supply boat only comes twice a week. If you are not done in two days, you'll be stuck here for a week." They hugged again and he was off.

Sunny immediately went upstairs to the closet where she stored her art and supplies. Everything was as she left it. What a relief; the task of packing was going to be easy. The park workers had neatly stacked her personal stuff in a corner. She was happy to have her travel wardrobe back. She was more comfortable in her "hippie outfit" than the clothes she recently purchased.

She spent the rest of the day packing and moving her art materials to the first floor so she could more easily transport it to the park skiff. She folded and packed her clothes in her duffel. As the sun was descending toward the horizon, she walked to the lee shore hoping to see the green flash. She checked on how the old boat house had survived.

When she reached the beach, she was thrilled to see that the sand was moving and a boil of baby sea turtles was emerging from their sandy nest. It was a reaffirmation that nature persists. In spite of the downed trees and wrack line of debris, in spite of the erosion of dunes, these miniature turtles were showing that life endures. Natural cycles might be interrupted, but life goes on, demonstrating resilience.

These creatures have a lineage that far exceed the tenure of humanity and they will likely survive after humanity departs. With giddy delight, she watched their scramble toward the ocean, to begin a new generation.

The sun set as a big orange ball being consumed by the distant horizon. She didn't see the green flash, but that didn't matter. She was rewarded and happy to have experienced seeing the turtle march. She walked back to the keeper's house in the blissful twilight afterglow of the sunset.

Since the park supply boat would not be back for another day, Sunny decided to treat herself to a day of solitude exploring the post-storm landscape of Loggerhead. She could call Bob and return today to spend the night at the guest quarters of the fort because she was packed and ready. Instead, she decided to stay in the solitude of the key to wander the places she had visited during her daily walks.
She carried a trash bag with her and picked up litter. She was amazed at the amount of flotsam that had accumulated in the month since she had left the island. There was so much that she decided to be selective in removing the most egregious insults to her island. She collected the vile plastic and left the metal and glass bottles. Some ropes and nets were too much for her to handle, so she tried to expose them in the hope that park staff or future volunteers would be able to remove the debris.

She spent a pleasant day of reflection and introspection. She even saw benefit to the toppled Australian pine forest. The non-native trees had been overwhelming the native plant community. Now that most of them were down, this was a chance for the Park Service to embark on a restoration of the coastal plants and get rid of these invasive trees.

At night, the moon was waning, and the sky was the magnificent canopy she had enjoyed so much during her stay on the island. The only thing she regretted was not having a bottle of wine to toast the Milky Way.

As the sun came up over the fort the next morning, she knew she would have to call Ranger Bob. Somber, she surveyed her desert island and made the radio call to be picked up. She hated to leave Loggerhead Key. It was imprinted on her soul.

A couple of hours later, Bob came to Loggerhead Key in the park skiff to pick her up and take her back to the fort. Bob and Sunny loaded her duffel, easel, and art portfolio case, boxed and wrapped in plastic, into the boat and then backed off the beach. They arrived at the fort in time to meet the supply boat that Sunny would hitch a ride back to Key West on. Fort Jefferson and the Dry Tortugas disappeared in the wake as the supply boat left the beach on Garden Key.

On the 4-hour ride back to Key West, Sunny thought, "Everything is working out great. I survived the hurricane. I have my art. The Keys are recovering. Matvey is OK and I am on my way home. I'll see Chris soon." As the boat arrived in Key West, Sunny was in the sunshine, ever the optimist, with better days ahead.

NINETEEN

At the resort at Girón, things were back to normal operation. Guests were arriving for their all-inclusive vacation week or leaving from their week in a tropical paradise. The tourism officials had visited to conduct their own investigation of Evelyn's assault and dismissed the incident as unpreventable.

Behind the scenes, rumors were still rampant among the staff. Matvey was gone without a trace. He must have been the perpetrator. Even the employees who had befriended Matvey had unanswered questions. Some thought he might have been taken by the police. Others suspected he was hiding in the Zapata Swamp. Nearly every day the police would stop by the resort to speak with Maria la Gorda and ask for Matvey. If he was already in custody there would be no reason for the police visits, unless it was the secret interior ministry that had captured him. Then Matvey might disappear without a trace.

Privately, La Jefa Maria was worried. She had helped Matvey and feared that he might be discovered and, if interrogated, he could implicate her. She hoped he escaped. She worried a bit about Evelyn, not so much about her injury, but whether the assault would taint Girón Beach Club Resort as a dangerous destination. La Jefa increased the emphasis on guest safety with the security staff and belittled them that they had allowed the assault to occur.

She wanted to reach out to Evelyn, but there was really no way to find her. In the days after the assault, she called the hospital to check on her status. When the nurse reported she was getting better, Maria stopped calling.

Evelyn recovered well from her head trauma. After spending a couple weeks in the hospital ward, she was eager and ready to be released. While the medical care was good, being in a ward with 11 other patients, with a variety of maladies, was not like the private or semi-private rooms she was familiar with. Something was always going on, disturbing her rest. Sometimes it was a patient groaning in pain, or maybe it was a family member crying during a visit, or it was an emergency. The nurses were always coming and going, cackling like hens, at all hours of the day and night.

Still, the hospital had healed her and she was thankful for that. During her stay, she had several more visits from Inspector Costa. She hoped she did not reveal too much about herself and her activities while she was under the influence of the pain medications. As she was now more self-aware and in control, she was more careful and guarded about what she told him.

While lying in her hospital bed, Evelyn would close her eyes and try to recall what had happened when she was with Matvey. Bit by bit she added pieces to the story. She was certain he had taken the cross. But, as hard as she tried to recall details, she couldn't remember the attack. She remembered nothing after seeing Matvey holding the cross and how angry she was. Now, she was still angry, mostly at him, but also with herself for having casual sex with a kid. She hoped that the crucifix of the saint was long gone and no one had discovered anything that might implicate her.

On the day she was released from hospital, Yolanda came to pick her up. Even though she couldn't afford it, Yolanda had rented a car to collect Evelyn and her things. In a practical sense, she had no clothes since she arrived at the hospital wearing only a bathrobe. While the nurses provided her with some things to wear upon her discharge from the medical center, they were cobbled together pieces and ill-filling, not her usual impeccable fashion.

Now Evelyn planned to leave Cuba as quickly as possible to go to New York, London, or even Miami. She'd take the earliest flight she could get to wherever it was going. It didn't matter.

She had no money or credit cards, nothing, only the donated clothes on her back. With a little vanity, she tried to make herself as presentable as possible.

When he last visited her, Inspector Carlos had told Evelyn she could get her things at the police station when she was released, so Yolanda drove Evelyn to Cienfuegos. The inspector took her to a cramped interview room and sat opposite her.

"Your things will be brought here soon. I wanted to see if you remembered anything else about what happened in Girón."

Evelyn was nervous, wanting to just leave. She didn't know or remember all that she might have already shared with Inspector Costa on the multiple times he visited her in the hospital.

Evelyn responded that she couldn't think of anything else. Her memory was still foggy about her last night at Girón. "I am still in a fog. It's a bit in shock that one day I was fine and then I wake up in a medical facility. I recall going to Girón to spend a few days to relax and enjoy the beach before I had to return to Havana."

"Did you go to Trinidad before arriving at Girón?" Costa knew she hadn't.

"I don't think so," she said, not wanting to be caught in something that could be checked out.

A couple of police officers brought her things and placed them on the table. They laid her crated art on the floor.

Inspector Costa said, "Let's look at what we have," wanting to see if he could glean any more information by reviewing her belongings with her. "You will need to sign a receipt and tell us if anything is missing."

Continuing, he added, "I am sorry to tell you, but we believe you were attacked and assaulted. We all are sorry that this has happened to you. It is so rare to have this kind of thing happen to visitors to our country."

Evelyn wiped her eye, saying "I suppose I am unlucky." Because her head had been clearing over the time she was laying in her hospital bed, she knew that she and Matvey were together consensually and he choked her after taking the cross. But she didn't tell Costa this because she didn't want Matvey to be found. If he was caught with the cross, it would lead straight back to her.

"I don't remember anything except I was grabbed from behind and passed out. I woke up in hospital. I think I was out of my mind for days." She started reaching for her bagged-up belongings. But Inspector Costa insisted they carefully review the contents together. He had a handwritten inventory of what the police had taken from her room. Slowly, they compared the list with the physical objects, checking them off, item by item. He was a little embarrassed when he held up her lingerie and undergarments.

Among her possessions, she had substantial currency, some Barclays Bank and American Express credit cards, and a few pieces of jewelry. Costa asked "Does this seem like all your valuables? Do you think anything is missing?"

Evelyn answered quickly, "No, this seems like everything." Costa thought this lady can't remember details, but she knew immediately nothing was missing. Something is a little off. He kept a poker face and continued to review the contents.

After what seemed to be hours looking over her belongings, it all seemed to be there and Evelyn signed the receipt. She was in a hurry to get out of there and, frankly, didn't care if something was missing. She was about to gather her luggage and return to join Yolanda, who was waiting patiently outside, when Costa said, "We are not finished. There is the artwork in this crate. We need to be sure it is all there." Evelyn was exasperated and sat back in the chair as he lifted the box onto the table and opened the top using a screwdriver.

From what she could surmise, she had not revealed anything about the cross in earlier conversations because the inspector never mentioned it. His main concern seemed to be about the old paintings she had purchased for export. She knew she needed to pass them by Cuban authorities to get permission to leave the country with them. But it wasn't just a formality. It was likely that an inspection of the works would be needed. And, once authorities saw what she had in the crate it would either lead to their return to the original owner or, worse, confiscation and storage in the immense collection of art imprisoned in the archive. She reasoned, in her own mind, that the loss of the antique art was a small problem compared to the stolen relic.

Painting by painting, Evelyn told Costa about the origin and tried to bore him with details on the style, artist, and subject. She hoped that by revealing too much information, he would get tired and speed up the review.

When he came to the old paintings, she was less forthcoming. She said she couldn't exactly remember where she purchased this one or that one or anything about the artists or vintage. They were simply representative of the colonial or imperialist art style, prevalent before the Revolution. She explained that the pieces are appreciated by interior decorators in the UK to hang in formal settings. She told the inspector that the old paintings are not very good and some are damaged. She would say anything to devalue the old pieces so he wouldn't scrutinize them further.

Once he had completed the painstakingly slow review of the crate containing art, Inspector Costa said, "I will need to hold your crate until the Ministry of Culture sends a representative to look at these. I'm sure there will be no problem, but I can't give them to you now." Evelyn knew immediately that she would lose the paintings, certainly the valuable old paintings. The contemporary art might be released, but they were of minimal value. At least, she was not caught in Customs at the shipping port or in the airport. She knew no crime had yet been committed. It would only be a crime if the art was destined to be exported without a permit. Only the name, Jean-Pierre Gladstone, Port Au Prince Haiti, written on the crate indicated the art was meant to leave Cuba. But not yet.

It was pretty clear to Inspector Costa that Evelyn was up to something devious and she was not the pure academic art historian that she represented herself to be. He knew she had been with a man by the reports from the hospital. He wondered if she might have an accomplice she was protecting. He also was very curious about the whereabouts of Matvey, who had been missing since the incident.

"I will see that your package is delivered to you. Do you have an address in Havana where you will be staying?" asked Inspector Costa.

"Oh, let me ask Yolanda if I may stay with her. .... aah, never mind, I am going to the Hotel Nacional on the Malecón. I don't want to inconvenience the professor any more than I already have."

She was out the door with her luggage and purse. She couldn't get to the car fast enough. She didn't even delay long enough to change back into her own clothes, out of the ill-fitting garments the nurses had given her.

She was about to get into Yolanda's rental car when Inspector Costa appeared at the edge of the parking lot. He hollered to Evelyn, "Stop!"

Evelyn panicked, thinking, "What now?" She waited until Costa approached her before asking, "Yes?" He handed her her passport, with a wry smile, saying, "You will be needing this, won't you?" Evelyn nodded her head in acknowledgment, took her passport and quickly got into the car before the inspector could call her back again. As Yolanda pulled away, he gave Evelyn a slight wave goodbye.

On the drive back to Havana, Evelyn conversed with Yolanda about her horrible experience, thanking her profusely for being such a good, generous friend. Evelyn gave her money for the rental car. Yolanda didn't want to accept it, but knew she must because she could not afford the expense. Reluctantly, she accepted the money. Evelyn was creative and evasive in answering Yolanda's questions, particularly when she was questioned about why she was in Girón and not Trinidad.

They drove up to the imposing entrance to the Hotel Nacional. Gold leafed statues lined the landscaped entrance driveway. A uniformed hotel doorman opened her door and accompanied them to the front desk where Evelyn checked in. A bellman took her bags to her room while she and Yolanda went out to the lawn to sit for a few minutes. Evelyn ordered a coffee and asked Yolanda if she would like wine or a mojito. They sat for a while taking in the vista of the bay and traffic racing by on the roadway below the bluff where the hotel was perched. The view was magnificent with a panorama that overlooked the bay from the fort at the harbor entrance to the terminus of the Malecón.

After a short time, Evelyn asked to excuse herself, saying she needed to go to bed and rest. She thanked Yolanda again for her kindness. They hugged and Yolanda cried. Actually, she was eager to use the phone and hotel internet to search for a flight out of Cuba. With Costa's questions about her art and not knowing if Matvey had been caught with the cross, it was best for her to get out of reach of the Cuban authorities, as quickly as possible.

Evelyn looked out of the window of her historic room, thinking that freedom from the Cuban authorities was a mere 90 miles to the north. Close, but so far away. She knew she needed to wait, get on the plane and clear U.S. Customs, and then she would be beyond the reach of Inspector Costa.

Evelyn found a seat on a flight leaving the airport in the morning. She made arrangements to check out of the hotel early and depart for Miami. From Miami she could more easily get to New York or the UK. It was a relief that she would soon be a safe distance away from Cuba. She knew she would have to abandon her art, even if Inspector Costa ever did forward it to her at the hotel. It was a small loss compared to facing charges for trafficking antiquities.

It was a fitful night for her. She worried about oversleeping, worried about getting charged with a crime, and worried about the deception she had inflicted upon Yolanda. She hoped Yolanda would not get ensnared in the investigation. Yolanda had only acted professionally in her capacity as an archivist.

Evelyn woke abruptly and looked at the bedside alarm. She was up early and dismissed the alarm setting. Washing her face, she inspected her forehead. The contusion had diminished but the remnant bump was still tender. The laceration was healing, leaving a fresh scar from the cut and stitches at her hair line. She combed her bangs to cover the scar. As she looked at herself in the mirror, she thought a new hair style would easily hide this insult to her perfection.

Even though she was earlier than she needed to be to catch her flight, she wanted to get moving, reasoning that the earlier she got to the airport, the earlier she would be away from her present sticky situation. Evelyn called for a bellhop to come assist with her luggage. At the front desk she asked to check out.

The clerk pulled a note from the cubby-grid that held messages for each room. The desk clerk unfolded it and read out load, "Please notify me when Professor Evelyn Griffin checks out of the hotel, signed Inspector Carlos Costa, Cienfuegos Policia. There is a phone number. Would you like to call him from our house phone?"

Evelyn was startled, "Oh no, please. I will call him later to tell him I am moving to another hotel to be closer to the art gallery in Old Havana. I will let him know the new phone number of where I am staying when I get there." She snatched the note from the somewhat surprised desk clerk.

Evelyn hoped that this would buy her enough time to get to the airport, clear the exit procedures and get on the plane to Miami. She caught up with the bellhop, hailed a taxi and was off to José Martí International Airport.

Evelyn moved quickly to check in for her flight. Thankfully, it would be on time. She checked her luggage, knowing it would be inspected for contraband before being loaded on the plane. Obviously, she now had nothing that was prohibited. She purchased a bottle of water and stood in line to exchange her Cuban pesos for a currency she could use. Then, she lined up to have her exit interview with the immigration officials. Evelyn was close to freedom. Once she cleared the booth she would be in the international no-man's land – not yet in another country, but technically not in Cuba either. She would be just a bit safer from the reach of the Cuban police.

She approached the booth and handed her UK passport to the immigration officer. The official looked at her and compared her glamorous passport picture to her plain, unmade-up face. He looked at his computer monitor and checked a notebook. "Un momento. Espere aquí, por favor." He motioned with his hand to stop and left the booth. A few minutes later, a uniformed matronly officer, obviously a supervisor, approached her from the international side of the immigration booth. She gently took Evelyn's arm and asked, "Would you please come with me?" in perfect English. The booth officer handed her passport back to her and spoke the only English he knew, "Have a nice flight."

The matron took her to a desk at the side of the immigration booths and asked Evelyn to sit. "May I have your passport?" Evelyn handed it to her. "Evelyn Griffin, this is you?" Noting the passport picture was a little different from her present plain-Jane appearance, Evelyn nodded.

The officer picked up the phone and dialed a call. Evelyn could hear a faint ringing and a muted voice answer. The supervisor spoke, "This is Immigration Sergeant Lourdes Gomez, at José Martí International Airport. I have Evelyn Griffin here with me." She paused and reached out with the phone handset to Evelyn. "He wants to speak with you."

"Buenos dias Evelyn. This is Inspector Carlos Costa at the Cienfuegos Police Station. I was afraid I might miss you." Evelyn gasped. He continued, "This morning I called the Hotel Nacional and found out you were leaving. I did not want to have you leave without saying good bye and offer apologies for your assault at Girón."

Evelyn was confused and scared. He was obviously playing her.

Costa continued, "I was afraid if you left Cuba, I would not be able to get your box of paintings to you. The antiquities authorities looked at your paintings and they are approved for export. If you are leaving now, what should I do with them? How will I get them to you?"

She thought for a moment and said, "Thank you so much," in her best, pretentious, insincere British accent. "I will make arrangements for them to be picked up at your station if you will be so kind as to keep them for a few days until I can get a shipping company contracted?"

"Of course. It will be no problem, but it would be so much easier if you could return to Cienfuegos and take them with you. I would hate for them to get damaged or stolen here at the police station. It might be easier for you to get them shipped out of our port to, where is it? Oh, Port Au Prince, Haiti."

Evelyn was certain this was a delay to keep her there. He was tracking her for something. Maybe the art, hopefully not the cross.

"Thank you, but no, I have to get on the plane. Please keep my package safe until I can get it worked out. I will try to do it as fast as possible. I will let you know my address, soon. I have your number. And, Inspector Costa, I really appreciate all that you have done for me and hope you will find my assailant. Thank you, un millon de gracias! Adios cuidate."

She stood and asked the matronly Sergeant, "May I go?" The supervisor bowed her head and smiled. "Yes, of course. We hope you will visit Cuba again soon. Safe flight."

As she looked out the window of the plane as it flew over the city, she saw the broad Malecón roadway, the Hotel Nacional and the iconic lighthouse in the Morro-Cabañas fort at the entrance to Havana Harbor. She was relieved but melancholy. Goodbye, my beloved Cuba. Goodbye.

TWENTY

Matvey was determined to make the best of his time at the Cassiopea estate. He was grateful that he had a place to stay and a job to earn a little money. Henry and Sunny were helping him with clothes and food and even a wallet for his earnings. He felt safe and, best of all, he was out of danger from being caught in Cuba and sent to prison for murder. He felt guilt over Evelyn's death. It haunted him that she died. He did not mean to kill her. He only wanted her to stop screaming. If she had only let him explain that he wasn't stealing the cross.

Every day, Matvey woke with the sunrise. Sunny had given him an alarm clock radio but he didn't need it. It was useful to tell time and, at night, he would try to tune in a Cuban radio station.

Every day, except Sunday, when Henry would take the truck to church in the Bahama Village, Matvey worked with Henry on tasks around the estate. The hurricane clean-up was over, but the rock wall and patio project had begun and was a big job.

They carefully placed rocks along a string line to keep the wall straight. Each rock was positioned to wedge against another. A chisel hammer was used to chip away at the rocks that went outside of the lines so the wall was kept straight. The top of the wall was capped with concrete mortar, and smoothed by hand. Henry's hands were tough as leather from years of manual labor. Matvey found his hands burning and peeling after working with the caustic cement.

They worked well together. After a hard day collecting rocks and building on the wall, they would sit on the porch and split a six pack. Matvey was finding the work satisfying. It was making something that would last and he was proud of his efforts.

During one of their limes, Matvey asked Henry, "What does Cassiopea mean?" Henry replied "It's the name of an upside-down jellyfish. Mr. Abram told me he saw one when he visited the Keys when he was a young man. He thought it was beautiful with its tentacles swaying in the water, moving in and out. He said, 'I thought it was dying because it was upside-down.' So, he turned it over so it could swim away in the water.

"But Mr. Abram learned it wasn't dying. That was just the way the jellyfish lived. It lays on the bottom waving its tentacles to filter the water for food, taking whatever passed by. Mr. Abrams said it seemed like a good way to live, to lay back and take the opportunities that came your way. So that's how he decided to live his life and he must have made the most of the things that came his way, because he died a very rich man and found a good wife in Shelley."

Their conversation always seemed to drift back to the Dry Tortugas and Matvey wanting to get back to where he landed. He talked to Henry about the fabulous fishing they could have there. And the fort was amazing. He wanted to see it again. "Can't we go in your boat? It looks big enough. We could have a great time and catch lots of fish."

Henry was skeptical. "Matvey, it is a long way. Why would you want to go out on the ocean again after the Lord delivered you on your last trip?"

Matvey laid out his case, "We can watch the weather and not go in a hurricane! It's not so far for your boat. We could sleep on the floor of the boat. I saw a harbor there at the fort where we could anchor." Matvey pulled out a promotional tourist magazine with an article and pictures of Fort Jefferson and advertisements for the daily ferry tours, among the advertisements for restaurants and tours throughout the Keys.

After they finished their beers, they separated for the evening. Henry retired to read, sometimes a novel, often the Bible. He was a self-taught Biblical scholar as well as a self-taught naturalist. Henry had a whole library of field guides in the main house to select from.

Matvey spent his evenings listening to talk radio. It wasn't so much that he cared about the content. He was interested in learning better English. He listened a bit and then tried to repeat what he just heard. He was self-conscious about his English-speaking skills, wanting to be better at pronunciation. He also wished he was better at reading English.

Sunny set a date to leave Cassiopea and the Keys. She rented a car and packed her art for her trip to Bloomington. She planned to drive home and prepare her work for an art show to be scheduled later in the year, maybe December. She knew she had plenty of work to complete in her studio before she could mount a one-man show and she was anxious to get started as soon as possible.

On the night before she left, Matvey and Henry had a farewell party for her. They bought a key lime pie from the local bakery and a bottle of good rum. They set up a table and chairs on the new patio and party lights were hung on the new pergola that Matvey and Henry had built.

Matvey brought out his clock radio and tuned into a local radio station. Sometimes they even played a Cuban tune. When the song Chan Chan started, Matvey took Sunny's hand and drew her into dancing. She was not accomplished as a dancer, but moved well with the rhythm. Matvey, of course, had all the right dance moves and guided her expertly.

Matvey flirted with her all night, but she was aloof, seeming to not notice his advances. Her standoffishness was puzzling as Matvey was used to women being a little more receptive to his charms. He thought maybe it was because Henry was there and she didn't want to be promiscuous in front of Henry. Or, it could be that she was faithful to her beau, Chris, back in Indiana. Matvey felt a twinge of remorse that he had never been that committed to anyone, except his mother.

Matvey wanted to be with her. But he also respected her because she was so kind and free-spirited. On a slow dance, he tried to hold her tight, but she pulled back to a respectable distance and danced in a more formal position. He decided he would be a gentleman and not press her. Even though his seduction was not going to be successful, it was still fun for all of them. They were all feeling the influence of the rum and bittersweet departure.

Sunny drove away in the morning with her two favorite men standing in the drive watching her leave. Waving, they called out, "Safe travels. See you again soon!" Neither man knew when that might be because Sunny was a little eccentric and impulsive.

Henry said, "I'm going to miss that girl. She brought a lot of life to this place." Matvey agreed. "She is wonderful, like nobody I've ever met. She is so caring about others." Henry and Matvey returned to work on the rock wall. It was turning out well. The project was also clearing the grounds of lots of errant rocks that were strewn over the property. The two men estimated that together they had picked up thousands of rocks and wheel-barrowed them to the work site.

When picking up the coral and limestone rocks, Henry would check for lizards and toads. Not wanting to harm them, he would scoop them up in his hands and release them somewhere else that would be safe. In amazement, Matvey watched this large old man being so gentle and concerned. As they worked, Henry showed Matvey native plants telling him about medicinal uses or warning him which plants caused dangerous rashes.

"This is poisonwood. White-crowned pigeons can eat the berries, but this is poisonous! You will get a big rash on your skin from the juice!" While Matvey looked at the plant, Henry walked to a gumbo limbo tree, saying "If you do get the juice on you, wash it off, and rub the gumbo limbo wood on the place. It will cure the poison." Matvey was amazed at how much Henry knew about nature. "How did you learn this?" Henry said, "Some from my elders, some from Mr. and Mrs. Abram, a little on my own. You can learn a lot from nature, if you only look and listen."

They took their load of rocks back to the wall and started working again. It wasn't long before Matvey was talking about going to Dry Tortugas again, presenting a response against every objection Henry had. It was starting to make a change in Henry. Matvey was wearing him down to a point where Henry could actually consider that they might be able to go.

That night they joined together for dinner. They were missing Sunny. Henry made another Bahamian feast, frying small grunts, whole, only gutted, but with heads on. They devoured the fish. Matvey said, "If we caught big fish in the Dry Tortugas, we wouldn't have to pick the bones from these little ones." He grinned. Henry said, "OK, OK! We can go. I want you to know that it's a big trip for me and we'll have to be careful. Now, will you stop pestering me about the Dry Tortugas?" Matvey's grin grew to a big smile. He needed to be quiet now and trust Henry to make the arrangements.

Still apprehensive, over the next week or so, Henry started making preparations for a trip to the Dry Tortugas. He checked his boat and the motors. He bought a tarp that they could use for a shelter and made sure he had the USCG required equipment. He even purchased another set of emergency flares. At night, instead of reading, he studied the chart from Key West to Dry Tortugas and considered the options for a course. He did not want Matvey hovering while he figured it out.

Getting there was only half of the voyage. He had to get back. He would need enough gas and water because neither are available at the fort. He bought three 5-gallon jerry cans for extra gas and one for water. He sought information about the trip from others he knew who had made the trip. Henry was a cautious boater, capable in the nearshore waters, but not experienced offshore except for trolling in the Gulf Stream on calm days.

For the next week Henry and Matvey talked constantly about the plan and, finally, set a date, depending on the marine weather forecast. Matvey was overjoyed that he was on track to get back and recover his treasures.

TWENTY-ONE

Henry backed up the pick-up truck to hitch the boat trailer. Matvey cranked the jack stand to lift the tongue over the ball and then lowered it onto the trailer hitch. Henry shifted into park and went to the back of the truck to put on the chains and hook up the lights. Early in the morning, they would be off for the voyage to the Dry Tortugas. The cajoling and begging wore down Henry's reluctance to make such a long trip. Now, Henry was excited, if still apprehensive.

The Dry Tortugas is 70 miles west of Key West. It is not like crossing the Atlantic, but it is an intimidating distance for a small boat. Henry's Parker sport fisherman was solid, with two 150-horsepower Yamaha outboards. He kept it well maintained, cosmetically and mechanically. Henry wasn't worried so much about the boat being able to make the trip. He was more worried about navigation. Since the Dry Tortugas islands are the last keys in the archipelago, missing them on the trip out would mean the next stop is Mexico. That was definitely too far for the boat's fuel supply.

They had been preparing for a week by getting the boat ready and buying supplies for a three-day cruise. Henry purchased a gimbled compass to aid them in their voyage because, when he studied the marine charts, he noted there would be long distances between Cassiopea and Fort Jefferson without navigation markers and out of the sight of land.

Noticing Henry installing the compass on the Parker, Matvey asked, "Hey man, what are you doing? Can I help you?" He was always willing to help and often offering assistance, even in one-man tasks.

Henry chuckled, "Yes, buddy, you can help me when we are on the ocean. Pay close attention to this. It's a compass to help steer the course to the Tortugas and, I hope, show us the way to get back!"

The marine weather forecast was good. With the sunrise they would be on their way.

Matvey was exuberant about getting back to Fort Jefferson, but his real destination was Loggerhead Key. He had told Henry tall tales about fishing and the lighthouse to build Henry's enthusiasm. For his part, Henry was doing this for the fishing, but even more so he was doing it for Matvey, who seemed obsessed with Loggerhead Key.

They launched the boat, then motored out of Garrison Bight as the sun was coming up. It was easy to navigate the channel. They had a small handheld GPS that revealed the location of navigation markers with accurate latitude and longitude numbers they could plot on their paper chart. The excitement of the trip replaced the sea anxiety that developed in Matvey's psyche from his trip from Cuba that ended in the shipwreck. He was determined to get back to retrieve his buried treasure. He worried it might have been found, or washed away, or that he wouldn't be able to find it. Still, he was confident that he would find it and, by regaining the treasure, he would be on his way to a rich life in the U.S.

Henry kept a steady speed past the few islands that were near Key West. He had enough gas, but there was no sense in wasting fuel for speed that they didn't need. At 10 knots, in the favorable conditions they were experiencing, they would arrive in the early afternoon, with time to spare before sunset. The weather and seas were perfect. A gentle southeast breeze aided their speed and the waves were only 1-2 ft. A high-pressure bubble over the Keys would keep the weather like this for days.

They kept their eyes on the compass, trying to steer the course Henry had planned. Four hours out from Key West, the Marquesas Islands were to their south, clearly visible. Henry knew they were on track, maybe even a little ahead of schedule. The water was clear. They could see the sandy bottom 30 feet below the keel. Occasionally they passed over a darker patch of a coral head.

After the Marquesas, Rebecca Shoals marker was the next target. Then, after that, for a couple hours, they would be out of sight of land. From there to the Tortugas bank there was a channel that could kick up a bit if the weather was bad. It wasn't, so the seas didn't build any higher than 2-3 feet which was easily comfortable in Henry's boat.

When they spotted a thin line of land on the western horizon, they were both elated that they would make it. The thin line turned into an island, and then they were close enough to see the fort. They could even see the Loggerhead Key lighthouse, standing tall on the island beyond.

On the way a few other boats passed them on their way to the same destination. Many boats were larger than Henry's. They had only passed one sailboat heading west.

Henry and Matvey pulled up to the park dock to register with the Park Service and get instructions on where to anchor. They didn't have a tender, so this was their only way to get to the island. Since pleasure boats were not allowed to tie up for long, they moved to anchor in the shallow waters of the protected harbor east of the fort.

Matvey and Henry popped a beer and high-fived to celebrate their successful voyage. They relaxed and enjoyed the ambience. The fort was impressive. They noticed that the other boats, sailboats, trawlers, and yachts, in the anchorage were larger than Henry's. That made them even more proud to have been able to navigate and successfully arrive at Fort Jefferson.

As the sun set behind the fort, frigatebirds began leaving their aerial sweeps in the thermals over the fort, moving to roost on the spindly black mangroves on the island to the east. The wind went calm and the ocean was an undulating sheet of glass reflecting the colors of the sky. Matvey asked if Henry was hungry. In the excitement of reaching their destination, they had forgotten to eat. They broke out their prepackaged rations and washed them down with another beer.

Night blanketed the Tortugas in darkness. Anchor lights lit up on the boats, looking like stars. The stars overhead were twinkling and there was a hint of the Milky Way fading into view. They strung up a tarp to catch the dew and unrolled blankets to sleep on the open floor of the boat.

As they retired, Matvey said with emotion, "Thank you so much for bringing me here. You can't know how happy it makes my heart." The seasoned Bahamian replied, "You're welcome, buddy. Now go to sleep. We will fish tomorrow." Under the tarp hanging overhead, they fell asleep, rocked like babies in a cradle by a gentle sea motion.

Dawn brought seabirds to life. They both wakened to gulls and terns welcoming the new day. The sunrise was nearly as colorful as the sunset. The frigatebirds resumed their aerial acrobatics over the tall brick walls of Ft. Jefferson.

Henry and Matvey headed out to a reef a few miles off the fort. They dropped the anchor in a sand patch and drifted over the darker coral to fish the rock bottom. Henry opened their small bait cooler and recoiled at the putrid, milky green-brown soup his mullet was sloshing in. The ice had melted. But the mullets still made good bait. Pulling one out he fileted it on a cutting board.

They baited their hooks, dropped their lines until they went slack, then reeled in about three feet so the bait hovered just above the bottom. It wasn't long before one of the men got his first bite. Soon, they were in a competition to catch the first, the largest, and the most fish. But they were careful not to take more than they could keep cold in their larger ice chest. Soon, they were ready for lunch and the excursion to Loggerhead Key.

Henry beached the boat near the park dock on Loggerhead Key, which was still nothing more than pilings after the storm. He dragged the anchor high up on the shore not wanting the tide to take the boat and leave them stranded. Matvey could barely control his excitement and anticipation of getting to the monument to recover his strong box. He gobbled his sandwich and nervously waited for Henry to finish eating. It seemed Henry was in slow motion. Matvey told himself to be patient. To avoid being discovered and having more explaining to do than he wanted to do, he needed to visit his secret stash without Henry.

Sitting in the shade of a gumbo limbo that now had leaves, he told Henry, "Please excuse me for a minute. I have to go pee and walk back to where I arrived. It is something I'd like to do by myself." Henry waved him off, still savoring his sandwich. "Go ahead. Don't worry. I won't watch," grinning with a smile.

Matvey raced off on the path past the lighthouse keeper's house, stepping over the fallen casuarina tree trunks. Walking north on the beach he searched his memory for where the monument was located. Last time he was here, he was in a daze and being assisted by Sunny. It was hard to judge the distance. No matter, it was a small island and he was energized with determination to find his treasure.

He saw the top of the monument just behind the primary dune, about where he thought it might be. Racing up the loose sand slope, he fell to his knees and began digging at the concrete base of the marker. This time, he was not exhausted by digging the hole. Reaching down he felt a sharp pain on his finger and pulled his arm back to find a decent sized ghost crab firmly affixed to his index finger. Matvey had exposed the crab's burrow. The crab fought with his other claw to keep Matvey from extracting his digit.

Matvey shook it off. The crustacean had drawn blood! "Curse you, señor cangrejo. I am busy. Thank you for guarding my treasure," as the ghost crab scampered away.

After digging down 2 feet or so, Matvey touched the polyester backpack containing the metal box. It was still there! He carefully dug around the pack until it was loose enough to pull out without breaking it open.

He dusted off the sand, and tried the zipper. It was hopelessly fused with corrosion so Matvey ripped the bag apart at the seams. Inside the pack, the box was badly rusted on the outside. Opening it, he saw the assortment of earrings and jewels he had accumulated from his exploits, along with a little sand. He quickly scrambled through the container. Where was the cross? He moved the contents again. No cross. Clearly it was the largest thing in his treasure chest. It should be easy to see. Matvey laid out the torn day pack and emptied the contents onto the fabric.

There was no cross. Matvey sat back, on the sand, in disbelief. Thinking to himself, "Now I know why Sunny wouldn't take me with her when she returned to this island to get her things. It makes sense now. She must have returned to steal my cross. She saw me at the monument. I did not hear her, but she must have seen me bury the box."

He further convinced himself that Sunny had stolen his cross. It didn't make sense. In the days after the storm, Sunny had been good to him. She seemed like a nice person. But she was the only one who could have stolen the cross. The conflict haunted him. How could she betray him like this and take what was his? He had worked hard to keep the cross. It was his! Matvey was angry, and hurt.

He scooped his jewelry into a pile and carefully wrapped them in a piece of cloth he salvaged from the day pack. Then he flung the rusted box into the surf. He put his booty into his pocket.

He fumed all the way back to the lighthouse where he found Henry waiting at the door of the keeper's house. Henry smiled, "Everything come out all right? You really must have had to pee. Usually, it's the old men that take so long." Matvey feigned a smile, and mumbled, "Ja Ja Ja Ja."

"I'm sorry, Henry," Matvey apologized. "I have had enough of this island! Let's go!" Henry was surprised at how Matvey's mood had changed so fast. It was so contrary to the easy-going good-natured kid he had known for the past months.

Henry guessed maybe when he was off alone, he remembered the companions he lost in the shipwreck. Maybe he had seen their ghosts. It must have been something serious to change his mood so much. Henry did not want to ask him about it. If Matvey wanted to talk, he would. Henry backed off the joking.

They launched the boat from the beach. Matvey pushed out the bow and jumped on when they were in water deep enough to start the motors. Henry said, "Let's go fishing again. We still have room in the chest." Matvey was quiet for a bit, and said, "Maybe later. Let's go back to the fort until it gets cooler."

Back at the fort the ferry boat, *Miss Marathon*, was at the dock with a boatload of day-tripping visitors. The ferry boat carried passengers to the fort on long, day excursions. Loading in the morning at Key West's dock for the long ride out, tourists spend a few hours at the park and then board again for long ride back. Fortunately, the boat sells excess bags of ice to boaters and campers staying at the park. Henry bought two bags of ice from the ferry deckhand, saying, "Five dollars a bag! Can you believe it. $5.00 for a bag of ice – pirates!" He was only half joking, because the ice was of real value to someone who didn't have any. "I guess you can charge whatever you want when you are the only option."

Henry replenished the big chest and set to fileting the fish they caught earlier in the day, throwing the carcasses and guts overboard. Soon a large hammerhead arrived and circled the boat. It was escorted by a legion of remora, the fish that feed on the messy leftovers from a shark's violent feeding habits. To be ready for scraps, the remoras even attach themselves to the underside of the shark with a special suction cup on their heads. The shark circled several times and left, finding nothing more than a bloody scent in the water.

Matvey was unusually quiet, sitting sullenly at the bow of the boat staring off into the distance. He was still seething at being a victim of a thief. Henry wasn't going to let his moodiness prevent another fishing trip to the reef. He said, "Ok, Matvey, time to pull anchor. It's cooler now and I need to go fishing. That's what I came here for!"

Matvey dutifully pulled the anchor. He came to terms with his anger and the futility of being angry when there was nothing he could do about it. Matvey said, "Yes sir, mi capitan. Let's go catch fish!" This was more like the Matvey that Henry knew.

They fished the reef again with even better luck. They caught many fish allowing them to be selective in what they kept from their successful exploits. They were catching and keeping grouper, yellowtail snapper and no more grunts! Now they sought the larger fish that would make nice filets. They had enough fish for Henry to prepare using his Bahamian recipes. As the sun set, they headed back to the anchorage.

Two people in a dinghy came by to greet them. They were from a sailboat anchored nearby and introduced themselves, Marcy and George from Michigan. They were on a 32-foot boat. With his poor understanding of the North America geography, Matvey couldn't relate well to the long distance the couple had traveled to get to these remote islands.

As the couple sat in the dinghy, they exchanged pleasantries with Matvey and Henry, telling a few stories about their voyages getting to the Dry Tortugas. They brought some containers of food to share. Marcy said, "We don't have room for this in our refrigerator and thought maybe you would like it." Henry was graciously appreciative. "Yes, as you can see, we don't have a stove or cabin on our boat, so this will be better than another sandwich."

Marcy said, "We'll come back later for the Tupperware," and they sped off to their sailboat.

After dark they returned, and Henry said, "Please come on board. We have a bottle of rum, if you like rum. We can watch the stars for a bit."

Matvey retrieved the rum from the gear bag and found four plastic cups. Henry poured generous portions and toasted the sea and new friends. They all talked for hours, Marcy and George recounting their long trip cruising down to the Florida Keys, Henry regaling memories of Key West and the Bahamas, and Matvey sharing about life in Cuba. Before the sailors departed, they were all singing familiar tunes, *Guantanamera* and *Sloop John B*.

Marcy and George gathered their plastic containers and as they were pushing off, they said, "This is the best time we've ever had on our boat. I hope we can keep in touch." But all knew they never would see one another again.

The fishing, dinner, and drinking took Matvey's mind off of the cross and Sunny. Now, feeling loose from the rum, he pulled out a beer and sat back, in a melancholy mood.

"You know, Henry, you have been so good to me, to bring me out here. You have done so much for me by letting me work with you at Cassiopea. I really want to thank you, my friend." He lifted his beer in a toast to Henry.

Henry smiled, reaching for a beer himself. "It has been good to have you. I'm glad Sunny brought you to us. I couldn't have done so much without your help."

They sat in silence under the stars. The Milky Way was a star-speckled cloud in the dark sky. As Henry and Matvey looked out at the anchor lights on the other boats that were sharing the night with them, they wondered about where the boats came from and where they might go next.

"Let's hit the sack, my friend. We have an early start tomorrow to get back to Key West."

Matvey said, "Buenas noches, mi amigo." It was a good night, even if he would need to confront Sunny about the cross when he got back. But, for now, it was a good night

TWENTY-TWO

Henry and Matvey drove up to Marathon to the hardware store to pick up some special plumbing parts they needed for the cistern. They stopped at a convenience store for gas. Henry sent Matvey into the store to buy them each a Coke, thinking it would be good for Matvey to conduct a sales transaction by himself. Sooner or later, Matvey would be more on his own and not under his wing. After months of living in the U.S., Matvey was still impressed with the stock that stores had to sell. He marveled at the numerous choices for the same item.

In the convenience store, waiting in line to pay, he noticed a rack displaying the *Keynoter* weekly newspaper. What caught his eye was a photograph of Sunny and himself. On the front page, above the fold, the headline read "Artist Who Rescued Cuban to Exhibit." His eyes were fixed on the paper. He stepped out of line and picked up the paper. The cashier yelled, "Hey bud, you gonna pay for that! Or read it here? This ain't a libary."

Matvey didn't know how to respond. He nervously put the paper down. The clerk snapped, "It only costs a buck. Go ahead and buy it." He followed the clerk's instruction, putting the newspaper on the counter with the Cokes and handing the clerk a ten-dollar bill. After receiving the change, he walked out to the truck, trying to read the paper. His English reading skills were not as good as his conversation. Handing the paper to Henry, he said, "Look at this! It's me and Sunny!"

Henry started reading out loud.

"An Indiana artist who survived Hurricane Denise alone in the Dry Tortugas and rescued a shipwrecked Cuban refugee will be exhibiting her art work at the Key West Artist Studios and Gallery. The exhibit will showcase the drawings and paintings Sondra Kaye "Sunny" Griffin made while at Dry Tortugas National Park as part of the National Park Service "Artist in Residence Program" during the fall.

Griffin was on Loggerhead Key staying at the lighthouse for nearly 10 weeks before Hurricane Denise rapidly developed and hit the Lower Keys on September 15. The storm came so fast that the Park Service could not evacuate her so she sheltered in the historic lighthouse.

After the storm, Griffin found shipwrecked Cuban Matvey Valdez-Descon on the beach and cared for him until they could be brought to Key West by a rescue team. Four others on the boat that left Cuba in the storm were lost and are presumed dead.

Griffin's paintings and drawings feature the nature of the Dry Tortugas. She says of her work, "I am lucky to have had the opportunity to spend time on Loggerhead Key to observe and illustrate the diverse land and sea life at the national park. It was the thrill of my life."

Griffin received a BFA at Indiana University and a Masters in art history at Florida State University. Her exhibit is sponsored by art patron Shelley Abram and the Friends of the South Florida National Parks. An opening reception will be held next Wednesday at 6:00 PM. The artist will present a short lecture about her work at 7. The exhibit will run for a month. The gallery is open 10 AM to 6 PM Monday through Saturdays."

The caption on the photograph was "Indiana artist Sunny Griffin with Cuban refugee Matvey Valdez-Descon arriving at the U.S. Coast Guard Station, Key West, after Hurricane Denise."

There was another photograph of Sunny with one of her paintings next to the article.

Matvey asked, "Did you know about this?" Henry said he knew Mrs. Abram was coming to stay next week but she hadn't mentioned Sunny's exhibit.

Since returning from the fishing trip to the Dry Tortugas, every time he thought about Sunny, he would get angry and imagine in his head how, when she returned to Cassiopea, he would confront her about stealing the cross and get it back. For all he knew she would never be back, since she had the cross. He thought if Sunny comes back, I don't want her to find and take the jewels too. Now, according to the article in the paper, Sunny would be back. Now he would have his chance.

Matvey was staying in a small cottage at the Cassiopea compound. It was set up as a bunk house for the younger guests that Mr. and Mrs. Abrams would invite for short stays. It was also used as an overflow accommodation for the staff when extra housekeepers or kitchen help were needed for the special events the Abrams hosted at Cassiopea. Each of the two bedrooms had two bunkbeds so up to eight people could stay there.

The cabin was simple and austere but comfortable, patterned after a Bahamian dwelling, with the ceiling open to a common frame roof decked with Caribbean heart pine. Interior partitions separated the few rooms which included a small functional kitchen and a bathroom. Exterior walls were stuccoed coral rock, built strong to withstand tropical weather. The two cottages on the estate were a vestige of an earlier era when pioneering families first settled on the Key.

Matvey was happy to have the private place to himself, without the pressure of having to struggle with conversations in English. It was his retreat. Since the theft of the cross he didn't trust anyone. If Sunny could steal from him, anyone could, even Henry. He kept his cash with him at all times.

He decided the jewels needed to be reduced enough to fit in a small bag that he could carry in his pocket. He had his treasure well hidden, but he still didn't feel it was safe from discovery. He spent his evenings working on his jewelry while studying English. He borrowed the fishing tackle box to use the needle-nose pliers and small hooks inside. With these tools, he carefully extracted the jewels from their settings in earrings and pendants. He hid the gold settings back in the hiding place he had been using.

In the big house, in a kitchen catch-all drawer, Matvey found a purple velvet bag with a yellow tie, marked "Crown

Royale". He thought, "This will be perfect for my collection of precious stones and pearls. No one will miss this bag in this messy drawer."

The lack of information from Sunny about her coming to the Keys for the art exhibit added to Matvey's paranoic suspicions concerning her theft of the cross. Then, the day after he saw the article, the mail brought two envelopes to Cassiopea, one addressed to Matvey and the other to Henry. They were invitations to be guests of honor at the opening reception. Each invitation included a kind, personal note from Sunny. Reading the note helped Matvey be a little less suspicious but it didn't change his mind about her thievery.

Henry was disappointed that he wouldn't be able to attend. He was scheduled to present a sermon about the Bahamas and Turks and Caicos connections to Key West at his AME Church during the Wednesday service. He was committed to be there and could not cancel.

Henry said, "I'll drive you to Key West. But it'll be before the reception starts so I can get to church on time. Then, I'll pick you up later, after church. Maybe the shindig will still be going on and I can attend at least part of the reception." Matvey nodded as if he understood, but shindig was an unfamiliar word.

Mrs. Abram called Henry the same day the invitations came. She told him, "I'm bringing a friend to stay at Cassiopea and together we'll attend the reception. Because my friend will be staying in the guest house, Sunny and Chris won't be staying there. They found accommodations in Key West near the gallery. We'll arrive by charter jet by midday on the day of the reception. A limousine will be bringing us to Cassiopea.

Because the Mercedes was totaled by Hurricane Denise, I've arranged for a rental car to be delivered to the estate. Henry, please arrange for the cook to be at the estate and ask her to provision the kitchen for a big post-reception party. Maybe your new Cuban assistant can drive us to the reception since you wouldn't be able to take us."

Henry didn't think it was a good idea, even if Matvey could drive, telling Mrs. Abram, "That won't work, Mrs. Abram. He doesn't have a driver's license yet and I'm not sure how well he can drive. I'm dropping him off at Sunny's reception on my way to church, so you will be able to meet him there, if not before, when you arrive here."

Henry wanted everything to go well when Matvey met Mrs. Abram. She was very gracious and generous, but also very direct and strong-minded. Matvey had ingratiated himself to Sunny and himself, but Henry felt Matvey needed a little orientation to the protocol for the estate before he met Mrs. Abram.

Henry coached Matvey on what he should do when he was around Mrs. Abram. He explained that Matvey could be himself, but he should respect her privacy. Besides being polite and respectful, he should not try too hard. "If she wants something, she will ask. She is passionately interested in learning and you should not be offended by her boundless curiosity. She will probably want to know everything about you, but you shouldn't ask about her."

Henry said he loved Mrs. Abram. She and her husband took an interest in him when he was young and troubled. They and Jesus had saved him from a wasted life. Mr. Abram was a wealthy man and passed away a decade ago. Mrs.

Abram was devoted to her husband and continued building the paradise at Cassiopea in tribute to his memory. They both valued nature very much and mentored Henry to become a naturalist.

Mid-afternoon Shelley and her guest arrived at the estate in a chauffeured Lincoln Town Car. Henry and Matvey greeted them. She hugged Henry tightly. Then Henry introduced Matvey to Mrs. Abram. She said, "So nice to meet you, young man. I look forward to talking with you later in the week. I want hear all about your journey here and Cuba."

She went on, "This is my dear friend, Mrs. Anita Greene from Charlestown."

Anita Greene was the widow of Massachusetts's long-serving Senator Harmon Greene, a long-time friend of the Abrams. They had enjoyed traveling together as a foursome. Mr. Abram and Senator Greene were always talking finance and politics, while the ladies enjoyed discussions of art, literature, and fashion. Many nights they all would get together for a competitive evening of bridge. Now the two ladies were traveling alone, enjoying each other's company and reflecting on the memories of all their experiences together.

They all shook hands, then the two women went to their respective accommodations to prepare for Sunny's reception later that evening, followed by Henry and Matvey bringing their luggage. The limousine and chauffeur would return later to drive the two friends to the art gallery, since Henry wasn't available to drive the rental car that had been delivered earlier in the day.

At 4:30, Henry knocked on Matvey's door. Matvey was finished with his work removing the jewels from their settings.

He was dressed and ready to go. While his clothes were second-hand from Goodwill, he cut a presentable figure. Shopping at Goodwill had reignited his passion for fashion. The navy-blue sports coat fit his tall frame like a glove and accentuated his green eyes. He wore a light blue collared shirt, open at the neck, with no tie.

His jacket hid the bulge from his wallet, holding all of his cash, in the back pocket of his khaki pants. He kept the bag of jewels in the jacket pocket where he could easily check that they were still with him. As he stepped out of his door, he realized a little too late that he would have to keep his jacket on all night, no matter how humid and hot it was.

Matvey left with Henry. Once they arrived in Key West, Henry explained, "Until the doors open for the reception, you'll be on your own for a while. I hate to leave you here, but you can handle it, I'm sure." As Henry stopped his truck at the corner opposite the gallery, he pointed out where Matvey needed to go at six.

"Will you be okay?" Henry asked, treating him like a child on his first day of school. Matvey just smiled and closed the door. He watched Henry drive off in the truck to get to his church meeting.

Matvey was on his own for the first time. He didn't want to stand in front of the gallery and wait for the reception to begin, so he decided to walk on Duval Street until the reception. Then he could meet up with Sunny. He noted where the gallery was and then walked a few blocks, keeping track of his path. He didn't want to get lost.

He walked through the flow of tourists, following the crowd, past the t-shirt shops, bars and art galleries. It was similar to the tourist streets in Havana Vieja, except for the traffic. In Cuba, the streets like this were closed to cars.

In the open plaza by the ocean, people were assembled around various street performers. There were musicians, magicians, escape artists, and even a performance of trained house cats! Matvey wandered through the crowd to the edge of the water. Everyone was there to watch the sun set at the famous Mallory Square. Many were talking among themselves about how tonight would be perfect for seeing the "green flash," but Matvey didn't understand what that meant.

Boats were parading by the seawall, as the sun was getting lower in the sky. Many people were sitting on a big sailboat that looked like a pirate ship, with two masts and red sails and a big banner that read SUNSET CRUISES and a phone number. A large catamaran was loaded with partiers who were jiving and dancing to loud music. Small sailboats and jet skis were also going out to watch the sun set, while the commercial and charter fishing boats were returning to their docks at the end of the day.

He tried to read the names on the boats' sterns. There was *Party Barge* and *we bee windjammin!*, *Big Fish*, and *Baby Doll*. In particular, one fishing boat passing by caught his attention. *La Luna Grande* was painted on the transom. He thought, "That's like the name of the boat that brought me to the Dry Tortugas, but it's much bigger and newer, like the other fishing boats. I wish I had been on that boat instead of the old wood boat that sank."

Uneasy in the swarm of tourists at the pier, he felt that he had had enough wandering. Retracing his steps back to Duval Street, Matvey then strolled for a few blocks to the east.

Duval Street was a circus. Eccentric local characters were mixed with vacationers feeling liberated in the free atmosphere of Key West. He saw women wearing only body paint, men holding hands with other men, and middle-aged tourists gawking at the parade of people on the street and smelling the aroma of marijuana wafting in the tropical breeze. Loud Harley motorcycles rumbled down the street. It was like nothing Matvey had ever seen and he was ill-prepared for the cacophony. This was too much for him to process, so he stepped into an open-air bar where a Jimmy Buffett-like entertainer was crooning and playing guitar.

He sat on a stool at the bar. "Whacha havin' buddy?" the barkeep said as he laid down a napkin on the counter. He repeated, "Hey Bud, what can I get you?"

Matvey paused to comprehend what the gruff man had said, then he sputtered, "Er, ron, er, er, rum, please."

"How do you want it? With Coke? Ice? Neat? What kind?"

Matvey still didn't quite understand and he certainly didn't know brands. He declared, "No ice, only rum."

A little impatient at his indecision about the brand, the bartender decided for him, returning with a double shot, snapping, "That'll be eight." Matvey pulled cash from his pocket and laid it on the bar.

Being on his own without the guidance of Henry, the circus of Duval Street, and worry about seeing Sunny again had Matvey's head spinning. What would he say to her? What would she say to him? It all seemed so complicated and far beyond his experience. He sampled the rum and watched the promenade outside on the street.

Matvey ordered another rum while he sat and waited for the reception to start. He thought more about Sunny's betrayal and how he was shown in the newspaper. It made him angry all over again.

It seemed to be taking forever for the reception to begin, so he ordered a third rum. He was drinking rum like water, not sipping and savoring. He thought, "This rum isn't as good as Cuban rum, but it will do." He felt calmer now. When the singer finished his set, Matvey got up from the bar and started walking toward the art gallery.

A docent met him at the door and immediately gasped. "Oh my! You are the Cuban Sunny saved!" she exclaimed as she handed him a program. Her recognition only aggravated the anger he was already feeling. "So, I am just 'the Cuban'? Sunny didn't save me; she stole my cross!" he muttered to himself.

He went inside and nearly everyone was staring at him, or so it seemed. For those who didn't recognize him from the photo in the *Keynoter*, he was noticed because he stood out from the others who were more formally dressed and he was a handsome young man. He was self-conscious, feeling out of place and nervous.

Matvey noticed the bar set up in the reception room. The servers were more polite than the guy at the street saloon. Approaching the bar, he asked, "May I have a glass of rum?" They smiled, poured him a generous serving and picked up the tongs to add ice. He cautioned, "No, no ice please!" Then he retreated to a corner of the room and sipped his rum as he observed the guests, glancing away when he noticed them looking at him.

After ordering another rum, he left the bar, moving to the room where Sunny's art was hanging. He stood in a corner, waiting and watching.

He saw Mrs. Abram and Mrs. Greene arrive, to some fanfare. The crowd now turned their attention away from him to the wealthy philanthropist. People lined up to greet her and speak party pleasantries. After their procession through the impromptu receiving line, people turned their attention to viewing Sunny's art hanging on the gallery walls.

Shelley was always stylishly dressed, even for casual strolls around her island compound. Usually, on her strolls, she wore a tailored sundress and low heals that were not really suitable for the pea-rock gravel trail surfaces that wound throughout the property. She always had a matching purse on her arm. When she was on the trails, her Leitz binoculars were handy at all times so she could observe tropical birds to add to her life list. Her love of nature sustained her dedication to Cassiopea nearly as much as her devotion to the legacy of her husband. Her interest in nature was not shared by Mrs. Greene, but she was always patient with Shelley's obsession and feigned enthusiasm when Shelley saw something special.

Tonight, Shelley was dressed to the nines in a flowered two-piece ensemble that was a little out of date from today's fashion. But it looked good on her; she made it look stylish by the way she carried herself and the accessories she wore.

A clinking of a glass silenced the attendees. The gallery director announced, "Ladies and Gentlemen!" With a little more glass clinking, finally, there was silence. She continued, "Welcome and thank you for coming tonight! Please join us in the auditorium to welcome our featured artist, Sunny

Griffin. Sunny will be making a brief presentation about her work."

Folks started moving toward the auditorium. Matvey followed them in and stood at the back of the room while people found seats. The room was almost full. He did not want to sit in the audience. He preferred to lean against the wall in the back of the room with a few others who were standing. Security guards were standing nearby.

The director moved from the floor to the podium, "Thank you again for coming to this opening for a remarkably talented young lady. We would like to thank the Friends of South Florida National Parks and especially Mrs. Shelley Abram for sponsoring this exhibit." The crowd applauded politely but not really enough. The director continued, "For those who don't already know Mrs. Abram, please stand, Shelley. She is a great benefactor of this wonderful studio and gallery. We are so lucky to have her leadership." Mrs. Abram rose a little from her chair and gave a royalty hand wave and a nod to the seated attendees.

"Now it is my pleasure to introduce Sunny. Sunny studied art at Indiana University and was awarded a Master's degree from Florida State University. Sunny loves nature. She was selected for an art fellowship by the National Park Service to spend months in the Dry Tortugas. Well, I don't want to tell her story for her, so, let's all welcome Sondra Kaye 'Sunny' Griffin." To the clapping of the audience, Sunny approached the stage. Seeing Matvey in the back of the room, she waved at him and smiled, as she said, "Thank you." He glared back at her.

"I am so humbled to see all of you here tonight. I'd like to share some of my thoughts on my artwork and experiences at Loggerhead Key. But first I want to recognize my partner, Chris." Chris stood from her seat at the front of the room. Matvey was surprised. His attempts to flirt with Sunny were rejected because she was in a relationship with a woman! This revelation only added to his irritability, as it threatened his masculinity. His attitude about gay people had existed for a long time and was not to be undone simply by the government now allowing same gender relationships.

Sunny continued, "And I want to recognize my friend who was delivered to the shore after the terrible storm we endured, Matvey Valdez-Descon," pointing to him at the back of the room. "As many know I found Matvey washed up on the beach and I helped him to safety."

Immediately, Matvey burst out, "You are not my friend. You did not save me. I saved myself! You have betrayed me!" The audience gasped at the outburst. He continued, bolstered by the rum he had been guzzling for the past two hours. "You are not a good person. You are a thief and fraud." This was not the confrontation he had planned in his head. It was the confrontation the rum created. The attendees were disturbed and puzzled by his outburst.

The security officers standing nearby grabbed Matvey and took him out of the auditorium as he struggled against being removed. He had more to say to Sunny.

The situation was very awkward and upset Sunny. She paused, eventually saying to the audience, "I'm sorry for this. Please let me take a moment to collect my thoughts." She left the stage while most of the audience remained seated and perplexed. It was an unsettling situation for everyone.

The gallery director came back to the podium and asked for calm, begging folks to stay for the lecture. "Sunny will be back in a minute." She tried to lighten the mood, but her good humor fell flat.

The audience was very disquieted. This commotion was disturbing and a few people rose to scurry out of the gallery, including two gentlemen who were dressed in silk guayaberas.

Shelley and Mrs. Greene were upset with the horrendous breach of decorum that neither had ever experience before. They both sat quietly in their chairs and looked at each other, as if to ask, "What are we to do now?" They rarely were on their own without a staff member to intercede in the event of any unusual circumstance. Shelley grew angry and embarrassed that she had brought her friend to show off a young protégé and, instead, was exposing her to an unruly conflict. Shelley maintained her composure, but clutched her purse a bit tighter. She determined that, as a small senior woman, there was nothing she could do to exercise authority in this situation.

Sunny ran to the back of the auditorium where the security guards were still struggling with Matvey. He saw her and began berating her. "How could you betray me? How could you steal what was mine?" Sunny had no idea what he was talking about, but she could see that he was very agitated.

Holding back tears, she said, "Please calm down Matvey. I'm sure we can work out any problems. Please. Wait for me and we will make things right. I have to go now."

He broke the guards grip and stood in front of her, shaking his finger. "I trusted you. I never should have trusted you! You wanted it for yourself so bad? Why didn't you take it all?" The guards regained control and asked Sunny if they should call the sheriff.

"No! No! Please don't. I don't know what this is about, but I don't want Matvey to get in any trouble. He will be deported if he does."

Hearing this, Matvey immediately quieted down. Fear of government authorities had been infused in his psyche since he was a child. He found a little self-control, relaxing a bit. Sunny mustered her composure and said firmly, "Matvey, I will see you after this event. We can talk about whatever is the problem. I love you and don't want to lose your friendship." Irate, Matvey snapped, "OK, then maybe you can give it back to me. Maybe then we can be friends."

The guards took him to the exit and gave him a gentle shove toward the Duval Street sidewalk.

Then she returned to the podium to resume her presentation. She generously asked the audience to forgive Matvey, excusing his behavior as a result of the stress of being a refugee survivor of a horrible tragedy.

The two men who were in the lecture room were standing at the street corner. Seeing that the guards let Matvey go, they called to him, "Matvey, Matvey. We are security and you must come with us. You are in big trouble."

Matvey complied. One of the men motioned to a car waiting nearby. The car came to the curb, stopped abruptly, the door opened, and they placed him in the back seat, using the typical police procedure of guarding his head from the top of the car door opening. Although he was dulled from the alcohol, Matvey's thoughts were racing. "This doesn't seem like the police. There are no uniforms, no police car. But they act like the police. They act like they have authority." Buzzed from the rum, he offered no resistance. The two men got inside the car, one on each side of Matvey, with him in the middle.

Without any further word, they drove off, passing through the tourist district which was even more active at night, driving to the charter fishing dock. Matvey had a feeling they were also Cuban, maybe Cuban-American criminals. Once the car stopped, the men got out of the car and motioned for him to get out too. Sensing something was wrong, Matvey said, "What is this?" As he exited the car, he heard a voice answer, "Soon enough you will know." Then everything went dark.

As the reception ended, Henry arrived at the gallery. Approaching Henry in a perturbed state, Mrs. Abram said, "Henry, I want that young Cuban man off the property – immediately." The waiting chauffeur opened the Town Car door for her and Mrs. Greene and they were off. Sunny came out of the gallery to say goodbye to Shelley but Shelley was already gone. Henry was standing there confused. "What is going on?"

Sunny told him about Matvey's terrible outburst and how she didn't understand what he had been shouting at her about. She said she tried to calm him down and thought they could work it out if she and Chris came to the estate later and talked to him.

Henry interrupted Sunny, "That might not work. Mrs. Abram was very angry and ordered him out of Cassiopea.

I don't think she is in any mood to change her mind, so it would be best if we could find him and figure something else out."

Following closely behind Sunny, Chris caught the conversation between Sunny and Henry. She interjected, "He looked drunk to me. Not what I expected from all the good things you told me about him." Turning to Henry, Chris continued, "He really interrupted Sunny's show, but it certainly gave people something to talk about!"

Henry told the artist and her partner that he had dropped Matvey off an hour or so before the reception doors opened. He lamented that he should never have left Matvey alone, especially on Duval Street. "There's too much craziness here. Where is he now?"

"Well, I didn't see him leave. I had to return to make a speech about my art and the experiences I had at the park. After his yelling, it was a tough act to follow." Chris added, "You did well! I think the audience calmed down after the excitement and they seemed to connect with you." It was reassuring to Sunny, but Chris was always supportive.

"Well, the only problem is that Mrs. Abram doesn't want him back. At all. I don't even think he can come back tonight. Let's drive around and see if we can find him. I don't think he can get far on foot."

They went to their cars and started cruising the tourist areas, driving slowly by the open-air bars. They drove through old neighborhood side streets, scanning the sidewalks. They decided they could not call the Sheriff because any trouble with the law would not be good for Matvey. He could be returned to Cuba.

After two hours, they had no luck. He was nowhere to be found. The later into the night, the more unusual the island city was becoming. Party revelers were stumbling out on the sidewalks and vagrants wandered the old streets to scavenge for food and fodder to trade at a pawnshop. Late at night, Key West becomes more frightening than benignly eccentric.

The three searchers parked at Mallory Square and walked out to the pier. The mast lights on the sailboats in the anchorage sparkled on the calm waters. Henry, Chris, and Sunny decided they would just have to wait to see if he found his way back to the estate. They parted, promising to check in. In the morning, they could resume looking for Matvey. He couldn't get far without a car.

TWENTY-THREE

Matvey woke up on his side. Disoriented, it took a moment for him to realize he was constrained. He had thrown up and wreaked of rum and vomit. His hands were bound behind his back. His ankles were strapped together and his knees bent back. He was hog-tied with a rope tying his ankle bindings to zip ties on his wrists. He struggled for a minute, but quickly found it was pointless and painful. He couldn't see through the cloth over his head. His mouth was taped shut. Being contorted distracted him from the pain throbbing in his head.

He flopped around whatever floor he was on, thinking maybe he could get up on his knees. He tried to shout, but with his mouth taped, that was useless as well. Matvey was terrified to his core.

It was futile. He guessed he was not in the custody of the police. The last thing he remembered was sitting between two Cubans in the back seat of a big "Jeepon."

He tried to calm himself. He closed his eyes and breathed slowly. He felt a motion and heard a rumbling sound. "I am on a boat! It's moving. I am abducted! Those two Cubans have kidnapped me! Why?" He didn't know if he still had his money or the small bag of jewels. "Why would these guys take me?"

He didn't know where he was or what time it was. The engine rpm increased and the floor tilted, causing him to slide back a little on the inclining floor. The boat was bouncing over waves and he lifted and fell with each bounce. It seemed like hours, only listening to the sounds of waves beating on the boat's hull and the drone of an engine.

Finally, he heard a door hinge creak. Then he was being lifted to his knees, with someone on each side pulling him up under his arms. In Spanish, the guy on the left said, "Get up! It's time for you to confess." He heard laughter.

Matvey was being dragged, his knees scraping on the cabin sole. His captors were brutishly manhandling him. Now he could see a little light twinkling through pinholes in the fabric bag someone had placed over his head. He felt the warmth of the sun and smelled the ocean. Yes, he was on a boat.

The bag was pulled off his head. Fresh air flowed over his face. The bright sun hurt his dilated eyes. He squinted until they adjusted. On his knees, he could see the ocean over the coamings. It was ocean all around, with no land in sight. The same two men that were at the art gallery were standing over him, swaying with the motion of the boat.

Ripping the tape from his face, one Cuban said, "Go ahead. Call for help. Only the fishes will hear you."

The other man introduced himself. "I am Inspector Carlos Costa of the Cienfuegos Police Department. Do you know why I have taken you into custody?" Matvey shook his head no.

"Señor Matvey Valdez-Descon, I am placing you under arrest for the assault and rape of a woman at Girón Beach Club Resort. What do you have to say? We know you did these crimes."

Matvey was confused. He was in Florida, in the United States, and he was being arrested by the Cuban police?

Matvey said, "What? I did not rape the woman. It was her choice to be with me. I did not mean to kill her. It was an accident!"

Costa chuckled, "That may be, but your victim is still alive and recovered from the beating you gave her." Matvey didn't know if he should believe it, but, if true, it was a relief that he had not killed Evelyn. At least he would not go to jail for murder.

The second man chimed in, "Your problems are so much more serious, you despicable thief. You have committed a crime against the Revolution. I am Agent Fernández of the G2, assigned to capture the thief of our national patrimony and to charge you with crimes against the Revolution."

Matvey asked, "What crime?"

"You have stolen a valuable religious artifact from the Revolution and taken it out of Cuba. This is a serious crime, one that carries a larger punishment than your crimes at Girón."

Matvey protested, "I did not steal the relic! It was the English woman!"

"No worries, we will catch your accomplice if she returns to Cuba. We already have her collaborator, the art professor, Yolanda Lopez-Ballar, in prison." Matvey was puzzled. He did not know any professor named Yolanda.

Fernández smugly continued, "We may not need to wait for the thief to come back to Cuba. We have sent to our embassy in London papers for her arrest and extradition. The English art professor has violated so many Cuban and international laws about trafficking antiquities. I think Scotland Yard will get her.

Inspector Costa nudged Fernández and quipped, "So, Fernández, do we get to go to England to get her. I'd like to meet the Queen."

Agent Fernández furled his brow. "Costa, this is serious!" Then, grinning, he chuckled, "Coming to capture this criminal was our work, but also a nice vacation." Both men were a little giddy about their success in capturing a fugitive during a clandestine operation.

Costa said, "We were sent to bring you back to Cuba for justice. When the theft of the cross of Fray Bartolomé was discovered, the investigation became a national case and G2 Agent Oscar Fernández joined me in the investigation and the pursuit of you."

Matvey was perplexed. How could they know I was in the U.S. The quizzed look on his face led Costa to explain.

"Our sources in Florida saw a photograph of you in a newspaper and alerted the Interior Ministry. We have many eyes in the United States. I published a warrant for your arrest in Cienfuegos, but the Ministry of the Interior has precedence in your case. Agent Fernández and I were smuggled into Key

West to find you. It is no problem to get to Florida when you have an American fishing boat bring you from The Bahamas."

Fernández said, "That's enough! Give him the water and put him back down below. He will face the charges when he gets to Havana." Costa opened a bottle and held it to Matvey's mouth. He drank the water as it spilled down his chin.

Costa then cut the rope that tied his hands to his feet. Matvey could stand, and hop, with Costa's assistance, to the forward cabin, falling into a bunk. His hands and feet were still bound. The door closed. Matvey looked around, quickly realizing there was no way out. The cabin was bare and the portlights were not large enough to exit through. Matvey lay there pondering his future in Cuba. The criminal charges were bad, but Matvey was much more afraid of what the Ministry of Interior would do. The rumors of their brutality were legend in Cuba.

Two hours later, Matvey yelled "I have to urinate! Now! Please!" He banged on the door with his shoulder.

Inspector Costa brought Matvey back to the open deck and cut the zip ties on his wrists. "Go over the side and don't try anything!" He pulled the tail of his guayabera to reveal a holstered revolver.

The boat slowed to a stop, just drifting and rocking in a gentle sea while Matvey was pissing. The boat captain who had been steering from the flybridge backed down the ladder to the aft deck. When Matvey zipped his pants and turned back, Alvero was there, standing close and looking at him, with a long filet knife. Grabbing Matvey, he held the knife in one hand near Matvey's throat, just below his ear, while squeezing his throat with the other hand.

Matvey blinked and shook his head. He saw the knife and the grizzled old man. It took him a few seconds to locate the man's face in his memory. He gasped as he recognized the captain as the captain of the old wood boat that sank in the hurricane. He thought the captain of the La Luna was dead. Was he real or a ghost from hell?

Alvero's steely stare burned into Matvey. While he put up his hands in a motion submitting complete surrender, Matvey called, "Officers, please take me back to the cabin." He trusted the police, even the harsh Fernández, more than the crazed sea captain.

Fernández and Costa leaned back on the side of the boat. Their arms were folded against their chests. "I'm afraid we are in international waters and we have no authority here. The captain of this boat is in charge until we reach Cuban territory," Costa said.

Matvey was frightened and trembling in fear. Matvey was as frozen as he was on the boat during the hurricane when it wrecked. He reached to hold Alvero's wrists at bay. The old man was strong.

"I am Capitan Alvero Marin-Zayas. You forced your way onto my boat at Marina Hemingway. I was taking my daughter and her family to Florida. You were a stowaway. When we wrecked, you could have saved my grandson and daughter, but, no, you kept the life ring for yourself."

Matvey stuttered unintelligibly, "a... a... a, what...I did...I couldn't...how?

"You swam to the island and never looked back, but I saw you swimming away. I am an old man, but I made it to the island too. I wandered around the island until I saw you at that headstone, where I saw you bury your box. I was going to kill you then, but the woman found you, so I hid until she took you to the house. When I dug at the monument, I found the cross of Fray Bartolomé de las Casas. I left your trinkets, but knew I must return the cross to Cuba. It could not be yours!"

Matvey realized that he had made a mistake to blame Sunny. She was innocent and he had been mean to her. He regretted his tantrum, but now the knife at his neck was commanding his focus.

Alvero continued, his knife holding Matvey immobile. "I survived on coconuts and hid until you and the woman left the island. Then I found plenty to eat in the house for the next week. A fishing boat came. They were Cuban-Americanos. They took me to Key West to be with my charter boat friends."

"Without my La Luna it took me a long time to get back to Cuba to return the gold crucifix. I gave it to General Rodolfo Diego. The General ordered the Ministry of Interior investigation and arranged for this new boat. Then he asked me to bring these men to Key West to capture you. It is my honor! No, it is my pleasure to slit your throat, but I might decide to castrate you first."

Alvero tightened his grip, his knife holding Matvey immobile. "Enough!" Alvero yelled at himself as he shook his head. He was impatient with himself for explaining his ordeal. "I don't have to tell you anything! You do not deserve any explanation. You deserve only punishment and judgment from God!" Alvero strengthened his grip and pressed the knife harder against Matvey's neck, drawing a little blood.

Alvero raised his voice, "Now you will join my grandson in the Gulf Stream on your way to hell!"

As Alvero pulled his arm slightly back to lunge the knife into Matvey's neck, Matvey cried out, "NO! Officers, please!" Alvero paused, looking over to Fernández and Costa to see if they would intercede.

Fernández said, "It is the captain's decision. He is the authority here. Of course, Costa and I would have to report what we see, but it is up to him. He is the captain and we are not in Cuban waters."

Alvero glanced at them and grinned, looking for their consent.

Matvey cried an appeal, "No! Stop! Don't you care? You can't let him kill me! I did not kill his family, they died in the storm. There was nothing I could do."

This only made Alvero angrier. He was focused on making Matvey pay for the loss and pain he suffered since he observed his daughter, son-in-law, and beloved little grandson sink below the waves. Alvero wanted revenge, but he was sobered by the presence of the two cops.

Inspector Costa said with casual disregard, "We are at sea. The captain is in charge until we reach Cuba. The captain must decide, but for us .... What do you think Fernández? This scum is your prisoner first."

Fernández thought for a moment, "Now or later, you will face justice. Your fate in Cuba may be worse than dying here. You know, for me..." He added, with a sneering smile, "Me importa tres cojones," the rude Cuban idiom for "I don't care."

"Either way, Costa, we will return to Cuba with a criminal who will pay for his crimes. We'll have either a thief or the murderer of a thief."

If you enjoyed this book, try the sequel!

ADRIFT IN THE GULF STREAM
Matvey escapes his captors, but is alone in the Gulf Stream, drifting in the current. A sequel to *Across Florida Straits,* this book continues the story of Matvey, thief of antiquities and wanted for assault by Cuban authorities. Will he survive to find his way to a new life in The Bahamas and leave his past behind?

Other Books by Marvin Cook

HOUSEBOAT HERMIT OF THE EVERGLADES
Nefarious activities in the Everglades forge an unlikely friendship between Thompson, an old hermit living on a houseboat, and a burned-out and disillusioned National Park Service park ranger. Seeking a more peaceful wilderness and life changes, they migrate to North Florida's Nature Coast, encountering more adventures along the way.

CAN'T OUTRUN THE PAST
Enjoy the sequel to HOUSEBOAT HERMIT as trouble follows Thompson and Refuge Officer Bob Nelson, formerly a NPS Park Ranger, in North Florida's Big Bend wilderness. Unknown agents target Thompson to secure the secrets of his past only to be thwarted by the local sheriff and new friends.

DYSTOPIAN PARADISE

The story of Pilar, a young girl who is a force of nature, takes place in a future brought about by events occurring in modern times. Set in Florida and the Caribbean, Pilar ponders questions she cannot answer. What lies beyond the horizon?... Are we alone? When a ship appears in the distance her life takes a new path. In time, she discovers answers to some of her questions at Nueva Panacea.

THEY ALL CALLED HIM PINKY

Gold Award Winner, Florida Writers Association Royal Palm Literary Award

Written for children ages 8 and up, this book is illustrated with colorful images by Marvin Cook. The hero is a lone flamingo that visited St. Marks National Wildlife Refuge after a hurricane in 2018. Pinky makes new friends with many of the refuge's diverse bird species. The resident birds learn to accept Pinky, even though he is different. The story incorporates educational, moral and cultural lessons, with encouragement for kids to be the best they can be.